MW01242135

THE SPELLBOUND ABBEY

THE SPELLBOUND ABBEY

Mason Monteith

MASON MONTEITH

THE SPELLBOUND ABBEY

mason.r.monteith@gmail.com.
First paperback edition October 2022
Book design by Seventh Star Art
Map by Mason Monteith
ISBN 979-8-218-05286-7 (paperback)

Dedicated to everyone who believed in my writing beyond 'just being polite.'
To my family for motivating me to continue, to my friends, and to those who are no longer with me.
This is for you.

TABLE OF CONTENTS

Characters and Locations
Characters... I
Locations... V
World Map... VII
Prologue... 1
Part One, The Letter of Inheritance... 6
Ch. 1 The Pages Prior... 7
Ch. 2 On Hold... 29
Ch. 3 Long Overdue... 52
Ch. 4 Loose Pages... 60
Ch. 5 The Delivery... 68
Ch. 6 Recall... 79
Ch. 7 Book Return... 97
Ch. 8 Complete Annotations... 107
Ch. 9 Unpublished... 137
Part Two, No Page Unturned... 152
Ch. 10 The Database... 153
Ch. 11 Gathering Information... 167
Ch. 12 Primary Source... 177
Ch. 13 The Weight of Paper... 183
Ch. 14 Renewal... 196
Ch. 15 Bindings... 207
Ch. 16 Unabridged... 221
Ch. 17 Bookends... 227
Ch. 18 The Pages We Remove... 236
Ch. 19 Book Mend... 251
Ch. 20 Complications... 258

Ch. 21 Spilling Ink... 269
Ch. 22 Burning Pages... 290
Ch. 23 The Stories Left Untold... 305
Ch. 24 The Words that Remain... 309
Part III, Final Edition... 316
Ch. 25 Beyond the Books... 317
Ch. 26 Scale-Bound... 324
Ch. 27 Cutting Corners... 329
Ch. 28 Allowing the Past... 337
Ch. 29 ...To Affect the Future... 348
Ch. 30 Between the Lines... 360
Ch. 31 Behind the Cover... 368
Ch. 32 A Query... 381
Ch. 33 Hidden in Ashes... 395
Ch. 34 Rebound... 401
Ch. 35 Dedications... 411
Ch. 36 Archive... 421
Ch. 37 As it is Decreed... 435
Ch. 38 The End and the Beginning... 439
Ch. 39 Advisors Wards... 449
Ch. 40 Ghost Writer... 462
Acknowledgments... 469
About the Author... 471

CHARACTERS AND LOCATIONS

CHARACTERS

- Audrey Hughes: A young woman of the lower class, works at the local library to pay for her younger brothers to go to school. Audrey is a very curious young woman, and always seeks to learn more to teach her brothers and herself.
- Farah Davies: An upper-class woman who rules the district as a part of the board. She is older, and prefers to spend time relaxing at the library with her friend.
- Dominique: A young man visiting the district from out of town, oddly kind and stands out from others within the district.
- Julian Halloway: An upper-class members of the board, a cold controlling man.
- Priscilla Halloway: Wife to Julian, she is very mouse-like and timid. Priscilla keeps to herself and her writing most of the time.
- Vivienne Raithe: The most controlling member of the district board among the upper class. A refined and polished lady who always appears to have things under control.

- Mr. Hughes: Audrey's father. Mr. Hughes has been out of work since the border patrol was disbanded due to insufficient funds. Now that he is older and has bad eyesight and a poor leg, he has a hard time finding work.
- Mrs. Hughes: Audrey's mother. Mrs. Hughes was one of many to be hit by the unknown sickness within the district. While it doesn't seem to spread, no cure is known. She wastes much of their money on fake cures in an attempt to fix it herself.
- Fletcher and Remy Hughes: Audrey's two brothers. Smart but impressionable young boys, Audrey keeps a close eye on them when she can and tries to keep them on a good path.
- Esme Dayholt: Board member of the neighboring district, Broise. Esme is timid but tries to be productive and take care of things. She prefers to travel as opposed to staying home with her husband.
- Emmett Wingrave: Upperclassman who was once engaged to Audrey Hughes. Emmett is an arrogant and blunt young man, who needed to marry in order to get his own inheritance.
- Francis Bishop: Board member of the

neighboring district, Fayehun. Francis is a businessman at heart, and is only a member of the upper class by marriage.

- Prince Leon: The crown prince of Flaize, only recently allowed into his princely duties since his coming of age season.
- Advisor Odell Alborne: The advisor of the royal family, a cold and intense woman who once worked alongside the Flaize army as a general.

IV

LOCATIONS

• Dragnior: The homeland of the Dragonkin, creatures that can shift between the forms of various dragons, humans, and many other creatures. Little is known of this country, as it has been very closed off from humans for many years. • Flaize: The human country is divided into six districts. Founded centuries ago by Bryun F. Lumar, the hero from overseas who led his people to safer lands during a war from their homeland.

• District Yonnam - District insignia: Griffin as it represents protection and safety along the borders with the dragonkin. Yonnam was once the most proficient with its trained guards and patrolmen until less funding forced them to disband.

• District Broise - District Insignia: The sun, divinity and royalty. Broise is the leading producer of fine silks and is also the home of the church where holy magic is used. The usage of this magic is banned beyond the churches small uses of it, as it is difficult to contain.

- District Fayehun - District Insignia: Phoenix, Fayehun is the district of trade and is symbolic of the country's growth and prosperity.
- District Dyvast - District Insignia: Dragon, symbol of wisdom and hidden knowledge. After one of the dragonkin shared knowledge of magic with the humans in an attempt at peace between the peoples, this city became the capital of knowledge in the country.
- District Lunida - District Insignia: The Moon, Eternity and Immortality. The Capital District, named after the founder, Bryun Flaize Lumar. His symbolic insignia was the moon, as he was once a lunar knight before fleeing his home country.
- District Eighvale - District insignia: Hydra - Victory over enemies. After an eight headed hydra was killed by the hero Bryun here, the city of Eighvale was founded. Eighvale is a rural farming and fishing district, and is home to many who choose to explore the seas.

World Map

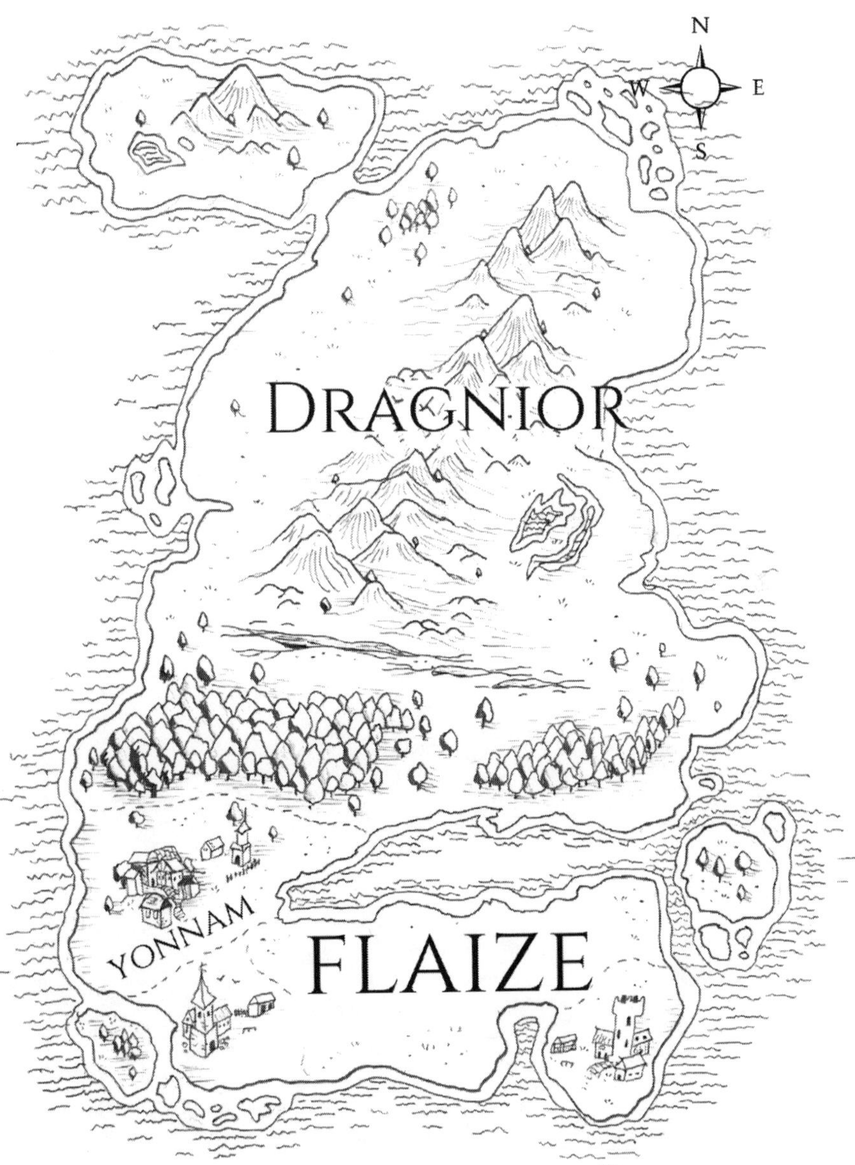

PROLOGUE
INCOMPLETE ANNOTATIONS

"...A will was found already filed with her lawyer, which places you as the sole beneficiary of everything she had. This includes her title, savings, place on the estate, and to her request, her place on the board...."
- A Fragment of an Inheritance Letter

Fine events are for fine people.

This was a fact.

I do not mean people who dress up and cover themselves in embellishments and riches - though that is the first thing that may come to mind, it isn't only that. The manners and aura of a person also matter, but most important are your family and your class.

Things that are out of one's control are the deciding factors of such things in life, on whether or not you would be at such a place. And, the worst thing is, being at such a grand event and causing a complication.

That's what I tell myself as I stand by a strange man in a room of even stranger people.

The man who stood by me is an outsider, an *intruder*. Though I remind myself that he is not very different from myself in the given situation, except of course, the way he got in is different.

Standing close, he seems smug, as though he's just gotten away with theft.

Like a Cheshire cat.

How did he get in here? And who is he?

Everyone watches, waiting for a word, an answer – *anything* to explain how this random man shoved his way into this exclusive event. Though it is not silent as people begin to whisper among themselves about the situation. I dig my nails into my palm as I look at the stranger.

"I'm Audrey's husband of course, here to be with my wife."

Husband? I look up at the man's face, having to double-check it. I must be imagining things, right? The man claiming to be my husband is someone I never expected to see here – or again at all.

He presses something into my hand, and I look down at it. A common flower from the area, a bright red Antirrhinum. A Snapdragon. I clench the flower in my hand, frowning at the meaning it carries.

"I wasn't aware that Ms. Hughes was married," a man states as loudly as possible, gaining him the attention of every person gathered in the elegant room.

My chest feels tight, and I am at a loss for words as the situation unfolds before me. The man is standing in front of me; he is the host of this... party of sorts. He seems angry, with his cold, silver eyes fixated upon me, and it makes my skin crawl.

I can't focus as it happens, as women's beaded skirts rustle as they lean in to whisper to each other, speaking in hushed but giggly voices while watching, with the men merely gruff in their boredom of the situation. So many eyes are on me, the strange man who's forced his way into the and the host who stands in a rage before me.

The stranger standing over my shoulder doesn't make the situation any better. His closeness makes me self-conscious, and I feel keenly aware of how close he is to my back. I dislike being near people, especially near strangers. Though I dare not react sharply, lest I give the people a reason to gossip. Instead, I dig my nails deeper into my hand, as a reminder to control myself.

Why is he saying this? The host surely knows that I have no husband- even the man claiming to be my husband should know this-

As I look around the room of finely dressed people staring, I realize they are not staring at me as much as they are waiting for the host to respond to the situation. He's baffled and seems taken aback.

I almost feel satisfied having confused him after how he's been treating me tonight. After being humiliated at this event, being belittled. Though I find myself momentarily satisfied, it is not enough at the moment to make me feel at ease.

I should not be here...

Looking down at my plain dress, I know I'm out of place. Everyone else knows it as well. Now with a man claiming to be my husband, I don't know what to do next.

Why did I come here?

Why couldn't I just leave the abbey alone?

PART ONE
THE
LETTER OF
INHERITANCE

I
THE PAGES PRIOR

"With word that Dragnior, the bordering country of our land, Flaize, is preparing for war, many people are wondering when they will be called to serve for King and country. With the spread of sickness, and the tensions spreading during this industrial revolution throughout the districts- should the Kind be preparing for war? Or dealing with the troubles within the borders?"
-Flaize Daily, Article by James T. Lilith

There are three things I already know to expect from today, because even though it is not that far into the morning, three things are definite.

1. There is bad news in the country
2. Papa is in a bad mood
3. I have to choose my words very carefully.

I can tell something bad has happened by the way my father taps his fingers on the table, reading his paper quietly as I dodge around where he sits at the table so I can cook. The kitchen is far too small, feeling more like the end of a hallway with counters, more so with the round dining table shoved into the corner. Cooking while he's in here is a pain, but I won't say anything. Especially not now.

Now, he isn't being too quiet - rather the sounds of his grumbling and huffing as he reads the paper have become such a regular occurrence that it's become like white noise to me.

"What's new today?" I ask cautiously, uncertain about whether or not I'm entering into a lecture or a conversation.

"Papa?"

"Haven't you read the paper?" he asks, not looking up. A pan-seared smell wafts into my nose. I turn to look at the stove.

Shoot. The eggs are already burning.

"I haven't had the time to," I say quickly, reaching for the pan. "What's in it?"

He finally puts the paper down and shifts in his seat as much as his bad leg allows him. "Audrey, there is talk of another war."

I freeze for a moment, before quickly scraping the slightly burnt food onto four, mismatched plates. It's not surprising, and it doesn't come as a shock to me either.

Though, I haven't even been too concerned, as arrogant as that may sound.

To not care about a war. Then again, any war talk has to be a rumor, but even rumors can put my father into a foul mood.

Our country is divided into six districts, founded centuries ago by Bryun F. Lumar, the hero from overseas who led his people to safer lands. All districts were under the rule of the royal lineage of Lumar, and I know that there have been tensions between us and the country our people came from but still. A *war?*

"A war with who? The state of things overseas has been improving." When my father doesn't respond, I continue. "Is it a war within the districts? Or-"

"With Dragnior," he states. I turn to glance at the paper and hit my hip on the edge of the counter as I do. I curse silently under my breath so father doesn't hear. *Dragnior*? I carefully scan the paper.

Dragnior: The homeland of the Dragonkin. The Dragonkin are creatures that can shift between their form of dragon to a variety of creatures, and in a few cases even humans. Little is known of Dragnior, as it has been very closed off from humans for many years. There was a peace treaty though. But even with that they don't trust us nor do we trust them.

It shouldn't come as a surprise though, we did invade their country. Though it was many years ago, before I was even born, that was a fact that would never change.

I continue gleaning words from the page over papa's shoulder, letting out a relieved sigh when I reach the end.

"It looks as though it is only a rumor," I conclude, handing him his plate of scrambled egg and bread. He grunts in thanks.

"Let's hope it stays a rumor."

"Even if it wasn't, you won't be called to serve because of your leg." As soon as the words slip out of my mouth, I regret them. I speak quickly to brush over them.

"You know, I only mean that you don't have to worry about it. Surely they won't call you to serve -" He pushes his plate away.

"They will Audrey- Now that the sickness has spread and we're already short on men in the district." I sigh, setting the other three plates at the seats around him. He's right. Even before the sickness began, young men were leaving the Yonnam District to go into magic trades throughout other districts or to go learn from the academy in the capital district.

We're lucky Fletcher and Remy are too young to serve. However, they're also too young to go into any trade to help the family. But what if they are really desperate for men? Fire isn't the only thing we would face against the Dragonkin...

They can hide within our people according to -

"Audrey!" Father's shout pulls me from my thoughts, and he looks at me with a frown, as though he can tell what's on my mind. But he can't, thankfully that was the one place safe from his cutting words. "I know it's been hard to find another suitor," he begins gruffly. That is, in fact, the farthest thing from what is on my mind. I feel my stomach turn as I already know where this conversation is headed.

Papa continues, oblivious to my avoidant expression. "Perhaps I should see about inviting the blacksmith's son for supper one day. He makes a fair amount, I'd wager. Especially with a war coming, it'll be a pretty honorable income for the cost of weapons."

I dip my head, trying to keep in check the rage in my tone. "I should go wake everyone for breakfast."

Quickly, I am out of the kitchen and heading down the narrow hallway. I feel my father's gaze piercing my back and I know he is angry at my avoidance of the subject. *When will he understand that I don't have time for that? Working to keep up with the cost of the boys' schooling...* If I stopped working even a day for romance, I'd never hear the end of it, even if it was for money. Besides, everyone is struggling right now.

Perhaps we wouldn't be, I think to myself, if I hadn't made that grave mistake.

I run my hands through my hair and shake my head, as though that simple action could ward away the bad thoughts.

Yet no matter how much time has passed, destroying my family's one way out by breaking off my engagement to the wealthy, yet uncouth Mr. Wingrave is something that always lingers in the back of my mind. Even if my intentions were once good, I know deep down that good intentions did not put food on the table or send my brothers to school.

I stop at a room with a painted door.

This is the room my brother's share, and the door is covered in flowers and many odd scribbles. This had once been my own bedroom, but once I was big enough and Fletcher and Remy were born, I had to make do with our old storage closet. While at first Fletcher had hated the flowers and wanted to paint over them, he never did because Remy started to like them.

I open the door and step inside. The two of them share one narrow bed. I step over and shake the two awake. *They're getting too big to share, and soon I'll have to scrounge up what meager savings I have and buy another one.* I try not to think of all the other uses of the cost of a bed as I look at my brothers.

At twelve, Fletcher is far too cocky for his own good. While Remy is ten, he is a quiet soul and takes more after me with his eagerness to learn.

"Fletcher, Remy, it's time for breakfast." I don't wait to watch as they sit up together, mumbling and rubbing the sleep from their eyes. I leave and continue to the last room in the hallway.

Opening the door, this time I am more careful to be quiet as I do. I look in to see mum asleep in her bed. It's small, only having enough room for mother and father, yet it looks gigantic nestled in the small room.

I can't bring myself to look directly at my mother's face, knowing that since the sickness got to her, I won't find that warm and familiar glow of my loved one.

"Mum, I made you breakfast..." My eyes land on the bottles. On a chair used as a nightstand next to mum sits five of them, two empty and the rest half filled despite being unopened. So, she has still been taking that.

How did she afford it? Did papa go through my things again?

I clench my hand into a fist as I look at the bottles of shimmering blue liquid.

Since the sudden appearance of the sickness within the Yonnam District, the sales of various magic solutions had become a booming business. Snake Oil.

The cures made through magic solutions and self-proclaimed 'miracles' did nothing to stop the sickness. Yet still, mum spends all of our savings on it. My stomach turns as I look at the five bottles.

Sold half empty, with how many she's already purchased... I try not to think of all of the problems that could be solved with that money.

Turning away, I return to the kitchen where Fletcher and Remy silently sit by papa as they wait for me. I try not to feel envious of how good they all look together. Papa with his gray blonde hair and my brothers with their matching blond bedhead. Like a matching tea set. I felt like the odd one out no matter how often I have been told that papa's hair used to be the same color as my own.

"Auddie?"

I turn to my brother when I hear him call me by my nickname. Only Fletcher and

Remy call me *Auddie*. Them, and nobody else.

"Yes?"

"Where is mum?" Remy asks.

I freeze for a moment, Remy has a concerned look on his face as he frowns.

"She is just... Tired is all." I catch my father's gaze, he frowns and shakes his head. He doesn't want me to say anything more to the boys. "Just let her rest, alright?" I grab my bag that sits next to the front door.

Fletcher doesn't need to be told twice as he begins eating immediately, Remy still stares at me and glances at my bag, confused.

"I thought you didn't work today?"

"Normally I wouldn't." I say as I put the bag on my shoulder. "I'm going into work and I might not be home until nightfall, so don't wait on me." Audrey walks away before her father can protest. Before anyone knew it, she was out the door.

I hardly even noticed the cold autumn wind at first, even though it blows straight through my blouse and cardigan. I wasn't dressed terribly well for the weather, but it wasn't bad either. A button down blouse, a loosely knit cardigan, and a long black skirt with boots normally would be enough, but this year fall came early. It was turning cold far sooner than normal as well.

Why does papa keep allowing her to buy into that?

The only way I know that they could be affording it, is if they already found my new stash...

I try not to remember the humiliation on my parents faces the first time I found out they took from me. While papa was guilty, and said as soon as he found work and mum recovered I would get paid back in full, mum was a different story. I owe it to her, she said.

She hasn't been the same since she got sick... *I should try to understand.*

But still- I already pay for the boys to go to school and pay for food from the market.

Instantly I feel guilty as my heart drops, I shouldn't think like this. *It's ungrateful of me.*

When will she understand it though, that the magic 'cures' aren't helping her?

They're killing *her.*

Perhaps even faster than the sickness is.

I myself standing on the cobblestone streets just outside my parents home. Though the houses and stores that line the roads around their home weren't extremely well kept, they couldn't be considered very dirty either. Still, my destination in comparison shows the difference between where I live and the class above our own. The upper class sectors.

While the two sectors of the district's city were extremely close, the differences were quite apparent in Yonnam's city.

As I continue down the road, I don't notice it much anymore. Though I remember the first time I was taken to the upper district it was a shock for me.

The brick buildings look almost too polished and clean, the light-posts all have working bulbs and light the streets at night, the plants and gardens off the street were well kept, and the shops at this end of town could afford to stay open through the sickness. Behind me there were more boarded up shops and closed up homes.

The two sides of the district shared one thing, and that was the fact that the streets were more often empty or only a few people would be out. While not everyone was susceptible to the sickness, and the doctors confirmed that it didn't spread, that did not stop the fear from spreading.

Though with less and less people going out into the streets, businesses were failing for quite obvious reasons.

I pass many ornate and luxurious looking homes and shops along the cobblestone streets, but my destination was deeper into the upper class section of the town. It is only when I see a large, ominous yet ornate gateway that I know that I am getting close to my destination.

The gate was one that was rarely seen open, if ever. Even before the sickness it was normally closed more than it was open. I never put much thought into it at the time, that was where the leaders of the district lived. The three head families.

The Davies, the Halloways, and the Raithes. Those three last names would be all I knew of the district rulers by this point.

What lay beyond that gloomy gateway was the Yonnam Abbey. Most of the people of the district would live their whole lives not knowing what lay beyond the gates, of course nothing other than what they were told. This led to many rumors and dramatic stories being told about what lies within. This is where the families that ruled the district lived. The upper class.

There were three ruling families, each family had one member running the board. The board also supposedly was kept in check by the upper class and their families, the only others to go within the abbey even now, but it didn't feel as though they were kept in check.

At least, not to the rest of the district. The Lords and Ladies of the abbey ruled the district as they deemed fit, and right now with everything going on it often felt like they didn't care for the rest of us.

I always felt sick as I passed the gate, I don't know why but there was something about it. Something... wrong.

I try to shake my head to ward off the bad feeling. It was just the rumors and stories getting to me. Nothing more than stories told to children to keep them from trying to sneak in.

If I could avoid it altogether I would, but it is on the path I had to take to work so I simply had to get over it.

Are they doing anything about the rumors? What do they even do in there anyways?

I sigh and continue past the gate. They probably do nothing useful...

Perhaps they are just trying to stay away from the sickness?

It had been months now- no. It had been perhaps years since a magic user had been summoned for the re-casting of the protection spells around the district. It was hard to tell, as each time had a longer gap between each re-cast. Not to mention that each magic user seemed less and less confident or qualified for the job.

Perhaps it is a shortage of magic users who can come out?

There is an urgent need for magic users to attend the academy-

Then again, it hasn't stopped any from coming to sell their 'elixirs and miracle cures'.

It doesn't matter right now, I can think about it all I want later. I tell myself this, though the moment my head hits the pillow I know I'll be too exhausted to unravel the mysteries of the district.

Finally, I stop as I reach the doorstep of my workplace. It was a rather small, yet elegant building. It was a cottage looking place, which was a little too large to be a home, though clearly it had at one point been used as a house.

With a large wooden sign hanging down from a chain attached to the roof, it read 'Heirloom Library.'

Well, I lied, it was supposed to say that but it didn't.

With the letters being worn over the years it read 'H i l m L i b a r y'.

It hardly mattered though, as anyone who came to the library had lived here long enough to be aware of what the building was used for.

This was once a house, very long ago, and once was considered very upper class. That was long ago, and since then the owner had expanded it into a public location.

Now, I work here, and *that* is no lie.

I push the door open and step inside, I am immediately greeted by the smell of dusty old books. Moments later an old gentleman walks into the room. He looks a lot like a raccoon with his shaggy hair and tired eyes. Mr. Abbot was his name.

He stops behind a counter with stacks of books upon it.

"Audrey, good to see you this morning." He glances around before leaning across the counter. "One of the upperclassmen just came by."

"Oh?" I feel my brows furrow as I sit my bag by him, "Did I just miss them?"

I look around, but there was nobody here. I began peering around the bookshelves but still, nobody. I turn back to Mr.Abbott quizzically.

He fixes his oddly small round glasses.

"No, no, they're just out back in the window room. It's that kinder lady, you know, the one who comes by to visit with you." He scratches his head for a moment.

"What was her name... Far- Fasha... Fahrah?"

"Lady Farah Davies?!"

Why is she already back again?

"Yes! Farah! She brought more books, I'm working on putting them all in our logs." The man says with a smile. "Go see about thanking her, then come help me out if you could."

I nod and quickly turn away, hurrying through the maze of oddly placed old bookshelves and dodging around book stacks on the floor until I reach a glass door. I stop for a moment, picking up a few books and putting them on the shelf as I glance through the door.

I've only met one person I'd *truly* call kind. At least, amongst the upperclassmen. No, I should say amongst most people I've met, regardless of class.

That one kind person was the Dowager Farah Davies.

She was the only person from the ruling families that Audrey had really met. Despite having told Audrey of having a personal library of her own within the Yonnam Abbey, she still came to the local one to visit her.

She was here three days ago, and she is starting to come more frequently -

Farah shouldn't be out this much. Not with this sickness - we don't even know if it can spread easily.

I open it and step out into a small room, where only one woman sat nearby.

This was the window room. The entire room was mostly taken up by the windows showing the lush garden kept behind the houses on the street, making it an excellent place to read. It was once a greenhouse, but had been repurposed when Mr. Abbot turned the place into a library. The room used to be busy, filled with people reading or having conversation with close friends about gossip from the capital. Since the sickness spread, it has been mostly unused.

There were two armchairs and a beautiful but old antique couch, as well as two small tables set up. It was a little crowded but still very cozy. The furniture here was far nicer than anything Audrey had at home.

At one of the tables a refined looking older woman sat reading a book, she had yet to look up, absorbed in the book she held, she did not react to Audrey's entrance. The lady was quite elderly, but still was extraordinarily beautiful. Her hair was braided into a tight bun with a few loose curls framing her face.

Her warm skin was glowing in the lighting that filtered through the windows, and she wore a very modest and elegant dress, which seems a bit much for a library visit.

It made me feel a little out of place with my hand me down skirt and blouse from my mum. I sit down at the table across from her.

"Good morning Farah," I greet her informally, and she lowers her book to look at me. She stares for a moment, as though she had to process who was speaking to her.

I notice a tiredness in her eyes.

Deep dark bags beneath her blue eyes were clear to see despite the makeup used to cover them up. Her eyes look hazy with exhaustion as well. Something was clearly wrong with her.

Her eyes just then light up as she recognizes me.

She smiles. "Audrey! I was just beginning to wonder when you would be arriving."

I frown, she speaks in a forced tone, as though she were struggling to sound happy. Why is she out again?

"Farah, what's wrong-"

"Did you have the next book in this series?" she says, holding up her book before I can finish speaking. "I believe I will be finished reading it before the end of the day."

"Yes, I have it ready on the counter for you," I say quickly.

She clearly doesn't want me to ask...

Should I push it?

I think about how I would speak with my father or mother, if it were either of them, pushing on a subject was not an option. Though it was neither of them in front of me at this moment.

"Farah..." I begin carefully. "Is there any reason you've been coming to the library more frequently?"

"What do you mean? I enjoy coming to the library to see you."

That comment makes me feel happy, but it also makes my heart drop.

A dual edged sword.

Does she really have nobody in the abbey willing to visit with her?

"I know, but- If you're ill shouldn't you rest? You look tired."

Tired was an understatement of how she looked, but Audrey wouldn't say it.

Farah laughs, "You're the only one to really notice and say anything about it."

She closes her book carefully with its bookmark in place and sits it down onto the table. "You see, the thing is, I can't sleep. I haven't been feeling much like myself and..."

She stops, her eyes no longer focused on anything as she is lost in thought.

"And?" I ask cautiously.

Quickly, Farah looks at me again.

"And, I simply must get out of the house more!" She chuckles.

I furrow my brows at her, "Is that all? Is there really nothing else wrong?"

"It's good to get fresh air when one doesn't feel well, dear Audrey."

I sigh, she was clearly keeping something from me, which was unusual.

Not for people to keep things from me, but for Farah to keep things from me.

Though, I didn't want to push it any further than I already had.

Audrey was never the kind to push things with people she cared about.

No matter how much she had wanted to. 'It's disrespectful to speak your mind.' is what one of the many things she learned growing up. She was far too blunt and honest as a child. Bluntness is not a virtue true of a lady. Audrey quickly shakes her head as though to ward off bad memories from coming back.

"Make sure you're taking care of yourself." I chide.

She chuckles, "That's very kind of you to care about my well being, dear

Audrey." Farah picks her book back up.

"Now, I won't keep you from your work, I'm sure Mr. Abbot would want help organizing the books I brought in from my collections. Just make sure to stop by and visit with me when you can." Farah says with a tired smile.

I nod, "Alright, I'll get you the book that comes after that one in just a bit as well." I say with a motion towards the book she held on the table. I stand up to leave, but I pause for a moment.

I wish she would tell me what's wrong... But I am glad she took the time to come and visit with me.

"Audrey, dear?"

At first, I had found it odd, being called dear by anyone was foreign. Even more so hearing it from someone of a higher class than I. But now I had gotten used to hearing her call me that.

"Yes, Farah?"

She half-smiles, "Thank you for always being here for me to visit with. I know not every young person wants to be around an older lady like me, so I appreciate that you've taken time for me until now."

Why does this sound... Final?

"Of course," I reply, "You're my closest friend after all. Thank you for continuing to visit." This time, Farah brightens up a little more as she gives her a big smile.

"Anytime dear."

2
ON HOLD

"...It is difficult to confirm the sighting of a Dragonkin unless they return to their natural form. Since they can take on the form of a man, woman, or child, it is next to impossible to confirm. Therefore the rumored 'sightings' are merely that. rumors..."
-A History in Magic: Creature Compendium

It had been many days since Farah's visit to the library. I didn't know whether this was a sign of her taking care of herself and listening to my words or a sign that she had gotten worse to the point where she couldn't visit. Either way waiting was required to see, but I couldn't shake this sinking feeling in my chest. The chilly weather outside didn't help either.

I sat in the kitchen with my father, it was already the afternoon. I find myself guilty at the time I've lost on my day off from the library. Mr. Abbot insisted I take a break, I even took a few books with me that I had been wanting to read. When I had woken up today though, I found the pages bland, and words looked like unintelligible scribbles upon those pages. I couldn't read. Well, I am capable- I just... Didn't have the focus to read like I wanted to. Papa had yet to look up from his paper, I sat holding a book that I had yet to lift up to read. Too busy overthinking.

Did she finally decide to listen and take care of herself by resting?

Or did she perhaps get worse?

Maybe I shouldn't have been so harsh last time I saw her...

"Papa? Can I ask you something?"

"Hm? Something the matter, Audrey?"

"It's just-" I stop.

No. I shouldn't bother him about my worries. He has enough to worry about trying to find work.

I quickly look over the paper he is reading.

"What do you think of the rumors involving the Dragonkin?" I begin awkwardly, "Do you really think they could be within Flaize districts?"

Papa sighs, "You and I both are worried about that then. The thing is... it's almost impossible to tell just by looking. Since hey can shift into a human form, unless we see them shift there is no way to find out." He puts his paper down. "I've only seen one in my life. When I used to be an officer of the borders before we started using magic for that job."

I frown. "You never told me you saw anything at the border."

"Well," He sighs, "I didn't want to scare you while you were so young."

"You'll tell me now though, right?"

"Yes, yes..." He puts his elbow on the table and leans forward as he begins to speak.

"It wasn't close, actually, I saw it from a great distance, thank goodness. I saw a small figure out on the hills past the woods that border our district. At first, I thought some young man was dared to go out there - I almost yelled out to it. It stood there for a long time before it just- it grew. It was almost the size of the hill as it extended its wings. It headed deeper into Dragnior, so I kept on patrolling... but just seeing the immense size of it was enough to kill any curiosity I had of crossing over. Not your mother though, she-"

He pauses for a moment and leans back in his seat.

"She what?"

It takes a long moment before father finally continues."This was- long before she began to fall ill. She wanted to come with me the next day to see for herself. Saying she didn't believe it was the size of the hillside. I never let her, of course, but I still thought it was humorous. Watching her eagerness at it all."

The two sit there in silence for a moment, reminiscing. Before her father stands up.

"I'm going to go check on your mother, since you're free today to pick up your brothers from school." With that he hobbles down the hall, leaving Audrey in the small kitchen by herself.

I sigh. There went any chance of reading. *Yes, I had not been reading but still* - I wish I had more choices in my free-time. That I'd have more motivation to do the things I wanted to do besides working for the family. I shake my head at my father's attitude. I always found myself wondering how I was so different from him. His way of thinking, his morals and emotions, even with looks. I did not feel like his daughter anymore.

What made us change so much?

I'd better get started on making my way over there then.

I stand from my seat at the table, pushing my own chair and father's chair in before heading to the door. Grabbing a long brown coat, I throw it on before opening the door and heading out into the cold.

Papa is always avoiding prolonged conversations.

Is he afraid? Does he think I will bring up the night I broke off the engagement?

The night that I had finally spoken against Mr. Wingrave was fuzzy. I don't recall how long it had taken me to get home, all I knew was that it had been dark when I reached the door. In the dim lighting from the street lamps,
a lush flower garden could be seen surrounding the entryway, Audrey carefully
stepped down the pathway to the door. It was late, later than it should have been when anyone would be getting home.

It is because of this that Audrey opened the door quietly. Slipping in without much of a sound. She leaned back against the door for a moment, taking that moment to breathe at last when she heard two hushed voices from the hall.

It's Mum... and... Papa?

Quietly, she shuffled across the room to the edge of the doorway that led to the hall, she stopped.

"Have they gotten back yet?" Mum said.
Audrey heard a gruff voice respond, it was her father. "No, and I hope they take their time."

"Honey, don't be so hard on yourself- another job will come."

He didn't get the job?

Father sighed as he leaned against the wall, her mother continued speaking. "We're lucky that Audrey caught that young man's attention, working in the upper class sector has its benefits."

"You're right," Her father chuckled, "I was surprised when he came here asking for her hand in marriage."

I felt my heart sink with every word, I slid down the wall and sat on the floor.

Any good feeling from moments ago was now gone.

"When they are married, Audrey's title will be better, and the money will be better for all of us." Her mother heaved as she spoke, sounding short on breath. "We can afford to keep sending the boy's to school without Audrey having to work to pay for it-"

She broke off from her sentence, into a terrible fit of coughing.

"Amelia? Darling?!"

Suddenly, the sound of glass shattering filled the hall. Audrey hurried to push to her feet and looked around the corner to find her father on his knees by her mother. A vase was broken beside her as a table was knocked down.

Papa looked up at Audrey, he knew she had heard and now she knew what they had been expecting of her, of the money she - no, they would get from her fiance.

A proper conversation would never happen to discuss what had happened that night.

I don't know whether it was- is better that way or not.

Mother had fallen ill, father had no work, and the boys were asleep, ready to go to school that next day. An education that could no longer be afforded without me continuing to work to pay for it.

I try to tell myself that this was out of my control, I couldn't have known she was hiding her illness from us. I didn't know that papa wouldn't get the job. I didn't know how badly we had needed that money.

I broke off the engagement, and broke off our one chance of getting the funds we needed to thrive.

Now, we would have to survive.

Looking back, I still don't know what to think, how different would my life be now if I had accepted Mr. Wingrave, flaws and all.

How much better would all of our lives have been?

The school was pretty far, it was the opposite way of her work and was closer to the town border than most places that she would visit. It also was like navigating a maze of streets to get to.

If it weren't so close to the border and was a little closer to home, I would trust that Fletcher and Remy could get home alright.

But it wasn't.

Still, out of the three schools in the district though, this was the most affordable one.

Audrey herself was not able to attend school for very long, once her brothers were born she had to stop attending just so that they had money to eat. She didn't want the same for them. So she had begun working at the library when she turned fifteen. Seven, and almost eight years ago now.

As I go down the many twists and turns of the various streets of the district, I reach the point of the town that was smaller and had more buildings with spaces from one another. It was the end of the more... city-like part of the district and made way for the more rural farming section. Tall buildings became smaller cottages to shacks and sheds alike. Nicer farms could be found at the borders with the other districts, but the border with Dragnior was a different story. Small plots for farming and gardens took up much space between houses, and roads gave way to dirt paths. The gardens didn't look as though they were doing too well, but considering the earlier cold front it was no big mystery as to why.

I round one last corner where the dirt roads open up to a big patio like area. The old patrolman building comes into sight. It was once where her father worked, but it has since become a school building.

Since the magic barriers were put up, shortly before her youngest brother was born, papa lost his job. No matter how much I wished they kept jobs open for the patrol officers, the district leaders saw no point in it. The magic barrier was a cheaper option then paying working men and women all year long. If the jobs had been kept open, perhaps my life would be very different. Magic barriers were nothing relatively new, though most districts did not use them until more recently at the decisions of the ruling houses of each district. I've never seen anything outside of Yonnam, so I wasn't sure how many other districts used that or if they still had patrolling officers or not.

As I walk to the school building, I notice that the front doors are already wide open. The only person around was the youngest lady teacher, who usually dismisses the children once their parents arrive. Her name was Ms. Padwell. I couldn't help but feel envious of her. She was a little younger than me, hardly twenty years old, but because she didn't have brothers to take care of or a father that didn't work, she could afford to work at the school for little pay.

The teacher spots me, and immediately looks confused. Which was the first bad sign.

I hurry over to her, feeling a little out of breath from the long and hurried walk.

"Did all of the children already leave?"

"Yes, your brothers told me that they had permission to leave without a pickup- they even brought this note-" Ms. Padwell pulls a note out of her pocket. I grab it, a little aggressively. It had her fathers signature on it.

Fletcher! I should never have taught him that...

When her father had been applying for jobs at a more frequent rate than he did now, he had Audrey help with applications by signing his name on applications, or on any bills they received. It was a lot of work for her at the time, so she also decided to teach Fletcher so she had more help.

I look up at Ms. Padwell, she has a concerned look on her face. I almost felt guilty for my feelings of envy moments ago. She was a good woman, and a hard worker. *She is just... luckier than I am.*

I shouldn't worry her about this, she has enough on her plate as it is.

"Ah yes, I forgot about that." I lie, "I'm sure they're home already. Thank you Ms. Padwell."

Ms. Padwell didn't look fully convinced, "Are you sure?"

I nod, "Yes, I'll just be going home now so I'll probably catch them on the way back."

"Also, not to push but..." Ms. Padwell pauses, as though searching for the right words. "When can we expect payment for this semester of the boy's schooling?"

I furrow my brows, "Did my father not bring it to you this morning?"

She shakes her head, and I grit my teeth.

That explains the bottles by mum's bed, and why he didn't want to pick up the boy's himself today.

Despite this, I smile, "I must have accidentally forgotten to give it to him, I'll have it to you soon enough." I begin to turn to leave, as I do she calls out, making me stop.

"Please give my offer further thought Audrey - You would make an excellent teaching assistant. I know the pay isn't good - but please keep it in consideration."

I nod and quickly turn and hurry back down the road. Afraid that if I stayed another

moment I would accept. I don't have the time to work here, I would learn a lot and it would be a dream - But it wouldn't be enough money. Either way, I don't have the time to dream. I would have to put that on hold. Perhaps one day
I would have the time, but right now, I have to find my brothers.

The sun was setting as Audrey still searched the streets for her brothers. After going home multiple times and not finding the shoes by the door, she took to the streets to find them. Continuously checking around the school, the center of town, even going all the way to her work to see if they had gone there. Fletcher and Remy were nowhere to be found.

Why would they fake a note?!

Did they plan to go somewhere?

I knew that the pair would never try to run away - Fletcher maybe for fun, but he wouldn't drag Remy into it.

So where could they be?!

I feel myself wearing down as I continuously walk up and down the cobblestone streets. My shoes, which are a size too small, were starting to wear on my feet from all of this walking.

They're nowhere!

I stop just a few streets away from the school. It is poorly lit as most lamp posts don't even work at this end of town.

There are also candle posts, but none seem to be lit.

It's getting dark, why hasn't anyone lit the candles yet?

I find myself beginning to call into question my own sense of direction as I spin and look at my surroundings.

Maybe I'm lost too.

Being there were very few places I actually went, it felt rather odd to go down all of the different streets I barely would go to. I shouldn't be too surprised that I could get lost, that's what I tell myself, anyways, it still felt foolish though.

I slowly walk to the nearest bench, feeling pain in my feet with every step. As I sit down I rest my fingers upon my temple as I think.

I glance around and realize that just a street over is the path to the school, I am already back here again.

I sigh.

How do I go home and explain this to papa -

That's when I finally hear a familiar voice.

"I think it's somewhere in this direction..." One voice says loudly.

Another quieter one can be heard moments later, “Fletcher, I’m pretty sure this is the street to school.”

Audrey jumps off of the bench. The voices were close. I turn to see two small figures appear from around the corner.

“Fletcher? Remy?!” Audrey hurries over to them, the two immediately brighten up when they see her.

“Auddie!”

I grab the two of them and pull them into a hug, leaning back I frown.

“Why in the world did you two think you could walk home- alone when you still don’t remember the path? Did you even think of what might happen being so close to the border -”

“I’m assuming you are their mother then?” A sharp voice comes from behind the two boys.

I look up, startled to see a young man standing there. I quickly stand up from hugging the boys, my shoulders tense and I try to force myself to relax.

How did I not notice him?

She quite obviously is dumbfounded as she looks the man over. Who is he? He didn’t look like anyone she had seen in town before. With amber upturned eyes, long red hair, deep sienna skin, and strange casual suit style he looks different than the typical man in the working class of the district. Though he didn't look upper class either.

"I'm their older sister actually," I correct after a moment of silence.

His face turns red, "Pardon me, I just assumed... Well, wrong."

"Were you with them?" I ask, trying to change the subject quickly.

Do I look old enough to be a mother?

Fletcher speaks up quickly, "He was trying to help us get home safe, but we all got lost- but only by a little bit!"

I look at the man, *they trusted a complete stranger to help them home?!*

We need to talk about this later but...

They're lucky he wasn't dangerous.

Thank God.

I cautiously dip my head to the stranger, "Thank you for keeping an eye on them."

The stranger flashes their teeth in a smile, it was both warm and off putting to me. I couldn't tell if my anxiousness came from my dislike of others, or if there is something off about this man. Either way, I found him unsettling.

"Of course. Do you mind if I walk with all of you home?"

"Are you sure- We're not keeping you from anything are we?"

I want to tell him to go away, we've been fine on our own. I've been fine on my own, but that would be too rude even for me.

"Considering all that's going on near the border at the moment, I'd feel better seeing you all get home safe before dark." He chuckles, as though he just told a little joke. Was he trying to make light of a dark situation?

"Ok, I'll lead the way then -"

As I start to walk, Remy nudges me. I cast a quick glance at him.

He mouths at her 'introduce yourself!' Making Audrey suddenly self conscious. Well, *more* self conscious is the better way to put it. I was thankful Fletcher didn't notice, he lacked tact about these types of things, much like I did at his age. Remy though, was very mature for his age, but I would never say that aloud, as I didn't want him to feel the need to grow up any faster.

"Oh, pardon me for not introducing myself-" I start awkwardly as they begin to head down the street, passing the men lighting the lanterns for the night. I try not to be annoyed with how late they are.

"My name is Audrey Hughes, and I'm sure Fletcher and Remy already introduced themselves," I look at the two boys. Remy nods, while Fletcher is clearly lost in his own little world.

"I'm Dominique Pascal, pleasure to meet you."

I shiver, there was something odd about his voice. It was almost too pleasant and silvery. It was different from those I had met within the district before.

You don't talk to many people though, I remind myself.

Even though she wants to stay silent, Audrey can't help but feel curious. Moments pass before she speaks up.

"You don't seem like you're from Yonnam." I begin, silently praying that I was not overstepping my boundaries in this conversation. "Did you recently move here from another district or...?"

What if he's one of those magic elixir peddlers?

"You could say that... I'm here with my family right now. I don't know if I'm going to stay here or just visit right now."

He furrows his brows. "This may sound odd but, I believe I saw you at the local library the other day. Do you work there?"

"Er, yes I do." Am I going to have to see him at work now?

At least Mr. Abbot would be there...

"Will you be going there often?" I begin picking at the hem of my coat. Suddenly acutely aware of my brothers snickering as they watch me fumble with my words.

That's right... This looks like I'm embarrassed or flustered to them.

They're too innocent to know how many ways this situation could turn wrong.

"I actually do." He glances over at her, "Perhaps you'll be seeing more of me."

It is at this moment that their father comes into sight. He was standing just outside the house waiting for them.

He looks anxious.

It was the first time in a while Audrey had seen him anywhere but inside the house at the table. I feel relieved at the distraction from the conversation, until I see the look on papa's face.

"It's getting late, what took you so long getting back?" He asks sternly, remaining calm enough. I know that his calmness is not from his own personality, but because he recognized a stranger was accompanying them.

If Dominique were not here, I knew the tone of this conversation would be far different. For the first time, I was grateful for this strange man's presence.

Here it comes. I think as I quickly try to summon the courage to answer.

As I open my mouth to answer, I hear a voice other than my own. Dominique steps forward.

"Pardon me, but I'm visiting family here and it seems Ms. Hughes and I lost track of time when we struck up a conversation."

She raises a brow at him, but says nothing.

Why is he helping?

When papa turns to me, I quickly smile and nod. I know how much worse it would be if I argued.

He breathes a relieved sigh, "I was worried something had happened. Is that all it was?" Father asks, looking at the boys. The two quickly nod, knowing that any other story would have meant trouble for them. Fletcher especially. I notice him holding his hand in his pocket. He probably still had a piece of dad's signature to copy.

Before father can say anything else, Dominique is backing away.

"Well, I'd best be hurrying home myself. I wish you all a good night."

With that he glances at Audrey one last time and smiles before he backs off and vanishes down another street. Gone from their sight.

"It's good to see you mingling with people your age. You should start focusing on making friends more, Auddie." He laughs heartily, I feel my gut twist at this comment, but I purse my lips together. I could see that papa was exhausted by the way he swayed from where he stood. So I begin to motion for the boys to hurry inside, pap continues speaking as they reach the door.

"Perhaps we will even see another engagement ring soon-"

I feel the exhaustion getting to me, and I can't keep quiet.

"My priorities are my work and taking care of the family." I snap. Immediately I feel dizzy.

I shouldn't have said that aloud, I bite my tongue, I should have kept my mouth shut.

"Audrey!"

"I am tired, I have to sleep so I can go to work in the morning."

Before he can say anything else, Audrey opens the door and ushers her brothers inside without another word.

I leave my shoes and coat by the door, and follow my brothers to their room. I shut the door quickly and turn to glare at the two of them, crouching down to their level.

"One of you better explain why your teacher handed me a note of excuse from having me walk you home."

Fletcher and Remy glance at each other.

"It was Remy's idea-"

"-Fletcher wrote it!"

I sigh, "I know Fletcher wrote it, but you went along with it." I wiggles my pointed finger at Remy. "I want to know why. Were you going to run off? Go mess with Mrs. Finkle's cat again? Well?!"

The two look down, before Remy finally speaks up.

"I knew today was your day off from work- I didn't want you to have to waste time coming for us since you already are doing so much."

Oh no.

I sit back, looking at Fletcher.

"Is that really why?"

He nods slowly.

"That's... Surprisingly, considerate of you. Both of you. But just think, what if that man earlier wasn't as kind as you two were being? Or what if the rumors of the dragonkin appearing were true? Do you know how worried I was when you weren't there?"

The two remain silent.

"We're all lucky that man didn't mention anything to papa," I pull them into a tight hug. "I understand you were trying to be helpful, but don't be doing that again, ok? It's ok to need me sometimes, you shouldn't have to grow up fast yet, alright?"

"Sorry Auddie."

I sit up, suddenly the weight of the day bearing down felt like too much as drowsiness began to creep in more.

"Alright, you two need to get to bed now, it's getting late."

"What about supper?" Fletcher asks.

"I - Didn't have time to make any since I was looking for you."

I can't let them go to sleep with empty stomachs...

"Go get some bread from the cabinet, I know I don't normally let you have it by itself- but considering today's events, it is fine. Go ahead."

The two rush by her, opening the door and heading into the kitchen. I stand up and walk across the hall to the storage closet, well, my bedroom.

It was a small space, being it used to be the pantry. It only had enough room for my narrow bed and a small chair used as a nightstand. Grabbing a match, I light the candle by the bedside before shutting the door. I sit on the bed and watch the flame flicker. I didn't want to think about the engagement again.

I know papa hates me for calling it off -

With a sigh I lay out on the bed, too tired to change.

What a lousy way to spend a day off.

Thank God for that man and his quick thinking, otherwise I would still be out there getting lectured for teaching Fletcher how to forge a signature.

Still, there was something odd about Dominique. Where was he from? He seemed very different from most people I've known.

How did I not notice him at the library? I've never heard that name in town either-

Who is he related to?

Pascal... How odd.

Farah might recognize the name.

I feel a pang in my gut as I realize how long it had been since I thought about her. Dominique was now lost in Audrey's mind as she fell asleep praying she would hear news on Farah's state in the morning at the library.

3
LONG OVERDUE

"...As Magic being used for more everyday purposes becomes more popular, there has been a rise in the prices of magic services since right now so few actually have mastered it and are licensed for its usage. Though many still pay for more 'dangerous' cheaper options..."
-Flaize Magic Academy Paper, Author Unknown

Weeks had passed since I had seen Farah at the library... Or at all to be completely honest. The trees were no longer the light yellow and greens as autumn was beginning, rather dull orange and bloody reds filled the streets as the leaves began to fall. I've never liked the season, well that is a lie. I did like the general feel of autumn. It just didn't last long, in the next month or two we would be experiencing a cold front.

I found myself worrying more, even at work. Mr.Abbot noticed, or at least I think he had. The library also noticed, as the organization was rather lacking in the past few days. Well, more so than the usual amount.

Mr. Abbot has stopped working and watches as Audrey struggles to work, his forehead creased as he furrows his brows.

"Is everything alright, Audrey?"

"Why wouldn't I be?" I reply after a moment, quickly trying to look busy.

"It's just," He begins slowly. "You've seemed on edge since the Dowager Farah's last visit. Are you worried?"

"Huh?" I pause and glance over at him for a moment, taking a second to process what he had just said. "Oh, yes. Do you think everything is alright? With Lady Davies, I mean?"

Mr. Abbot sighs, "I honestly don't know. I sure hope she is." He looks around them. "Without her, this library would have gone under long ago."

Audrey leans against the shelf. He is right. She has been our primary visitor, resource, and company for quite a while.

"Is there any way I can try to see her?" I say unknowingly aloud, looking over the books I had yet to shelf.

"See her? Like visit?" Mr. Abbot widens his eyes. "I haven't heard of anyone of our class entering the Abbey gate unless they worked there as servants."

I sigh, but stay silent as he continues to speak.

"No, I would wait a while longer. If she still doesn't visit again and we don't hear anything bad on the paper, then we'll think of something. Alright?" I nod, but say nothing as I am already lost in thought again.

Could it be that she got worse? What if-

What if she has what mum has?

I feel my stomach turn at the mere thought. I knew Farah had been doing worse the last few times I had seen her, but I never really considered the worst case- That it was the mystery sickness that came from nowhere.

If that's the case-

There must be something I can do for her.

"Ms. Hughes?"

"Yes?"

"You won't try anything dangerous, right?" Mr. Abbot said. "You're a hard worker, and a good young lady, I would be sad if anything had happened to you because of the abbey's doing."

"I won't, Mr. Abbot. You don't need to worry."

I did know Mr. Abbot was trying to help me calm down, but that didn't mean I had to agree with his answer.

I'll have to find a solution on my own, I decided that as I finished work that day. The library was in tip top shape with her newfound motivation that day.

I left work that day with a goal. The cold autumn air didn't even bother me without my coat, which I had forgotten at home. As I walk down the road. I stop at the abbey gates, looking through the ornate metal bars. Farah was there.

Within those walls somewhere. I need to be able to do something for her. There *must* be something I can do for her.

I can prepare a basket for her- something so she knows she is missed. I am sure she is waiting for the next book in that series she was reading- and some tea would help.

I turn away from the gate, hobbling down the street. It's been a while since my brothers got lost that day after school, but I still feel as though I haven't recovered.

For some reason, I'm not bouncing back as fast as I usually do.

I sigh, pausing in front of the general store. This will cost a pretty amount as well, but I do have some money to spend after skipping a few meals – not to mention the night I couldn't make supper.

It has been a while since I've prepared a gift for Farah, or anyone. I really haven't had the time.

I make my way into the store and the owner, a hefty older gentleman greets me promptly. I give him a little way before turning to look through the shelves. I'm comfortable around Farah and Mr. Abbot, but that's the extent of my extroversion.

I breathe out, relieved to be out of the shopkeeper's sight, but looking up, I notice a familiar face.

"This is a surprise," comes a silvery voice. "Hello again, Ms. Hughes."

I realize only too late that I had stepped in front of the stranger from the other day. I spun around to see Dominique Pascal with an amused expression on his face.

I feel my face flush as I quickly step away, putting some distance between the two of us.

"Sorry, I didn't see you there." She replies in a plain tone. It wasn't extremely obvious when she was embarrassed or awkward, as she generally was not super expressive or reactive to things, but even a rock could tell she was flustered by this encounter.

I was slightly surprised I didn't notice him, he stood out. With long fiery red hair, warm espresso toned skin, and thick brows raised as he looks amused by the situation. He was like a daisy in a field of tulips, he just stood out. His style was unlike the casual wear in Yonnam, wearing more of an industrial style of a vest with a collared button down, while most men in Yonnam wore overalls, trousers, or plain shirts - basically more practical work wear. Or at least, most men in Audrey's class dressed like that. It's that in spite of this he still manages to sneak up on her.

"It's pleasant to see you again, it's nice seeing a somewhat familiar face every now and then."

"Oh - How has your visit with your family been?"

"It's been... interesting, to say the least."

"Are you not enjoying your time in Yonnam?" I ask, wondering if perhaps he might explain why he was here and bothering me. I scan the shelves behind him as I wait for an answer, looking for something.

"It's hard to say - You know how checking up on people can be." He lets out a tired sigh. Before Audrey can say anything else, he smiles and side steps as he notices where my gaze had gone, "Running errands today?"

I slowly nod as I grab something off of the shelf, "I just got off of work and thought I'd grab some things on the way home." I grab a few more things, a tin of tea bags, a jar of honey, and a loaf of bread.

"Lovely, well I am sure you're eager to get home."

Good, now he will get back to his own life and me back to mine.

I assume he means to leave me be now, so I walk to the counter and set everything out for the shopkeeper, but Dominique follows. I glance over my shoulder to see what he was buying, but don't see him holding anything. I'm not given much time to think on it though.

When the man says the price, I feel my stomach drop. Did I hear him wrong?

Since when was it this expensive?

"But that's more than it was last week-"

"I'm sorry ma'am, but with the way the shop is running I need to raise my prices to stay open-"

"I'll pay for it." Dominique interrupts the shopkeep, he raises a brow at this, glancing back and forth between him and Audrey.

I quickly shake my head, "You don't have to do that."

"You're right, I want to." He says with a warm smile, he drops a few coins on the counter. The shopkeep takes them and nods, Audrey frowns at him and quickly puts the things into her bag before the pair leave the store. *Wonderful, now I owe him.*

Dominique steps down the stairs first and offers a hand for Audrey to carefully step down as well. I hesitantly take it and stop beside him.

"I can pay you back-"

"Don't worry about it," He says. I watch his expression for a moment. *Is he going to say I owe him dinner or something else now?*

But He says nothing else about the payment.

"Well, I won't keep you, as I am sure you are tired," He dips his head, "I'll be seeing you around, Ms. Hughes."

"Goodbye Mr. Pascal," I reply slowly, still processing what just happened.

I turn to walk away, but as I turn away I hear him call out.

"You can call me Dominique."

4
LOOSE PAGES

"...Are there variations within the Dragonkin race? Many reports and descriptions have been taken of Dragonkin, but no two sound the same. Some are described to have two to four legs, some with none at all. The only consistency in the description is its size. Could this be drawn up to be exaggerations due to fear, or do the Dragonkin have variations within their society..."
-A History in Magic: Creatures of Magic

The next few days I found myself feeling slightly less anxious. I had left the basket I had put together for Farah along with books and the things from the market at the servants gate to the abbey, where I had often seen the servants collecting mail from the delivery man. Even without a response from her, I felt a little more at ease as I did more than sit aside and wait for her. I even found myself humming along with Mr. Abbot as we worked at the front of the library, we almost had it back to pique condition with very few books left on the floor that needed to be shelved. Soon, I might even have time to straighten the shelves better.

Perhaps one day soon, I'll bring the boys up here.

Once they're on break from school, I'm sure they would enjoy a few of the books donated.

As I begin to work my way further back into the library, I hear a bell ring as the door opens. I didn't think much of it at the time, and ignored it as I kept working.

"Oh - I - Good Afternoon Madam! How may I help you today?"

Mr. Abbot speaking so formally?

I wonder who that could be.

Audrey continues shelving, continuing to listen to the exchange between the stranger and the library owner.

"I'm here to see a girl who works here, Annie?"

"Oh you must mean Ms. Hughes, and..." He pauses for a moment, hesitating to correct her. "Her name is Audrey."

The stranger merely huffs in response,

I can hear the clicking of her toe tapping on the floor.

Slowly, I peek around the edge of the shelf to see who was asking about me when I see her.

A very well dressed woman stood by the counter, with a man dressed in servants attire standing by the door. She wore a cream form fitting dress that was loose at the bottom and lay out on the floor around her heels, the coat with it had a large collar flipped out in an elegant manner, and the jewelry... She wore more expensive clothing than anything I had seen in my lifetime. It was even more extravagant than the things I had seen Farah in when she would visit.

She looks upper class -

Did Farah send her for me?

Without fully thinking, I step out.

"Hello, I'm Audrey."

When the woman's gaze turns on me, I feel a chill down my spine.

Her beauty was stunning, and almost scary.

Her round amber eyes narrow as she looks Audrey over, she flips her long wavy platinum hair over her shoulder, her eyebrows look too perfect, and her merlot colored lips are pursed.

"So you're Audrey, hm?" She looks her over with a hand on her hip, she doesn't seem pleased.

"Did Farah send you?" I ask hopefully.

"Farah? You mean the Dowager Farah Davies?" She raises a brow at my informal speaking.

I curse at myself silently before

continuing. "Only, it's been a while since she last visited. She comes so regularly so

I wanted to know if everything was... alright?"

The lady pauses, as though thinking over whether or not she wanted to answer her, before finally responding. "Lady Davies is at the Abbey resting. She will not be back for some time."

Resting -

What a relief!

That means she finally took my advice.

Audrey smiles and dips her head, "I hope she is well soon."

The lady continues to glance around, not saying anything else, leaving Audrey and Mr. Abbot to watch and wait.

A good few minutes pass before she turns to Audrey, "I'm looking for a rather specific book, though I cannot recall the title of it at the moment, could you show me around and help me find it?"

The woman steps towards me, waving off her servant as he begins to follow. He stands by the door waiting, not looking at anything in particular as the woman stops by me.

"Of course, I just need to know-"

Before I can even finish speaking the woman struts past me and further into the library. I glance at Mr. Abbot before hurrying after the woman.

"Who organizes this place?" She asks, turning to face me. I quickly stop so as not to run into her, taking a few steps back.

"I do, along with Mr. Abbot occasionally." I answer simply. I look at the shelves and begin motioning towards a few. "I don't know what type of book you're looking for but here we have our informative nonfiction, our practical guides and such. Next to it we have biographies and history books and -"

"Mhmm," The woman absentmindedly hums, "And what made you start working here? The location?"

I furrow my brows, "Well, the other library shut down long ago so this was the only place I could work and still be surrounded by books."

"Really? It isn't because this is the higher end of the city?" Before Audrey can respond she continues, "So you work here to gain knowledge as well as funding?"

I look at her for a moment before I nod, "That's... Not how I would put it but yes."

The woman frowns, but says nothing else as she walks away to another bookshelf. I hurry after her, dodging around a few books left on the floor next to fully stocked shelves.

"You asked me about Dowager Farah earlier, how do you know her?"

I stop by the woman who is standing in front of the last shelf in the hall, she faces the books but watches me out of the corner of her eyes.

"She visits the library often, so we speak when she comes by." I answer simply. As Audrey continues explaining the woman is merely watching her, eyes focused on every movement like a predator with prey. After a few more minutes of Audrey explaining the variety of shelves, she turns to face the strange woman.

"Did you have any ideas on where you might find this book?" I ask, noticing her striking eyes were still focused on me.

Did she hear any of that?

The woman shakes her head, "I don't think you have what I need."

She is asking a lot of questions... Did she even have a book in mind?

Or perhaps she didn't really care for my help? As though she could read my mind the woman grabs a book off of the shelf.

"This wasn't what I was looking for, but I believe I will check this out for some time."

The book cover had a butterfly on it, *"How to Pin and Mount Butterflies and moths."*

Interesting choice.

I reach out for it, "I can take it to the front for you..." The woman was already walking away, I have to hurry to follow her to the front where Mr. Abbot sat twiddling his thumbs waiting. She drops the book on the counter, "I'll be checking this book out."

While Mr. Abbot hurriedly grabs the book and begins to pull out the checkout card and she looks back at me.

"Audrey, yes?"

I nod, it was hard to meet her intense gaze and I felt the urge to look anywhere else.

"Hmm." She says nothing else as she checks out the book, only turning to her servant.

"Smith, it's time for us to leave this place." The servant doesn't say a word or even look up from the floor as he opens the door and steps aside as the woman storms out. When the door shuts, Mr. Abbot looks at Audrey.

"What exactly just happened?"

I furrow a brow, "You don't think Farah sent her?" When Mr. Abbot doesn't reply, I continue. "Now we know why we haven't seen her."

"I don't think that anyone on the board would come to simply say someone is ill... Not with the way she was eyeing you."

"What else could it be?"

He shrugs, "I don't know. Just be cautious for a while will you? For my sake at least?"

"Alright, I'll be cautious Mr. Abbot."

I go back to shelving the stack of books I had left behind, glancing over the titles then taking them to the correct general area that they would belong.

That was a little odd, but is it surprising?

She is upper class. The upper class really don't interact with us anymore.

I shrug, and try to focus on the books in front of me again.

But what if Mr. Abbot is right? Was there something off about her coming here? Should I have stepped out and introduced myself? Or should I have remained behind the shelves out of her cold gaze?

5
THE DELIVERY

"...There is no life without death, there is no death without life. It takes a long time to live, but no time to die. Do not mourn for those lost who lived after a time, for they are the lucky ones, and us, their witnesses..."
-The Poem's of the Kings Death

Any sense of calmness that I had felt before, however slight, was gone. It had been a week since the lady from the abbey had visited and still there was no word from Farah. I try to stay positive in front of Mr. Abbot at work, knowing that he was worried that I would try something crazy.

Though I couldn't stop worrying.

The hope I had when I left that basket was overshadowed by overthinking and stress.

I watch as my brothers play in the small park near the edge of town. Since nobody was really around other than a few of the same class passing by, it was calm enough for us to be here. It was getting chilly out, but despite that the warm sun rays through the park's golden colored trees made it bearable.

Watching them run around as they play with each other, I can't help but feel a little envious about how carefree they are. I wish I could still feel like that.

Maybe I should take that teaching job... I could work at the library in the evenings afterwards so I still make enough...

If I do that maybe one day I can-

"Ms. Hughes?"

I look over to see someone coming towards me. It was Dominique, again. His long hair was tied up today, and the shirt he wore a button up shirt had its sleeves rolled up, he also wore a vest with slacks, and his upturned eyes flash as they focus on her.

She stands up, clearly startled as she is pulled out of her thoughts.

"Dom - Mr. Pascal! Hello."

He did say I could call him Dominique but- If I get comfortable saying that and Fletcher hears- I'd never hear the end of it. I don't want him taking that back to papa.

He smiles as he stops next to me, "You can just call me Dominique, I really don't mind." He glances over at Fletcher and Remy. "Are you in charge of your brothers again today?"

I nod, "They behave themselves pretty well, but being close to the border and all... I prefer to be cautious."

"People are far less nervous in the other districts than they are here. Most people here stay inside more because of it." He sits and motions for me to sit beside him. I hesitate for a moment, glancing at the closeness of the two spots. I glance across the park at Fletcher and Remy.

They had better not cause me trouble for this...

I sit next to him carefully, ensuring there is still a slight bit of room between us on the small bench.

He's been friendly enough but...

Something still feels odd about him, familiar almost though still he is an absolute stranger...

It's only because he is from out of district, I tell myself. *It's nothing more.*

You're probably still on edge about Farah too.

I miss her - I wish I could tell her about Mr. Pascal and ask for her advice.

"Is there a reason why nobody sees anyone who runs the district?" he asks.

"You mean the board?" I ask, surprised by the sudden question. "I mean- They are the *upper class*, they tend to stick to themselves."

Dominique furrows his brows. "Strange. In the districts I've visited, most other leading classes tend to mingle with their people through events and parties and such. It's so-different here."

"Doesn't sound like it's a good difference." I say. "So you said family brought you here?"

He nods, "I originally thought that I'd just be visiting but right now I'm not sure. I could be staying for longer than I thought."

When he doesn't say anymore, I hesitate on pressing the matter. Still, I wonder what *'family'* situation could bring him here if he's been to far better districts than ours.

The two continue to converse back and forth for a while. Mostly small talk, being Audrey tries to ask questions to figure him out while he tries to steer the conversation into something less quizzical. This goes on until suddenly Dominique pipes up.

"You looked down earlier, is something the matter?"

I glance at him, eyes wide, making him put his hands up quickly.

"Don't worry, you don't have to tell me. You just looked deep in thought when I spotted you, I thought it almost rude to not ask."

"Was it that obvious?"

He nods.

Normally Audrey would simply blow this off and answer with a simple 'I'm fine.' Yet with everything going on, having someone asking about her made her feel obliged to answer. That, and the absence of Farah. Vulnerability is a dangerous thing. And Audrey was too worn down to consider any outcomes of her not keeping to herself.

"I'm just... Worried about a lot. A few people close to me have fallen ill, including a close friend of mine, Farah. We still don't really know what it is for one, and the other is - too far away so I'm not updated on her condition."

I feel my stomach turn as I don't tell him the whole story. It almost felt like I was lying to him.

But why tell him the whole story?

What about him makes me feel compelled to speak?

I stand up and grab my bag from off the ground.

"Anyway, I am sorry if I was being a downer on your day," I continue before he can respond. "I must be going now though."

He stands as well, before he can say anything in response I already am calling my brothers over.

"Don't worry about it, I appreciate you being comfortable enough to talk to me. Not many are."

I pause, turning to him to ask him to explain what he had said, but before I can ask

Fletcher and Remy were already hurrying over. The time to speak was gone. It was my own fault really, for trying to rush out of the conversation.

That didn't mean it wasn't annoying.

"I hope we will meet again soon," He says dipping his head, "Goodbye, Ms. Hughes." He then turns away and leaves me alone with my two brothers who both look at me quizzically.

"Was that the man from the other day?" Remy asks softly.

Fletcher frowns, "What did he want now?"

They really are too suspicious of their fellow man, they're too young to be like this.

"We were just talking," I say, giving Fletcher a playful shove, making him giggle. "Don't worry about it."

Before they can begin to make fun of the situation I begin to lead the way down the street, making them follow.

"Why are we going back already?" Remy asks.

"I need to start making supper." I answer simply as I lead the way. As we pass by others the two immediately get quiet. It only takes a few minutes, but the second they arrive home and they boys get through the door they find their energy again. Which also meant noise.

They rush over to their father, who unsurprisingly is at his usual seat at the table in the kitchen. The two start going off about their time in the park, and while papa listens he extends his hand to Audrey - holding something to her.

I didn't notice until I had slipped my shoes and coat off, so I hurry over to take it and glance it over.

A letter for me?

While I had seen an abundance of papers, old letters, bills, and other such things from the mail, I never saw anything directed at me, not to mention the quality of it.

I flip it and read the front. My eyes go wide.

Papa hushes the boys quickly, waving them off with his hand.

"Audrey, what exactly is that?"

"It's a letter from Yonnam Abbey." I answer, I flip it and begin to open it to ind the envelope had already been opened. Her brothers look astounded at her, they begin to crowd around her to see it.

Papa sighs at them, "Fletcher, Remy, go to your room for a bit."

The two hurriedly rush down the hall and into the room, Remy peaks out for a moment before shutting the door.

"I tried to read it," Papa begins. "Though the writing... was too fancy to be eligible to me."

I don't say anything to that, but I am relieved at the privacy, no matter how I got it.

"Now tell me, why would someone in the abbey write to *you.*"

I glance over at him, his hands are shaking, an angry expression on his face.

He expected the worst... Not just from the abbey, but the worst from me as well. Does he think this is because of Mr. Wingrave?

Mr. Wingrave was loosely related to those of the abbey, but he lived in the upper class end of town outside of the abbey. He probably was able to come and go from the abbey though, but I didn't think about that much. Until now.

"I - I don't know." I stammer, "I mean... An older lady from them used to visit the library but-"

"Is it something bad?"

I can't help but snort in spite of my nervousness."I wouldn't know yet. I sure hope not."

"Well come on," He says, sounding increasingly annoyed with my patience.

"Let's see what it says."

I open the envelope up and carefully pull out a thick letter, I unfold it.

It was an extremely gorgeous letter, with fine calligraphy in cursive writing. The only thing that was off were the dirty fingerprints left from papa's earlier reading attempt.

Dear Ms. Hughes,

Recently, Lady Farah Davies has passed away due to old age. We had her funeral weeks ago. A will was found already filed with her lawyer, Mr. Greene, which places you as the sole beneficiary of everything she had. This includes her title, savings, place on the estate, and to her request, her place on the board. This also includes anything left in her rooms and spaces found within the estate. We have already been through all the procedures to see if this will was sound and could stand by law in court.

We expect you at the Abbey by the end of the week.

Signed,

Lord Julian Halloway

It didn't take me long to read the letter, it was the news that I had been waiting to hear. Though that wasn't all. I place the letter down in front of papa, who still stares at it, as though he can glean some information from it.

She's dead? But... She can't be. It says from old age, but it couldn't have been... If anything took her it was her illness but... Did they think I was unaware of it?

"Well? What was it for?"

I take in a shaky breath, trying to calm myself and keep my composure.

I glance over at papa, he seems anxious to know.

He doesn't need more on his plate with mum's condition and his own.

"Far - the Dowager Farah Davies was a friend of mine. She visited my workplace often and, well," I sigh. "She's leaving me everything, papa."

His eyes go wide, "Audrey that's excellent news! You finally have a chance to do something beyond the library!"

He jumps out of his seat and pulls me into a hug, but I don't hug him back. I didn't have it in me. He backs away. "Ever since your fiance - *ex* fiance...Er, Mr. Wingrave... Well, since that situation, I was worried nothing else would go right- but I was wrong! Finally something is going right in my life!"

His life?

"Isn't it?" I reply weakly.

Is it?

I don't deserve anything she had.

This was never something that was meant to happen.

I need to get away and think.

My father looks at me, with a confused look on his face as he waits for my response.

I smile through a clenched jaw, grinding my teeth.

"It is wonderful news, papa."

6
RECALL

"...With the recent death of one of the board members, Lady Farah Davies, being announced in the papers we begin to wonder who will take her place on the board. Someone else of the three families here or someone from another district being brought in..."
-Yonnam Gossip Papers, Author Unknown

Every second that passed was like a prick in my skin. Time slipping by was pushing me closer and closer to the end of the week.

To the deadline.

There is only one day before the set day that I would have to go to the abbey, but I wasn't going to. Instead, I tried to think of what my next action should be. I had spent less and less time at home, as every time I would be there so would papa.

He would bombard me with questions about the inheritance, but not so much for my sake- but for his own.

"How *much* will you receive?"

"Will we be able to move in with you?"

"You won't leave us behind, right?"

"Why don't you just go now?"

How do I tell him I don't want to accept it? That I'm not going to?

That I can't *accept it?*

I can't... Right?

Surely there was a mistake. Farah may have liked my company, but even she couldn't leave something so important to a lower class woman. Especially not me, I am not deserving of that title within the community. *Lady Audrey Hughes.* I could almost laugh at the thought.

Am I being selfish though?

What about mum?

Could this not help her?

And Fletcher and Remy, and even papa. This could be better for them- and even me.

I could afford higher education - No, it would be dishonorable to use her money for my own gain.

"Ms. Hughes?"

I stand up fast, I look around and realize I was still sitting in the window room of the library. Mr. Abbot is peeking through the doorway.

"Is everything alright?" He says as he slowly steps into the room. "Only, I recently heard about what happened to Lady Davies and... Wanted to check in with you."

I smile at him. *It's kind of him to check in.*

"I appreciate your thoughtfulness Mr. Abbot, but I'll be alright. So don't worry about me."

Despite my answer, Mr. Abbot walks into the room and sits beside me. I look at him, confused.

"Listen, I know you're not much one for friends. Farah was one of the few you called a friend, and I know she considered you one too." He lets out a deep breath.

"It's ok to mourn for her, you know. You have to let it all out eventually if you want to appear calm as you try to be."

I look at him, and shake my head. "I just don't want to cause more problems for my family."

"And you won't. I honestly think I can say you're the least problematic person I know. Trust me, I am an expert on problematic, my wife would - *could* have told you all about that." He shakes his head and chuckles, reliving past memories for a moment. He pats her on the back before standing up. "And don't forget, I'm here for you too if you need another friend. Alright?"

I feel as though I could cry,

I *should* cry.

I've been a burden on everyone.

But no tears came forth.

I. Feel. Empty.

"Thank you." Is the simple response I can give.

There is no emotion behind the words as I lose myself in my thoughts.

A jingle can be heard suddenly, the front door of the library had been opened.

"Now, rest here as long as you like. When you decide you want to get back to the old grind I'm sure I can find something for you to do." He chuckles at himself before heading out of the window room, leaving me to be by myself again.

Slowly, I get up and look through the window leading to inside a minute after he left. I can see Mr. Abbot hurrying to greet a guest.

It is Dominique, though at that time, I don't really process it.

Instead, I am lost in my thoughts.

Thinking about the inheritance, Mr. Abbot's words, Farah - only everything.

He's right. Farah was a good friend to me.

I don't know why she would leave everything to me but -

She did.

I sit back down and rest my head on the arm of the couch. I close my eyes and think about how often Farah would sit beside me and speak with me when I needed to take a breather from re-shelving books and organizing the library. *What made her believe it was worth leaving everything to me? Was she aware- did she know she was soon going to die?* I remember thinking about how often she dismissed my worrying about her sickness.

Did she know even then?

But still why?

Why me? The librarian who suggested books and sometimes spoke with her?

I still might not accept it but perhaps - I should still at least go and see what the others have to say about it. Maybe it was a mistake.

Or maybe she had a reason to put me in this position.

I stand up, treading across the old flooring and opening the door to go back into the library.

I don't have time to sit around and think all day.

I still need to work, I haven't accepted the inheritance yet, so I can't slack off. Not even a little.

I still might not accept it but perhaps - I should still at least go and see what the others have to say about it. Maybe it was a mistake.

Or maybe she had a reason to put me in this position.

I stand up, treading across the old flooring and opening the door to go back into the library.

I don't have time to sit around and think all day.

I still need to work, I haven't accepted the inheritance yet, so I can't slack off. Not even a little.

By the time I had left the library the sun was starting to set. Hopping down the front steps and onto the sidewalk, I have to stop myself from following the regular path home. Papa was probably in the kitchen at his regular spot at the table, waiting for me to cook supper and be calm about being bombarding with questions and guilt as to why I wasn't scurrying like a rat to this position that was dropped into my lap.

No matter how I tried to look at it, I couldn't think of an appealing reason to go home.

Fletcher and Remy will be fine for one night. I tell myself. They know what to do if something happens to me.

I stop at the gates of the Yonnam Abbey, staring inside.

The path leading to it was so long that the building itself wasn't visible with the many trees and gardens lining the road. As it got darker, it didn't help the visibility. It felt ominous to look at, despite how grand it must seem to others.

Most people in the town would live wondering what lies behind the gates.

Only I had the opportunity to actually go inside.

Perhaps I won't go...

I did cherish the time I had with Farah, she was a good friend. Despite our differences, I wouldn't trade the time I knew her for anything in the world.

But me? Going through the gates as one of the people who live in the abbey?

Who guides the district?

I don't belong there.

Do I belong where I am now though? In this cycle?

I'm not so sure anymore.

I turn away from the gate, not sure about the results of my choice, but the choice feeling definite in my heart and mind. I didn't know where I was going, but I began walking down the street when I heard loud footsteps coming towards me.

"Ms. Hughes!"

Dominique appears from the shadows by the abbey, stopping a few feet away he heaves as he leans over for a moment.

How long has he been running? I wonder as I look him over. He looks exhausted, but he smiles.

"We've been seeing a lot of each other recently," I say with a slight sigh, it's hard to sound happy today.

I almost feel exhausted as I watch him catch his breath and regain his composure.

"I've been looking for you -" He says as he holds a letter out to me. "- Got this letter I had to deliver, directly to your hands only."

Looking at it, I can't help but feel deja vu. It looks exactly like the letter of inheritance's envelope. I grab it, a little more aggressively than intended and glance at the top.

It's...

From Farah?!

How -

I look up at Dominique, he raises a brow at my expression, "*Where* did you get this!"

"I - Was helping... My family with the mail deliveries today. This was left behind and I found it earlier."

He puts his hands in his pockets and waits, like he was wanting to see me read it.

Mail? The family who dealt with mail in town did not have the last name Pascal?

Perhaps he is a distant relative? Or related by some other way.

Placing the letter into my apron, I look back at him. I didn't want to read its contents in the presence of others. *I have seen Dominique quite a bit, and he seems trustworthy... but still...*

It's something I better wait and face alone.

I try to push the letter to the back of my mind, but I feel keenly aware of the lightweight object in my pocket.

I look up at Mr. Pascal, *I was a little too aggressive wasn't I? Mr. Abbot was right.*

I'm not very open with making friends. *Wouldn't Farah want me to try?* Even though I didn't see a point in it from a logical point of view, I felt guilty thinking that.

I shouldn't waste time on friends.

"Would you like me to walk you home?" He asks.

"Ah, actually I'm going to - to the pub. Yes, there."

Hopefully that doesn't sound like I came up with that on the spot.

Dominique looks surprised. "Oh, do you

drink?" He asks.

I begin to lead the way down the road with Mr. Pascal at my side, I shake my head.

While Audrey was old enough to go to the pub like most her age did, she didn't have any interest in drinking. Seeing as it would burn through any of her earnings.

When the choices came to drinking or saving money for her brother's education, she knew which choice made more sense.

"I don't, and I'm not hungry... but it's the only place that can stay open to this hour anymore." When Dominique still looks confused, I continue. "I'm not ready to go home yet."

"Do you mind my accompanying you? Yours was the last letter I had to deliver today, so I'm not in a rush to go anywhere else tonight."

I nod, "I don't mind company." This was a lie, I usually minded having company. Though Dominique was somewhat a reminder of father's expectations, I didn't mind as much. Not as much as I would with any other strange man.

I know I need to be less closed off. This isn't the same as the situation with Mr. Wingrave, Dominique has been kind. I know papa would expect romance if I were to go out with a man, but right now that is the last thing on my mind. I just needed some company.

Though papa already likes him...

Why am I getting so worked up about this? It's not like this is a date, and you don't need to be talking to him.

But wouldn't Farah want you to try?

What do *I* want? I sigh quietly at that question. I didn't know the answer.

How about starting with some company?

Dominique raises a brow, but says nothing. It doesn't take much longer before the pair reach the pub. There were quite a few in town, but this was the only one open at this hour. It also was fairly busy. As we step inside, we are immediately met by the loud buzz and chatter of conversation and laughter from the many people in the bar. In spite of the town feeling fairly dead during the day, it didn't stop people from coming out for a drink in the evening.

A small booth to the side was the only clean table left open.

"Go ahead and sit without me, I'll be over in a moment." Dominique says, flashing his white teeth in a smile before he walks over to the bar. I watch him for a moment. He speaks to the bartender, it looks like he is asking a lot of questions as the bartender seems a little off put and only talks in short spurts.

I shrugged it off, maybe he didn't know much about this bar? Or he knew the bartender and was catching up? Either way, I sit down at the booth.

After a moment of fidgeting in her seat and wondering if she looked as tired as she felt, Audrey decides to get her mind off of it and reaches for the letter. She pulls it out of her apron pocket.

I guess now is as good a time as any to check it out.

If I leave it for later I'll lose my mind wondering about it.

Glancing over at Dominique again, he seemed like he was going to take a little while. Hands quivering, I pull the paper out of the envelope, unfolding the paper. I begin to read.

Dearest Audrey,

I write this as my intended will, with Mr. Greene as my witness. My will is the sole expression of my intentions concerning all my property, my title, and my place on the board and within Yonnam Abbey. Should anything I say in this letter conflict with, or seem to conflict with, any provision of my will, the will shall be followed.

I have requested that it is ensured that you will receive this letter should anything happen to me.

Audrey, the reason I have given you everything is because the fact stands that I have no children. My husband died many years ago, and I don't want anything left to the others of the board to find a replacement for me from somewhere else.

But please, if you find that any personal or family concerns mean that it makes sense to not accept — know that I wouldn't judge you. I understand I would be throwing a lot at you. If you're mourning my death, this is a lot to take in. Just know I leave it to you because I know you are strong, and that you can make a better difference in the world in this position, more so than working in the library. Remember I wish you all of the best, and I am eternally grateful for your friendship during my final years.

Signed,

Farah Davies.

I nearly hit the end of the letter when Dominique appears, two menus in hand. Audrey inhales her breath and sits up. She quickly puts the letter back into her pocket while he sits down.

"I wasn't sure if you were wanting food or drink so I brought this for you just in case-" When he sees the expression on my face he stops. "Is everything alright?"

I nod, quickly regaining my composure. At least, I thought I did.

Shaking hands and quivering lips didn't really seem composed, but it would have to do.

"Everything is alright, why do you ask?"

"Just making sure," he replies coolly. Dominique looks as though he didn't believe me, but he says nothing else on the subject as he pushes a menu across the table. "You sure you don't want to eat something? You look pale."

I shake my head at it and push it back to him. "I'll just get some water in a bit, thanks."

With that he takes the menus and pushes them off to the side, not looking at it for himself. Instead staring at me with concern apparent on his face.

I glance around the room as the noises get continuously louder.

It is then that Audrey spots a familiar face.

"Oh, there's our normal delivery man, Mr. Howard." I steal a glance at Dominique, who looks around the room as though he couldn't recognize who I was talking about.

Didn't he say he was with family delivering mail when he found that letter?

I've been so down and focused on myself - I know next to nothing about the man that sat across from me.

I take a deep breath before speaking, "So... I never asked, how are you related to the Howards?"

"Oh, he's just a cousin." He says simply. "I'll see him later tonight when we head home."

This was too much. Too overwhelming. First the letter, then Dominique somehow having it and not even recognizing people he claimed to be related to.

I don't trust him.

I need to get out of here.

The sounds in the room feel amplified in my ears as I slide to the edge of my seat, I feel myself growing extremely tired. Like I was experiencing an adrenaline dump after reading that letter.

Well, exhausted was the better way to put it. Like I hadn't slept in years.

I can't let that letter affect me so much -

I don't want Dominique to see me exhausted.

"I need to -" I break off from my question as I began coughing.

This is too much. Something is off with me, and then that letter...

I quickly glance around until my eyes stop upon the exit.

I need to leave.

"I actually am getting quite... tired. I'm going to be going home now."

I stand to leave, but so does Dominique.

"Do you need me to walk with you? You don't look so good -"

"No!" When I look up to see the concerned look on his face I half smile to reassure him.

I can't have him catch on that I've recognized something is off...

He might follow me.

"Thank you for your concern, but don't worry. I'll be fine after some rest." I dip my head, "Goodnight, Dominique."

With that, I quickly step away, getting to the exit. I hurry out into the dimly lit streets. The lanterns were already lit, and the sun was gone. Despite needing to leave from suddenly feeling ill, I couldn't help but feel bad. That could have been my last chance to get to know Dominique better, *but did I want to? If he was willing to lie about knowing the mailman?*

Despite all of my thoughts and feelings against him, I still felt a small pang of guilt. *Was I overthinking? Was I sabotaging my own chances at a friend because of my untrusting nature?*

I begin to walk down the road, *papa would be in bed by now and -*

"Audrey Hughes," A stranger calls out. I look back, across from the pub, a man stood waiting. They stare through narrowed eyes as they glance her over. They wore servants' clothes.

Are they from the abbey?

He steps towards me, and I don't know whether to run or listen. I don't have a choice as I am too exhausted to do much.

"I am Mr. Smith. I work at the Yonnam Abbey, I was sent to retrieve you."

I frown, "I thought I had until -"

"I believe the families would prefer to have you there tonight, to use tomorrow speaking with you." He motions to the direction back to the abbey. "If you could so kindly follow me?"

I pause for a moment, glancing over my shoulder at the pub.

This is all happening so fast-

Farah, I wish you could have talked to me before doing all of this.

Despite her exhaustion, Audrey still does not know how to say no.

"Lead the way."

7
BOOK RETURN

"...After the death of Lady Farah Davies, rumors are going around as to who will take her place in the running of the district. Will there be major changes in the next few months? Or will Yonnam remain the same for some time..."
-Yonnam Gossip Papers, Author Unknown

It feels as though centuries pass on the long walk up the path leading to the abbey. It was probably a very nice walk, considering the scenery around them. But as it was dark out, Audrey had already been on her feet for a larger portion of the day. It was a rather painful and strenuous walk.
I find myself struggling to stifle my coughing as I walk along with the servant. He casts weary glances over his shoulder every now and then, but says nothing of it.

As soon as the abbey comes into view though, all of my aches and pains are momentarily forgotten.

It was a grand building. Grand, yet ominous. It was far larger than any home, or building for that matter that I had ever seen before. Standing in the middle of a large field on its own, with multiple levels and many windows looking out. The architecture was extremely detailed and extravagant. It was almost too much to take in. It was well lit even in the night with the many lamp posts and lights on it.

For a moment, I could almost understand why they never left the place, and wondered why Farah did.

I always had asked her that, why did she leave the abbey to come to the small library? Was it awful there? What was it like? How did you always have new books to bring and donate with you? Farah would only laugh and tell me about how large of a place it was, and how it was large and lonely at times while our small library was comfortable and homely to her.

Audrey feels an ache in her chest as she looks at the building.

I never thought I would see this place, especially without you here.

"We will be entering through the servants hall," the man speaks so suddenly it makes me jump. "So as to not cause a fuss until tomorrow. As I am sure you can understand." Mr. Smith states simply as they turn off of the main road and away from the entrance towards the side of the abbey.

The side entrance wasn't as grand as the front entryway. It reminds me more of my own home front but much cleaner. A brick fence went around the sides of the door, but it had no gate. I follow as we walk through onto a stone pathway to the entrance door.

Mr. Smith opens the door and motions for me to go inside first. I dip my head and hurry through before stepping aside so he can continue to lead through the abbey. Ahead was a long hallway which led to many different rooms. I glance around as I follow him down the hallway.

I stop for a moment. If *this is the servants; entryway, what does the rest of this place look like?*

"This way Ms. Hughes."

I am taken out of my thoughts by the gruff voice of Mr. Smith. Smiling awkwardly, I hurry to continue to follow him down the hall.

"I'll be taking you to the late Lady Farah's room, don't worry -" He glances at me over his shoulder. "It is not very far into the abbey, so you shouldn't ever get lost. I also made sure the maids thoroughly cleaned it before you would arrive."

Many questions run through my mind. *Was she ill? Was it the sickness that was unidentifiable? Is that why it was crucial to mention cleaning?*

Despite all of these thoughts I mutter a quick response. “Er - Thank you.”

Continuing to follow him up a flight of stairs, I follow him through a doorway. Suddenly the surroundings have changed, from a simple servants hall to a grand hallway, even taller and wider than the kitchen at home. The walls had fine detailed prints upon them, the wooden flooring was mostly covered by long patterned rugs that didn’t reach the sides of the hall, and many paintings covered the pretty walls themselves.

Mr. Smith continues to lead me down the hallway past many ornate doors until he suddenly stops at one.

“This would be your room, Ms. Hughes.”

I nod, “Thank you, Mr. Smith.” I open the door and step inside.

As I turn and shut it behind me, I can hear Mr. Smith’s footsteps grow distant as he goes back to the servants section.

I take a deep breath before I turn to look around the room, the room itself was far bigger than her own. Possibly comparable to the size of their whole house. The walls were an emerald color, the furniture all made of beautiful warmly colored wood carved into curved and detailed pieces, and the bed itself took up most of the room.

This was Farah's room?

I notice a few things in the room which remind me of her, despite the room having been 'cleaned' before my arrival.

The books that I had recommended to her are left in a small bookshelf near the nightstand, one was even left on the vanity table. A pair of glasses sat on a table, and hung on the open dresser door was one of Farah's favorite dresses.

Spotting a small secretary desk, I notice it is closed. I walk over to it and pull open the drawers. It had been emptied out, all that remained were blank envelopes and empty pages along with a quill and ink.

I'm not too surprised. This is probably where they found the letter she wrote for me.

There must be someone kind within this house, I'm honestly still surprised they had sent her final letter to me. Or even told me about the inheritance at all.

I sit on the bed, looking around at the room.

There was a lot to take in. I begin to lie down on the bed when I spot a small time shoved between the mattress and the headboard. Like someone tried to hide it here.

I kick off my shoes and crawl across the large bed towards it. I slowly grab it, and look it over. *This is...*

I cried on my way to work, I was only sixteen and though at this point I was expected to work, I felt like a small child walking down the street. Walking past others on the street I felt tiny in comparison. With frail small arms and a skinny torso I knew was much too small for my age. Not one person stopped on the street to even acknowledge my tears.

Which was exactly what I wanted.

Carrying my over sized bag, I sobbed as I tried to forget just moments ago at home. The constant yelling, mum and papa constantly taking and selling any of my remaining schoolbooks from the year prior, I had only managed to keep one thing, and it was a very foolish thing to have kept. I peered into my bag, to make sure it had still been where I placed it as I stopped in front of the library. I knew I was lucky it was still there.

While my father was out of the house more, claiming to be searching for work, I saw him at the pub from time to time coming out as I hurried to work. My mother on the other hand was always at home, watching my two little brothers and taking more and more of my things to sell to afford to send

Fletcher and Remy to school. I let out a relieved sigh that mum hadn't thought to look into my work bag.

That was my one safe place now. Rubbing my eyes I pushed my way into the library, hurting past Mr. Abbot so he couldn't see how puffed up my eyes were.

"I'm going to the window room to clean!" I called out.

"Wait!" Mr. Abbot called, "Someone is in there -"

But I didn't hear him as I was already pulling the door open, I stepped inside to see an older woman quickly look up, her eyes were red and puffy as well.

"Ah, hello dear," The woman said quickly, dabbing at her eyes with a handkerchief. "I didn't realize anyone else would be coming to read here, I'll go -"

"No, it's fine! I just work here is all." I quickly said as I began to back away, I looked at the table in front of the woman, she had no books with her and had tears welling up in her eyes. I slowly stepped forward, "May I ask what's wrong?"

The woman looked up at her and chuckled softly, "Just going through tough times is all, deary."

I looked at her for a moment before it clicked.

Wasn't Mr. Abbot telling me about a woman who came by for a place to be sad?

I stood there for a moment, debating my next action before I pulled my prized possession out of the bag, placing it on the table in front of the woman.

"Here, you should have this, it's lucky."

"Are you sure?" She asked, looking at it.

It was a small plush, it looked old and worn, but not dirty. A small salamander with huge button eyes. A child's toy that Audrey had held onto for many years. Even her parents had forgotten where it came from, but she kept it all the same.

"That it's lucky?" I asked. "I know it's silly, but it had helped me pass my exams with full marks."

"Then won't you need it this upcoming school year?"

I looked down for a moment, tears welled up in my eyes again.

"Do you no longer attend an academy?"

I shook my head and began to back away.

"Wait! I didn't mean to offend you but... I was taught at a wonderful school."

I looked back at the woman.

"Perhaps I can teach you?" The woman asks, "It won't be the same as your old schooling, but I can come by in the evenings or when you work and teach you what I know."

I widened my eyes at her offer, "Really? You would do that?"

She nodded, "How about we both use the lucky plush by studying together?"

I hurried over and sat by the woman again, "Can we start after my work today!?"

"Of course! But first, what's your name, dear?"

"Audrey Hughes, nice to meet you." I quickly bowed a little, making the woman giggle. The woman dips her head in return, warm eyes sparkling as she looks at my big smile.

"I'm Farah Davies, I look forward to teaching you all I can."

Audrey pulls the object into the light. It is the tiny salamander plush.

It wasn't much, but it was that small gift that had started the friendship between the two.

She kept it over all of these years?

This worn down old thing?

I look around the room, she came from a place as magnificent as this, with the finest life one could live, and she still had chosen me.

To teach me, comfort me, and be a friend when I needed one most.

I held it close as I lay out on the bed.

It is only now that I can finally cry over the death of my best friend.

8
COMPLETE ANNOTATIONS

"...The King's advisor has finally announced that due to public angst over the border situation, that they would be sending knights to stay and guard the border along with the barrier of the border district, Yonnam..."
-Flaize Daily, Article by Anonymous

There is nothing unusual about waking up in a room and not knowing where you are. More often than not, it's simply just going to take a moment to process that you actually are somewhere you know. This was not the case.

Waking up in an unfamiliar, but an extraordinary room, I felt my heart drop as I rubbed the sleep from my eyes. Looking at the bed in the daylight, I realize that the bed could fit at least four more of me. The room in general looks very different than it had the night before when the servants had let me in and left me here for the night.

I sit up, frowning.

What am I supposed to do now? Should I go

find that servant -

As though summoned by my thoughts, a quiet knock comes from the door. I sit up a little more, looking down, I realize I had never gotten under the covers- or even changed for that matter.

"Ms. Hughes? Are you awake?"

I quickly jump off of the bed and hurry over to the door, lightly pulling it open. I am met by a woman not much younger than myself. She has perfectly groomed blonde hair pulled up into a tight bun, her fair skin is covered in freckles, and she has very round eyes and a small button nose.

She looks at me and smiles. She wore a simple black dress that was corset tight below her chest, and the skirt is low but shoes worn black dress shoes. It was a maid dress, but it was not a regular maid dress, this was a ladies maid.

The maid curtsies and dips her head, "Miss- *Lady* Hughes, I am here to help you get dressed and lead you to the library, where the Lord and Lady Holloway are waiting for you."

While I did not know much about the upper class, I was slightly aware of the various titles that the servants must call the men and women of the ruling district house. It was no surprise how little I knew, this was the first time I had been even beyond the gates of the district ruling house. The Yonnam Abbey, of the District Yonnam.

Most of the people of the district would live their whole lives not knowing what lay beyond the gates other than what they were told. The upper class controlled that, as much as they could anyway. No one could have foreseen a low-class woman like Audrey getting beyond the gates.

The maid passes by, making a beeline towards the overly sized wardrobe that took up a good corner of the room.

"The Dowager was around your size, so I am sure something here can work until we get your measurements..."

I clench my teeth as I hear her name, awkwardly I follow the maid across the room.

"So, what is your name? Or what should I call you?" I ask.

The maid pulls a dress out and smiles, "My name is Anita Paxton, you can call me Paxton. Lady's Maids are usually called by their surnames." She places the dress out onto the bed and places shoes on the floor beside it. "Now I only ask this because... you're new here, but would you like me to help you change?"

I feel my face flush immediately as I suddenly feel very conscious of my body. I shake my head, "I'd prefer to dress myself, thank you."

"I'll step out for a moment then, let me know when to come back in so I can help you with your hair and jewelry."

Before I could protest, Paxton was already around the room and out the door. The shadow from her shoes could still be seen under the doorway as she waits.

Quickly I take my clothes off, I struggle for a moment to get the dress on. Loosening the corset ribbon in the back I finally manage to get it on.

I'll have to ask Paxton to tighten this for me.

I'm going to have to get used to the idea of others dressing me if I'm to stay here...

Did Farah have to as well?

Audrey turns and looks in the mirror. She had never seen this dress on Farah, but the style reminded Audrey of her. It wasn't too overboard with embellishments and decorations. It didn't even reach the floor as it hit just at her ankles. It was a looser fitting dress, other than the torso, and it was a pale almost misty shade of green. It was odd seeing her plain face, tired round hazel eyes, and messy long toffee colored hair along with something Farah would wear so effortlessly.

I frown at my reflection.

I wonder what she would say about this dress on me.

I slip on the shoes and open the bedroom door again, letting Ms. Paxton back inside. She immediately goes to tie up the back of the dress tight, making me gasp in surprise.

"This color looks excellent on you, Ms. Hughes." She goes over to the vanity table and pulls out a chair, motioning for me to sit.

When I do, Ms. Paxton immediately starts comparing different necklaces. Holding them up to my neck.

"I think for today we will go with something comfortable, but elegant."

It felt odd, having my hair pulled and braided up into a bun. The few hairs left down around my face made it not completely unbearable, but it still felt wrong compared to the usual style. Or usual non style. Normally I would leave it down, and on the rare occasion I would take the time to carefully brush it out.

Following Ms. Paxton through the great halls of the abbey, it was difficult to not slow the pace and just admire it all in the light of day. The halls open up as they reach a large staircase, Audrey has to follow her down slowly as she wears the new heels.

At the bottom of the stairs, Ms. Paxton opens a large door and steps aside for me to walk through.

I take a deep breath before I step through.

It was a massive library, Audrey can't help but gape in awe at it.

When she was young she had thought the local library could be considered massive with several shelves in an old house with books not filling every shelf. It was huge to her at the time. But now that she stood in the abbey library she realized the local one could not even compare.

The shelves reach all the way to the top of the ceilings, with sliding ladders on each. A large area run with burgundy and gold patterns fills the room and covers almost all of the flooring, and various desks and antique couches were placed around with room to spare.

Two people sit at a table nearby, both immediately stand as I enter the room.

The door shuts behind me, making me tense up a little more.

The man begins walking over to her, and I feel my heartbeat quicken. "Ah, she is here at last! You must be Ms. Hughes.

Farah's *favored* of the people." He dips his head respectfully, which eases my anxieties slightly. Even with the calming gesture, his words carry a sharpness I can't help but note.

"We were wondering when you would decide to come to the abbey, I was beginning to worry you had not received the letter at the beginning of the week." The man continues on.

I can't help but look him over. He was tall, had fine features, his hair was nicer styled than any man I had seen prior, well perhaps besides Dominique, being a dark color with fine swept curtain bangs, and he wore a three piece suit that was well pressed and tailored. His silver eyes pierce her as he stares intensely. *Silver eyes?* His eye color looks like the reflection on knives or jewelry- *I've only ever read about such a character.* I think that perhaps I would have liked his character in a novel or story, but the man that stood before me I found to be handsome. Not quite in an attractive way, but rather an intimidating type of beauty.

I dip my head to him. Feeling uncomfortable, I decide to resort to pleasantries. "Nice to meet you." My voice cracks slightly. *Perfect.* I bite my tongue.

He says nothing to this, merely beckoning

the woman behind him over.

She complies and hurries to stand by his side. She was rather gorgeously dressed, but she had softer features than the man. Her eyes round and a soft brown, her lighter hair was dainty the way it was braided up with a few curls hanging down, she wore a dress fitting to her appearance as it was very loose and more innocent looking being a creamy floral gown, she is a pretty woman, but mostly I notice how she looks nervous.

Painstakingly so.

It sounds wrong, but I felt a little better that I wasn't the only one feeling anxious in this situation.

Audrey's shoulders slightly relax at this.

"I'm Julian Halloway, and this is my wife, Lady Priscilla." He says, flashing a fine toothed grin.

Priscilla curtsies as he introduces her, and I give her a small smile.

"So, it's straight to business I'm afraid." Lord Julian says, walking back over to the table they had stood at with his wife following like a shadow.

After a moment, I slowly follow the two across the room, looking at the table covered in papers they are looking over.

The man places his hands onto the edge and leans on the table, looking down among all of the neatly laid out pages.

"We've been corresponding with the late Dowager Farah's lawyer, over her intended will." He says, glancing over at me. "It seems she wrapped it up tight, she had multiple witnesses to this and even had it all done many months ago."

While I nod when he looks up at me, I can't help but frown as he looks away.

It sounds as though they were trying to find a way to undo it... I glance up at Lord Julian's face, *his expression is more relaxed than perplexed. Or perhaps I am reading too far into things?*

"Were you at all aware of her leaving this to you? Or did you by chance suggest anything of a will in any of your conversations?"

They're... Interrogating me? I quickly try to think of something to say - Afraid that they are trying to get me to answer quickly without thinking.

I shake my head, "I had no clue she would even think to leave me anything. Honestly, it was never a thought that would cross my mind." Lord Julian narrows his eyes and watches me for a moment before looking back down to the papers.

His sigh is loud.

That's the truth -

"It's going to be difficult going from your position to hers, she did not have a whole lot of work. Mostly agreeing or disagreeing with things on the board, signing papers, that sort of deal-"

What?

Considering her position, surely she did more than that?

Even in her older age... She always spoke of having a great amount of work when she wasn't visiting.

Watching the way Lord Julian looks over the papers instead of at me while he speaks, with his wife merely looks down at the floor behind him I can't tell if I am overthinking or not. This did feel odd.

This situation is odd. I remind myself.

"- So until you're properly trained in the tasks you will have to do, I will have my wife in charge of the Dowager's work." When he meets my gaze he is unflinching as he continues. "Don't worry, most of the training at first will be simple reading before you begin working alongside my wife and I. We're all trying to learn this as we go as this... *situation* is different from the usual we deal with her."

I don't say anything to argue with him, I don't know how I even could argue at this point. Yet still, I feel a small tug in my chest. *Something here is... off putting.*

"So what happens next?" I ask.

"We're holding an event tonight, a dinner... party of sorts. Every member of the board will be there as well as a few visiting from the neighboring district of Broise." He sits up and pulls his hands off of the table. "It's nothing too much, we will have dinner, then go through to the sitting room and mingle for a while before everyone goes up for the night. No need to worry about dressing up or putting on a show of things, it's fairly casual." He raises a brow as he looks at me. "Have you been to a dinner party before, Ms. Hughes?"

I try to meet his gaze, but his unflinching stare is rather intense. *Surely he can tell I have not?* I think to myself as I shake my head meekly.

"It's simple really," He begins, "We will greet the guests in the main hall and converse until the dinner is ready. We will be seated in the dining room where you are expected to speak primarily to those closest to you, though some might address others from across the table. Afterwards we will go through to the sitting room for drinks by the fire before everyone decides to go to their room for the night." He smirks when Audrey's eyes go wide. "So nothing too much, at least not compared to our other events."

Lord Julian then nods at his wife, and she steps aside and pulls a rope on the wall.

"What about..." I feel my voice die in my throat as Lord Julian turns back to me.

Moments later a servant enters the room.

"Did you have any other questions?" He asks coolly.

I glance at the servant. "Just... What about my family? Will I be able to bring them to the abbey as well?" *I know they're all at home just waiting to hear something... anything about what's going to happen now.*

He sighs, "I'm afraid we couldn't make that work. While we do have many rooms, I'm afraid they're all filled up by my family."

"But I saw a few empty rooms-"

"Yes, most everyone is at the capital right now, as the young prince has finally reached eighteen every district has most of the family members go to the celebrations." He pauses, but continues before I have the chance to respond. "Do you think it would be fair to give your family a room only for my own family to return to somebody else in the beds?"

I began to open my mouth to respond, but Lord Jullian's attention was already away from me.

"I have Mrs. Fink here to help you get on what things you need to learn to... shall we say catch up, before tonight." He dips his head at me, "And with that I'll leave you to it. See you tonight, Ms. Hughes."

With that, Lord Julian and Lady Priscilla leave me alone with 'Mrs. Fink'.

The lady walks over and immediately begins pulling books out onto another table, waving me over as she pulls out a chair for me.

I hesitate for a moment, and as I sit down as she drops a heavy stack on the table.

"Read these, by tonight." She states sharply, before walking over the stand by the doorway.

Where she stood watching through narrowed beady eyes.

This isn't what I expected. Not at all.

After spending hours and hours reading Audrey finally got a quarter of the way through the stack of books. None of them were anything that could actually tell her what she needed to know of Farah's position within the District house.

Most of them were school books, things she had already learned. Even skimming them took forever, and I read fairly quickly. Keeping a book open on the table, and my head angled down. I glance up at Ms. Fink, who has yet to stop staring since I've started reading. I found herself almost too nervous to stop reading.

Surely I can read from the shelves? Something - newer to me?

I begin to stand and walk towards a shelf when the lady watching suddenly shouts.

"Have you finished reading the books provided?"

I'm sorry - What?

Audrey opens her mouth to respond when suddenly the door suddenly opens making Audrey jump. She looks up to see a very sharp looking woman had entered, and it was the same woman who had visited her at the local library just before Audrey received the inheritance letter.

Her platinum hair was pulled up and braided into a bun with a few curls framing her face, she wore a rather showy beaded dress, with wide straps that laid elegantly on her shoulders showing her collarbone, and a skirt that just hit halfway down her shins that show off her tall black heels. Her whole look was extravagant and intimidating, but most noticeable were her oddly sharp amber eyes. She was not the type of woman who could have been easily forgotten, and her cold aura contrasts and stands out in the warm and comfortable library.

She steps into the room and immediately turns to look at me, Ms. Paxton stands behind her.

"So I can see Julian already has you settled in," She remarks coolly as she strides across the room. She has an icy aura, and appears calm and collected as she stops beside the table, placing a hand on the pile of books as she glances over what was chosen for me, tapping her sharp, clean nails on the cover. She focuses on the larger stack that I had left untouched.

"At this rate, it's going to be a while before you can perform the duties that came along with your... miracle of a title."

"I'm a fast learner, there shouldn't be any problem." I retort after a moment, surprising myself and making the woman chuckle slightly.

"No need to be on the defense, *dear*." She turns back to the door, "Paxton is here to retrieve you and your books and take you to your room, where you are to get ready for tonight's dinner."

As the woman begins to walk away she calls back, "Make sure not to dress like your class. This is an upper class event after all."

Wait - Get ready for dinner now? It's not that late in the day surely? Did Lord Julian not say that it would be more casual? Perhaps she just meant not the clothes I arrived in...

I glance out the window nearby to see clear bright skies. It was probably hardly past noon.

This makes no sense. I sigh quietly as Paxton hurries over and begins collecting the books.

"Oh!" I quickly am pulled out of my thoughts, "Let me help!" I began grabbing books before Paxton could get them all.

"Oh - there's no need-" Paxton tries to argue, but I had already collected the rest of the books. Paxton casts an anxious glance at the other servant in the room before leading the pair out of the library.

"Thank you," She mumbles quietly as soon as they reach the stairs.mI smile as I follow the maid back to the room. Well, *my* room.

I'm not going to learn much here - Not unless I can get books off of the shelves of my own picking.

After I had changed, Paxton had left

me alone in the room. Considering how far away dinner should be, I had decided to snoop around a little more. *There surely had to be something else left behind for me... right?*

I struggle to bend down or crouch in the form fitting corset dress, still I check underneath every piece of furniture. Even as I carefully slide underneath the bed. I find nothing.

It took a bit of time, but as I get out from under the bed and finally manage to get up I dust myself off. Glad to be alone but still feeling embarrassed. Hopefully, I didn't look like the awkward mess I felt like.

There really wasn't any dust down there...

They clean really well- the servants that is.

If there was anything else left to me by Farah, surely they would have left it for me... Right?

Looking back at the large stack of books left for me, I walk to the pile and grab one off of the top. Skimming it, I find nothing of any importance.

So I moved onto the next book, devouring the pages one by one and still found nothing useful. Mere children's lessons in manners, and history of the district. It was the sort of thing I learned back when I still was able to attend school.

This continues for a while until I'm back at the part of the stack I had finished in the library. Angrily I toss the last book down and glance about the room.

I know that Farah did more than this... They must think I am a fool that doesn't understand basic manners and writing.

Why didn't Farah do anything- or even *say* anything to prepare me for this? The others clearly don't want another person displacing the balance they have here.

So why? Why did she want me here in her place?

I should go speak with Lord Julian, he would know anything else I need to know.

I can't shy away from asking what needs to be asked here.

For Farah's sake-

I turn the door handle and it stops. It does not click open. Trying a few more times, it takes a moment for reality to sink in.

They had locked me in my room.

I step back from the door, looking down at it with my mouth agape.

Surely it was a mistake - Why would they lock me in here -

Moments later, I can hear as the servants are coming up the stairs from the servants hall, I step towards the door.

Pressing my hands against it and slowly leaning forward to press my ear to the cold wooden door.

I could hear chatter, though it was not the servants, but even further away. From the great hall entrance of the abbey.

Are they trying to keep me out of sight?

I feel my heart drop. I had always expected rudeness and harshness of others in the district. It was a cruel life in the lower class. Though even there, this was beyond anything I had experienced.

I feel myself grow hot as I begin to panic.

How long will they keep me here? Should I be trying to escape? Perhaps I can spy a servant from the window to help me?

If that doesn't work...

I hurry to the window and carefully unbolt it, opening it up wide. I can hear the servants outside, but they are just out of sight. The sky was just starting to get darker as the sun began to set. Placing my hands on the windowsill, I lean out to try to see around the corner of the building.

Suddenly, a brightly colored lizard runs up my arm. Shivers go up my spine as I fall back, trying to swat it away. When suddenly it was gone. I spin around and scan the room for it as I carefully half shut the window behind me, but the creature is gone.

I searched the room again, this time for the small amphibian that was now surely stuck somewhere with me. I then look at the door.

Did it crawl underneath?

It's probably deep within the abbey by now.

I can't help but chuckle, knowing that it has more freedom than me. At least, right now.

As I start to lean down to peer underneath the door, footsteps can be heard from the other side. I jump away at the sound of a key rattling and being pushed into the lock. The door opens, and I am met with the concerned face of Paxton. She doesn't quite meet my gaze as she speaks.

"If you could please follow me, Lady Hughes, they are ready for you now." The maid said nothing of the locked door, and quite honestly, I was afraid to ask. As I follow her down the halls I can already hear many loud and boisterous conversations happening in the main hall as people began arriving and are being welcomed by the board.

I feel anxious as I follow her back down the stairs and all of the people gathered come into sight. It was a large room, so it wasn't crowded. Yet still, there were many finely dressed people speaking to each other. It looks as though while most people had just arrived, many were speaking long before now. Past pleasantries and introductions and into deeper conversations.

If it was an accident... She would have said something. Was I left to come later for a reason?

If so... Is this reason safe, or something foul?

As I reach the bottom of the stairs, I realize Paxton has disappeared. I look around, there are many different kinds of people. I didn't know who to talk to, or how I should be speaking, as I didn't know the titles or places of a majority of these people. Most likely it was almost all family of the board members, they didn't all run the district- but still. It was all overwhelming.

I glance down at my own clothes and back to those around me. The dress I wore was very fancy in comparison to what I normally would wear, but it was far plainer than anything else in the room. I wore a floral dress that fit very much like Paxton's dress, as it is a corset fit on my torso and a loose skirt. The women all wore extravagant and elegant dresses, various cap sleeved or sleeveless gowns with beads or tassels that sway with every movement, the men wore structured suits with white bow ties that match their button-ups underneath the suit jacket and wore impossibly shiny loafers. I stood out in this crowd, and not in a good way.

My face feels hot as I see people stare and lean in towards each other to talk.

My ears burn as I realize they are talking about me.

After a moment, I notice as a servant enters the room from another doorway.

Nobody else seems to notice him as he stops beside Lord Julian and the woman from earlier and whispers something to them.

"May I have everyone's attention!" Lord Julian says loudly, making everyone in the room quiet almost instantaneously.

I wish my brothers would listen that well, I think to myself. Slightly smiling at the thought.

I feel my gut twist as I think of my brothers, but that moment does not last as I am pulled away from any thoughts as Lord Julian continues to speak.

"May I invite you all to make your way to the dining room, they're ready for us." At that everyone begins to follow them through the doorway from which Mr. Smith came. Audrey follows from the rear.

As I enter the room, I am met by odd lighting, a long and full dining table, and many servants.

I look at the lighting for a moment.

That isn't a fire -

Then what is it?

Electricity? I've heard of it in higher-end districts but... I've never seen it used in a house.

Shaking my head, I quickly take my place at the nearest seat. As soon as I do, Lord Julian pipes up, "Ms. Hughes, your seat is by Lady Priscilla, not there."

I feel my face flush as I quickly stand, only now did I notice the name cards hidden behind the luxurious plates. I glance at the name of the seat I was in.

Mr. Wingrave...

That sounds familiar.

I curse under my breath as others around laugh. Feeling the urge to speak up and say something - anything in response is shoved down as I look around at the many faces that watch.

I hurry around the table to sit beside Lady Priscilla, who quietly greets me, I sit down. I notice the pleased look on the sharp woman from earlier. *This isn't just a dinner.*

This is a game of some sort.

At this point, everyone had been seated, and three servants began carrying different plates of food around, lowering it enough to allow each person to choose what they wanted. As they reach me, I find it very nerve wracking as I carefully use the utensils to get a small portion of chicken cooked in a way I had never seen before.

Is someone watching me? I feel keenly aware of a certain gaze on me, I glance up and I'm met with a familiar glaring gaze.

A rather pompous looking young man, in an expensive suit far too tightly cut, as though he was trying to show off his figure. It takes a moment for me to recognize him.

Mr. Wingrave?!

It's Emmett Wingrave!

"So now that everyone is settled, let me introduce to you Ms. Hughes." Lord Julian motions to where I sat as the next servant leans down and shows a plate of mushrooms stuffed with a variety of things. I am very careful to place a few on her plate as Lord Julian continues speaking. Keenly aware of the many eyes upon me.

"Ms. Hughes will be taking the place of the late Dowager Davies, as most of you know already."

"How very kind of Lady Davies," A slightly older lady says from across the table. "To give someone of a low class a chance to move up in the world." Most people at the table snicker at this, even though the lady did not seem to have any ill intentions with her comment. Many lean in to those who sat near them to have their own conversations about it. Perhaps I should do this as well? I look around, Lady Priscilla did get placed next to me.

Perhaps I should take this chance to speak with her?

"So, Lady Priscilla, what exactly do you do?"

She looks startled at her being spoken too, like a mouse spotted by a cat. She glances over at me.

"Well, actually I don't do much with the board usually... I actually write for th-" Her gaze moves past me and she quickly looks back down at her plate while eating.

With a look around, I realize many people were still glaring. With my speaking to Lady Priscilla it turned their gazes upon her as well.

I knew it would be odd suddenly moving up in title but...

Is it really this unheard of?

This...

Disturbing to people? What do they think I'm going to do?

Poison their minds? Make them all poor?

It doesn't help anything that Mr. Wingrave was looking both pleased with my discomfort, but irritated by my presence at the same time.

Most at the table were relatives of the board members. Almost all lived under this roof. The only ones who were not focused on Audrey as intensely as others were those visiting from out of district.

Audrey focuses on cutting her food and eating it without conversing. When she takes a bite of her food, her eyes widen slightly. Amazed by the difference of food that they ate here.

I hear someone snicker across the table, looking up to see a larger balding man watching.

"So, Ms. Hughes." He says haughtily. "What exactly did you do before Lady Davies left you her position?"

I put the fork down, thrilled for a question I could finally answer. "I was a librarian at th-"

"A librarian?!" Someone else exclaims.

"Goodness, I didn't realize just how different of a person the late Dowager Davies had chosen." The woman speaking looks to Lord Julian. "Mr. Halloway-"

Wait... Are they not calling each other by their titles? Is there a reason for this?

Once Lord Julian has turned to the woman

she continues, "Do we know why she was chosen?" She asks.

Why not just ask me?

He doesn't really know either -

"The late Lady Davies was a kind woman who loved books and charity, there is no need to question it any further." Lord Julian answers with a simple smile. He raises a glass up.

I feel myself grow hot with embarrassment as the table laughs.

He was right about her, but what is he playing at?

Is he trying to make me feel out of place? Is he afraid? Why would he be?

Hours go by as the conversation shifts away from her and Audrey is forgotten enough to be allowed to eat the rest of her meal in peace. It was the most food I had been able to eat in years, I can't help but feel guilty as I thought of the family at home.

I just need to stay here for them, eventually I'll be able to send home the inheritance money and maybe even move them here but -

Is that not counterproductive? My ex fiance - I didn't want a man like him around Fletcher and Remy.

Wouldn't this be the same?

Looking around the table, at the many people who watch her through gleaming eyes like wolves in the hunt, I realize these are not people my brothers should grow up around.

My plate is almost spotless clean, but not completely when Lord Julian suddenly stands.

"Shall we go through now?" He says it as though it were a question, but nobody answers as everyone stands and follows him out of the room. I push my chair back and stand to follow, noticing how the servants pull out the chairs for all of the other ladies.

With a sigh, I follow the crowd into another room. This one was very similar to the library being it was pretty large and had many different seating areas. Mostly armchairs and couches. I notice the bar off to the side where a servant is preparing drinks. I was not the type to drink, I usually despised the idea as I knew my family had a history of being angry when drunk. That, and considering how much it cost, but with how the night was going thus far though, it seems like a good idea.

At this rate, tonight may be an exception for me. I think as I watch the man preparing drinks for those who went to stand by the counter.

As groups form and people begin talking

among themselves, I look around for a conversation to join. *Perhaps with Priscilla? Or that lady who spoke of me earlier?*

She doesn't even have the time to make a choice as it is made for her. A bald man in an overly tight suit is coming her way. Audrey's heart drops as she realizes it is Mr. Wingrave making his way towards her.

"Ironic to see you here."

I frown at him, he may look better physically then he did before when he had an overabundance of food to stuff himself with, but his attitude had not changed.

I'm surprised they let you in the gate.

I want to insult him aloud, to not hold myself back and tell him what I think. I can't.

Last time I saw him, papa was begging for him to take me back. I'm sure he knows that I am still unmarried as well.

"You're lucky that old woman took pity on you," He says with a wicked grin. "If it weren't for her dying pity, I would have been right about your future."

Before Audrey can open her mouth to speak, a servant stumbles into the room panting.

"I'll be seeing you around, Audrey." He hisses before sliding off to stand by a petite and loud woman who wore too much jewelry

and too much blush.
All conversations have stopped, or quiet down as everyone stares at the servant.

"Charles? What is the meaning of this?" Lord Julian asks.

The man looks out of breath, "Sir, there is a man in the main hall - he says he's -"
Suddenly someone pushes their way past the servant and strides into the room.

"Who are you? How did you get in here -" Lord Julian follows the man who walks straight past him. The man's gaze was fixated upon Audrey.
I freeze as he stops by me, wrapping an arm around me.

"I'm Audrey's husband of course, and I'm here to be with my wife."

Husband?!

I look up at the man's face, having to double check it, I must be imagining things. *Right?*

But I wasn't.

The man claiming to be my husband was someone I never expected to see here - or again at all.

It was Dominique Pascal

9
UNPUBLISHED

"... The King has been funding the Magic Academy for years, but now he is making it urgent to get more students. Therefore a few requirements have been changed for those who can get in, making it easier for the majority to get in, even when lacking in typical magic abilities..."

-Flaize Magic Academy Paper

"I wasn't aware that *Ms. Hughes was married.*" Lord Julian states loudly, glancing at Audrey for a confirmation that this man was who he claimed to be.

I look at the expression on Lord Julian's face, he seems taken aback, and a little *concerned* even.

I then turn to Dominique.

Why is he saying this?!

Better yet how did he know I was here- that this was tonight!

I look around at all of the eyes upon me.

I can't give them more to use against me! I'm already the fool of the hour...

If I act confused this could get worse.

Audrey opens her mouth to speak, but struggles to say something.

I can't leave it! I need to say something!

I glance over at Mr. Wingrave, his face is beet red and the irritation on his face is almost too delightful.

He would be wrong. Wrong about telling me I'd be a spinster forever.

Wrong about me never amounting to anything.

Spite is a powerful thing.

I put a hand on Dominique's arm, feeling sick as I do. "That's because it was only recently..." I trail off and look up at him, waiting for him to continue.

Dominique places a hand on mine, and I can't tell if it is reassuring or not as my legs feel wobbly.

He doesn't skip a beat. "We were keeping things under the wraps with all of the stress about the border lately, and didn't want to make a fuss. That's why Audrey has kept her last name, *for now.*"

Lord Julian grits his teeth, but says nothing. He waves the servant away, turning back to the group.

"Everyone go back to your conversations, nothing of any matter just a simple invitation error is all."

Everyone accepts this and goes back to their chatter, casting glances at Dominique and I every now and then.

"Why are you here -"

"Hold that thought," Dominique interrupts her. "Thank you for going along, but we cannot speak about it here." The two spot Lord Julian making his way over. "Just keep it up and I promise to explain later."

Lord Julian stops by Dominique, "I'm afraid I haven't had the pleasure, I'm Julian Halloway. You are?" He extends a hand to him.

"Dominique Madlocke," he says, shaking his hand. He doesn't flinch at Lord Julian's intense gaze.

"What exactly do you do, if you don't mind my asking?" Lord Julian asks.

"I used to serve as a knight, for one of the upper districts -" He replies calmly. "I decided to change things up and come
visit family in Yonnam. Then, I met Ms. Hughes and here we are." He looks at Lord Julian. "Now what *exactly* is it you do?"

Lord Julian smiles, flashing teeth. "I'm on the board, I help with the running of Yonnam District."

"And what exactly, on the board, do you do in particular?"

Lord Julian seems irritated by all of the questions, but with all of the eyes upon them he begrudgingly answers. "I watch where the funds are used, and mostly sign papers. Nothing too interesting to discuss at an event like tonight." He laughs slightly, it sounds forced.

"We look forward to discussing it with you at a later time then," Dominique says with a bold smile.

The corners of Lord Julian's lips curve down slightly at this, but he quickly regains his composure and smiles coolly at him. "I must get back to speaking with my guests from the Broise District." He nods at the woman who was kinder about my sudden rise in ranking. Dipping his head he backs away and begins to go back to his group but is stopped along the way by another person.

As soon as he is out of earshot, Dominique turns to me.

"You heard our story, so now - Are you ready to mingle?" He extends his hand to me.

"What do you mean -" As I take his hand he holds it tight and begins walking across the room, I have to hurry to follow.

How does he know so much-

It's like he has been here the whole night...

Has he?

I try to think back, to a servant's face perhaps, someone hiding in the shadows, anything but I can't recall any time seeing him.

I look ahead to the woman he was walking towards, she is middle aged and had a very warm style about her. With honey-blonde hair that was cut above her shoulder, warm tan skin, and a sunnier style she appeared welcoming. It takes me a moment to realize this was the woman who spoke of Farah's kindness during dinner.

The two stop by the Broise District board member, who turns to face them.

She smiles at me, "Oh, hello Ms. Hughes! Or is it Mrs. Hughes -" she glances Dominique over quickly.

Is there a reason nobody calls me Lady Hughes? Will I not gain the title until I am put into my role here? Or is it common to speak informally among the upper class?

"It's still Ms. Hughes for now, and this is my - husband." The word feels foreign on my tongue as I say it. It takes me a moment to recall his current name.

"Dominique Madlocke. We're keeping our... marriage under the wraps until things calm down for my family." I reply slowly.

The lady claps her hands together quietly, "How considerate!" Quickly she puts a hand up to her mouth. "Goodness, I'm afraid I have yet to introduce myself. I'm Esme Dayholt from the neighboring Broise District,you can call me Mrs. Dayholt. I'm sad to say my husband was unable to make it as he's become strangely ill all of a sudden." She still smiles despite the news she carried in her words, not seemingly in the slightest upset about her husband not coming with her.

Ill? Is it the same thing around our district? No - You're probably overthinking it.

Don't project.

"I'm sorry to hear that, I hope you can return home to him soon enough." I say sadly, thinking of mum at home.

Does she even know I am gone?

"Thank you for that. I'm sure he will be fine, but it's just odd. None of the doctors could figure out what was wrong. They just said he should stay home and rest."

That's the same with mum, and Farah couldn't figure what was wrong with her either... I just assumed because she was older -

Is this all connected?

"How exactly have things been in Broise?" Dominique asks boldly. my heart beats fast with everything he says or does. Like one wrong step could break the facade.

"Well, to be completely honest the rumors going around about the border have been rather difficult to control. That's actually why we're here. So we can return with news of how the border is being controlled."

"And what do you think of it?"

Mrs. Dayholt pauses for a moment to think before she replies. "I'm not quite sure yet. I have been told that it was recently that a magic user has come to recast the barrier spells around the district. I have yet to hear much more than this though."

Recent? It's been a rather long time since the last one -

"Hm, Audrey dearest," Dominique says dramatically. "When was the last time you saw the magic user in town?"

I see what he's playing at now.

He means to undermine the board.

Is this why he was here?

Is Dominique from a district against Yonnam?

Or is he working alone?

I don't know if this is a good move.... But he does have a point. I feel myself relax slightly as I stand next to Dominique.

"It's actually been quite some time since he's last been around. He's been due for quite a while as well..."

Mrs. Dayholt looks concerned, "And are there any officers patrolling the borders of the district? I never saw any on my way in."

Dominique shakes his head, "There haven't been any in a while. I believe we've been mostly reliant upon the barrier spells."

"Intriguing." Mrs. Dayholt said. "Thank you for informing me, now if you'll excuse me, there are a few other people I'd like to speak with before tonight ends. Including Lady Vivienne." She dips her head at Audrey. "It was a pleasure meeting you, Ms.- Lady Hughes."

Watching as she walks away to another woman, I huff as I see who.

So that's Lady Vivienne.

It was the lady who had visited me in the library here, and in town.

So that's her name then? Vivienne?

"Do you still not drink, Ms. Hughes?" Dominique asks, motioning towards the table.

"Tonight I'll make an exception -" leaning in towards Dominique, I whisper. "- But remember, I expect answers as soon as possible."

"I can give you answers later tonight," He says with a grin.

I scowl at this, making him chuckle.

"I meant nothing odd by that. Now what did you think I meant, I wonder?"

Disgusting.

I don't respond to his comment, instead I

make my way over to the bar, hoping he does not see my flushed face. That last comment was reason enough to drink something-anything tonight.

"What can I get you - Ms. Hug - Lady Hughes." The bar-tending servant stutters and he struggles to find the correct title to call her. I smile, knowing that the couple near the bar were watching. Waiting for me to slip up.

Is this really how it's going to be? I have to watch every step, word, or movement?

I thought it was bad enough having to tiptoe around papa but this -

This is a whole other level.

It takes me a moment to recall the only drink I had ever tried. It was with Farah long ago. She had snuck out a bottle of it with glasses to the library to drink while we talked. I didn't have much, but I didn't recall disliking it.

"I'll just have a glass of pinot noir," I answer. Breathing a quiet relieved sigh as the people stop staring.

As the man hands me a glass very lightly filled with a shimmering red liquid I take the lightest sip of it. Remembering how Farah had laughed when she gulped it down like it was regular juice.

I'm glad I learned my lesson then in the

company of a friend, glancing around at the many people around her. I try not to think about how bad it would have looked if I had done that again here.

As I finish sipping on the drink, I notice that more and more people begin leaving. Dominique is suddenly at my side again.

"Would you like to request for us to go up now?"

"You're coming too?" I ask, placing the glass down on the bar by the servant, quietly thanking him.

When the servant furrows a brow, Dominique laughs heartily, "Ah, you always make me laugh, my darling."

Once the servant has turned his attention elsewhere Dominique leans in.
"I need to be able to stay here, you don't have to worry that I'll try anything. I'm not here for that."

Audrey's face turns red at his implications.

"You'd better explain yourself when we go out then." I huff under my breath.

Audrey slowly and carefully watches her foot placement in her heels as she walks over to Lord Julian, he glances at her from the side. Stopping his conversation as she nears him. The others he spoke with stop as well.

"We were just coming over to say we're

going up for the night and -"
Lord Julian grins, "Ah I'm sure you wanted us to find a place for Mr. Madlocke to stay for the night. Since you two are still keeping it under the wraps, as you put it, am I right?"

I need to be able to question him!

Will I really have to wait? Didn't he say there were no extra rooms - He was lying then!

"Ms. Hughes, may I speak with you for a moment in private?" Lord Julian asks.

Oh no - Did he figure it out already?

I dip my head, casting an annoyed glance at Dominique; I turn away from him and find the exit to the room, which leads right back into the main hall.

Lord Julian follows me out into the hall where we are alone.

"Is that man really your husband?" He asks, stepping closer. His eyes are cold, and all of his charming charisma seemingly dissipated into the air. Replaced by a sharp and aggressive aura.

I take a step back, nodding. "Yes, it was only recently, and like he said- we're keeping it quiet for now."

"You just seem so... anxious." He says in a silvery tone. "Then again, this is your first event here." He backs up a bit, the tenseness in the air eases. Lord Julian smiles, his social energy returns. "We have a few more events coming up, so you'll get used to things easily enough."

He no longer seems to be paying attention to me, already looking to go back to the event. "You can go ahead and go up, Ms. Hughes, I'll have a servant find a room for your husband." He turns away and begins making his way back to the party. Clearly done with their little conversation.

I find that my head is spinning, I have to use all of my focus on walking up the stairs and not tripping in the heels I was wearing. *Where exactly was my room again?*

When I reach the top of the stairs, I see two figures standing aside out of the light.

A couple?

"Hello?" I call out, making the two turn.

It was Mrs. Dayholt and Lady Vivienne. Dayholt seems tense, but as soon as she sees that it was me, she relaxes slightly. Lady Vivienne not as much, her cold gaze upon me.

"Is everything alright?"

"Yes," Vivienne replies swiftly. "Mrs. Dayholt wanted to discuss some personal business tonight, and I thought it... inappropriate to do so in the company of the parts of the family here for a socializing event."

I nod, looking at Mrs. Dayholt's widened eyes. She looks like a deer that spotted a predator.

Is she in trouble?

"Well, I was just going to bed. Mrs. Dayholt you seem tired as well, I hope you will go to sleep soon too."

She quickly nods, "Yes, I think I'll do just that." She glances at Vivienne. "The servants showed me to my room earlier, I think I can find my way."

Mrs. Dayholt begins to walk the other direction, I glance at Vivienne, at the way she watches Esme walk away.

Was there something off?

I quickly begin making my way to Farah's old room before Vivienne can turn her cold attention back on me.

Quickly, I open the door and go inside before closing it behind me.

I let out a relieved sigh, taking a moment to catch my breath as I lean against the door.

Alone at last!

My head is spinning.

One day. *Only one day here and I already see that everyone is against me.*

What does Dominique want?

Why is he here?

The interactions with Mrs. Dayholt. How he questioned her about the rumors, the districts, and the borders.

Why was he so interested in all of that? WHO is he really?

Dominique Pascal? Or Dominique Madlocke?

Or is it neither?

I really need to be able to question him later.

I need to know how he knew I would be coming here... even before I did.

PART TWO
NO PAGE UNTURNED

IO
THE DATABASE

"...Reports of more and more magic users dropping out of the academy due to loss of powers has been increasing dramatically. Not only this, but magic barriers are needing constant re-casts as they are now falling down within days. What could be causing the sudden loss of magic in four districts..."

-The Flaize Spells Paper, Article by S. S. Lilith

I wasn't given much time to think that next morning as I am swept up in a whirlwind by Paxton and a few maids ready to clean the room for the day. I am barely awake as I get dressed, have my hair done, and follow my Lady's maid to the dining hall for breakfast.

I only feel half awake as I look at the room in the daylight. It felt like a completely different room, the dining table much shorter now with only a few people sitting at it. By the time I was fully awake, Paxton had shut the door behind me. I look at those who sit at the table, Dominique was not among them.

Lord Julian was not yet here either. It was just Lady Vivienne, Lady Priscilla, Mrs. Dayholt, and a gentleman I had yet to meet.

That's right... Mr. Wingrave lives in the upper class end of the city.

He shouldn't be up here too much - Right?

I sit down, silently thanking God as nobody corrects me on my seating choice.

I am a few seats away from Vivienne. I notice food was placed out on the table, so I reach forward and begin grabbing things and setting it on my own plate.

"So... Where is everyone else?" I ask after a moment.

Vivienne sighs, which warrants a quick glance from Mrs. Dayholt. "Lord Julian and your husband are speaking in the library, and most everyone else has yet to be woken. Schedules are apparently different in Broise."

Mrs. Dayholt frowns at this but says nothing as she continues to eat.

What happened between them?

Did Mrs. Dayholt confront Vivienne about it and not Lord Julian? Why? Thinking back to how I found the two last night, it didn't seem as though the two were arguing. In fact, it didn't even feel as though there was any animosity or even slight irritation between the two. Perhaps quite the opposite.

Does that mean Vivienne makes most of the decisions around here? But it seems more like Lord Julian does, after all he carried most of the dinner

conversations on his own. So Lord Julian might not be the head around here -
But Lord Julian is talking to Dominique in the library -

I feel my stomach turning, but I force myself to take another bite.

What if he was the test?

By going along with his little facade, what if that means they can exile me?

It had been a long time since an exile in any district.

Yet still, the controlling groups of each district still held the powers to do so. I had only seen it happen once, when I was very little. Father would tell me, "*Audrey, if you stop learning and studying that will be you.*" He had intended it to be funny, but it had scared me at the time.

Surely it would be just me right?

Or would my family be included?

I place the fork down next to the plate, *we know so little about the Dragonkin despite sharing a border.* Despite past 'peace treaties'.

Would we even last very long?

Suddenly two figures enter the room.

I look over to see Lord Julian and Dominique.

"Whenever you're ready to continue your studies *Ms.* Hughes, the library is now open for you." Lord Julian says with a warm smile. Nodding at this, I look at Dominique. He appears slightly irritated, but before I can even think to ask, he catches the confused expression on my face and quickly brightens up. Dominique sits across from me at the table.

I squint at him, and he simply smiles as he begins putting food on his plate. Humming to himself.

I wish I had the chance to speak with him more before all of this... Then I'd better understand what he is doing here in Yonnam.

I'm not sure I can believe much of what he says... I hope he won't lie to me.

Looking at Lord Julian, she can't tell what had transpired between the two as he is already back to his composed self.

Though he sits next to his wife Lady Priscilla, he doesn't say a word to her. Instead speaking with Vivienne.

The two really haven't interacted much since I arrived...

I finish my food after a few more minutes, but wait a while longer. Watching to see if anyone else will get up first.

Last night Lord Julian stood and then everyone left -

Is it the same now -

Suddenly Vivienne stood up.
"I have some business to attend to in my office, so I'll leave you all to it then."

Quickly, Mrs. Dayholt stands as well. "I'll join you."

Vivienne quickly casts a concerned glance between her and Audrey, but says nothing to stop her as she strides out of the room without another word, Esme
following at her tail. The sound of heels clicking grows distant after a moment.

I guess that means I should be free to leave as well?

I wait a moment before finally, I sit my fork down and stand.

"Where are you going?" Dominique asks quickly.

I glance between him and Lord Julian, he doesn't seem to be paying much attention at the moment.

"The library, I have some things I need to read through."

He puts his fork down, "I'll come with you." He hurries to my side and we leave the room with Lord Julian's sharp gaze piercing our backs.

I lead the way to the library, beginning to grab for the door but Dominique beats her there and holds it open.

"Ladies first."

His eyes are bright as he smiles at her warmly, I feel unsure of his kindness as I wearily step through the doorway. I glance around, there are no servants in the room at the time. *Perfect.*

I turn on Dominique quickly.

"Who are you, really?" I hiss under my breath. "Why have you been suddenly speaking to me? And how did you know to follow me here?"

Dominique puts his hands up and raises a brow. Looking more bemused than intimidated. Which only irritates me more.

"Slow down a bit there, you should still be careful with what you say, *darling*-"

"Don't call me that when we're alone." I retort.

"Why did you go along with this then, if you don't at least trust me a *little*?"

I sigh, "I couldn't- I couldn't handle having another reason to be the talk of the night... It was already going pretty awful, even before you arrived. Now tell me-" I step closer to him, making him back up. "*Who* are *you*?"

"Even if I told you, you're not going to believe it." He says, rolling his eyes.

"Try me."

He stares at me for a moment, as though he

expected me to back down. When I wait though, he sighs.

"I'm from another district, that much is true." He begins." I'm here because of rumors about how it was being run here." He sighs, "I didn't approach you because of this - well, what I'm saying is it's a coincidence... I socialized with most of the town actually. When I found that letter here I -"

"Found? So it wasn't lost with the mail -" I rest my head in my hand. "So you're not related to anyone in town either, but that's not a big surprise out of everything. Then how did you get the letter?"

"I snuck in - *doesn't matter how* - and heard of things being disposed of discreetly. Most of them were just old letters on paying to get mages here, or letters of affairs, but then there was that older lady's letter to you." He looks up at me, "Now do you understand why you were my perfect chance at getting in?"

I feel like he is telling me everything...

Or at least almost everything. But right now this is really the best bet.

It's this or work by myself.

And I'm not so sure how much I can do right now.

"Alright, well now that I'm stuck with you, what's the plan?"

He scoffs, "Harsh words for someone shy." I roll my eyes at him as he continues. "I need to find out what they're hiding here... Something is causing a great magic failure from here to the surrounding area, and I'm not sure what it is."

Audrey looks up at him, only just noticing how odd the colors in his eyes were. They were brown, which wasn't unusual, but they had flecks of varying tones of gold and black within them. She wasn't awestruck, but she felt as though she had heard something about magic association being visible in appearances once. Before she could think too deeply on it, Dominique begins to speak.

"We need to get you into your position of power, fast." He continues, not noticing my eyes fixated upon his. "Aren't you curious as to what's been going on here? Yonnam *is* the primary district where this sickness has been spreading. Broise is the next closest one, and Mrs. Dayton even told us her husband was ill with doctors unable to understand why."

As he focuses on me, I quickly look away. "So you really believe it is something here?" I ask.

I knew more and more people have been falling ill, but since mum started buying that 'magic cure' from magic academy dropouts I assumed it was being caused - or at least made worse by that.

There is about two months left now isn't there?

Thinking of my mother at home, I feel my heart stop. Was she still progressing as their neighbor had? Or was there a chance that she had more time being younger and healthier when she first got sick?

The sickness was strange. Some people had it last years, others dropped dead within months. The death rate overall was still fairly low, and remained within a few districts. Which is why there was so little alarm over it.

"There may be a source," Dominique continues. "I've been tracking it for a while and everything points to something here in District Yonnam. I believe it could be either someone, or something causing it intentionally."

"Do you think... If whatever the source was here was destroyed, would it allow people in the area to recover?"

"I can't say for sure, I don't know what the cause might be." He says solemnly. "But I do think the cause is somewhere here."

Perhaps it's worse than I originally thought here. How many times have I passed the Abbey and felt something... wrong in the air. *Could he be right? Is the source of the illness somewhere here?*

"Why are you telling me all of this?"

"You're the only one new to the Abbey, so I know you aren't in with anyone here... well, not yet anyways. I need someone else who can help me here."

I frown, "That can't be it. It seems like you can handle yourself fairly we -" I stop as he unbuttons the top few buttons on his shirt. "What are you doing -"

I stop as he pulls his shirt aside to reveal a purple and gold branching pattern appearing on his chest.

It's just like mum's marking... I remember seeing purple and gold lines going up her mother's collarbone. At first she had tried to hide them, and until she could no longer stand, no one had really known that she was struggling.

"I can't do this alone, because I've already been affected by the sickness."

I back away quickly, making Dominique fix his shirt again.

"Don't worry, it hasn't spread anymore and you can't get it from being near me - just the source. Otherwise this would be spreading like wildfire through the districts."

There is a chance I might already have it then... Maybe it takes longer to affect some people then? I think to myself.

Should I tell him?

No.

Why burden him with my own problems when instead we can work to find a solution?

But still...

"Then... You're trying to find it to save yourself?"

He shakes his head, "That's... not why I started my search, I picked it up along the way." He chuckles awkwardly, and when he sees that I'm about to speak he continues, interrupting. "For now though- tell me why Lord Julian took the job intended for you, and is giving it to his mouse of a wife?" He begins to walk over to the nearest table with chairs. I follow him.

"He said I should be properly trained first-" I begin, as he pulls out a chair and motions for me to sit. "Perhaps it's better that my family couldn't be moved here..."

"Your mother would probably pass the moment she reaches the abbey. *If* the source is here."

"You know my mother is ill? How?"

"I spoke to your father while you were out, he caught me on the street and wanted to... chat."

I snort. *Hopefully he isn't trying to marry me off to any man.*

"I know I can't bring them here, but still. They need money, and with me not there to work..."

"Once we can get you into your position, I'll help with negotiating having your inheritance sent home to your family."

I frown, surprised by his kind tone, but even more surprised that he seemed to already have this planned.

He is so kind to me, and has yet to dismiss anything I say and yet... He is not very open about his reasons to be here. What made him start *searching for this source?*

"Since then all he's done is given me books to read. None of them have been useful, to be completely honest." As I sit in the chair, Dominique sits next to me. "How exactly do you expect me to be able to get this role back? I can't just read a few books and then ask nicely."

"Exactly, you won't." Dominique grins, "I'll help you learn, then you'll take it back."

It had been hours and hours of reading books with Dominique. I enjoy reading, though I constantly would stop to wonder how much of this sort of thing Farah had to deal with and then still have the time and energy to come and visit me.

"So far what we have in short -" I begin, making Dominique look up from the papers he was skimming. "- Farah was supposed to be in charge of watching funds, reviewing the other's decisions and signing papers to ensure that everyone was in agreement, and performing activities for the public?"

"That's most of it, she was supposed to be what held everyone together and kept things in order. I find it odd that she didn't seem to do much of it. In fact it seems that as she got older she delegated more and more tasks between Lord Julian and Lady Vivienne."

I sigh, laying my head onto the table. "So then if there is a source here, Farah might not have known... There must be something that clearly states the roles and descriptions of what I am going to have to do."

Dominique nods, "I believe they are hiding a majority of it from you- that they even hid it from Farah somehow."

He glances at me, "I know there are a few more parties and events this week since other districts have been sending people to check the border district with all of the rumors going on. Lord Julian mentioned it when he interrogated me earlier."

"What do we do with that?"

"Easy, we need to get information, and cause a scene."

II
GATHERING INFORMATION

"...The King's soldiers are seemingly more active, as residents in the central district of Alant have been reporting multiple sightings of larger squadrons in training. But this was not normal training..."
-Flaize Daily

After three days of reading along with dinners and awkward conversations with people who didn't really care for what I had to say, I finally felt as though it was paying off.

Or at least, I felt like I was getting used to the way things ran in the abbey. Whether or not it was 'paying off' was another story entirely.

After every dinner, the guests and hosts would gather in the sitting room for drinks and conversation. Since this is more open than the table it was better for listening into conversations and conversing freely. The dinner table would be good - if it weren't for the seating arrangement always sitting Priscilla at my side. Who had become too afraid to speak to me.

I think of this as I keep catching her eyes on me as I stand by Mrs. Dayholt and a few others in the sitting room.

I don't know what to think of her.

Lord Julian is very clear on where he stands with my being here, Vivienne seems irritated but nothing more, but Priscilla -

I can't even begin to tell what is wrong with her.

She almost reminds me of -

"I think I will be staying a little while longer," Mrs. Dayholt says to the small group of women, I glance at her, frowning. "How come?" I ask.

"Well, V - *Lady* Vivienne is hosting a tea party soon and I'd rather not miss it."

She almost called her by the first name again.

Another woman speaks up, "Shouldn't you be getting back to your husband?"

Before I - or anyone for that matter can say anything in response, Mrs.Dayholt looks past us as though her attentions are elsewhere.

"I'm so sorry, but I feel a little faint. I believe now I should say my goodbyes and go up to my room."

She hurries away, far quicker than a faint

person should.

A tea party...

Perhaps that will be important?

Or is it just a place for gossip?

I watch her as she goes - the door to the great hall had just shut. It was almost as though she were following someone.
Most of the members of the Broise district board members would be leaving tonight, and now Mrs. Dayholt was staying behind.

She has been leaving the dinners and events rather early though. I think as she leaves the room. The women around me go back to gossiping, hardly noticing me.

"Did you see that?" One woman says, "Mrs. Dayholt didn't even respond to my question!"

Is she getting ill?

Mrs. Dayholt hasn't been here for very long, is the sickness taking hold in people that quickly?

Will it take ahold of me quickly as well?

"Well, she *is* in an arranged marriage," Another replies. "It isn't a big surprise she isn't rushing to be by his side."

The woman nods, "I met Mr. Dayholt, he is no social man, that's for sure. Even if he *were* healthy he tends to stay in the Broise Manor."

Avoiding her husband? Or staying here for a reason...

I shake my head, I don't even say goodnight to the women I stood by, as they are too enthralled by talk of the prince's coming of age ceremonies at the capital.

Mrs. Dayholt has been kind to me, so should I be snooping?

I needed to leave early as well. Except I knew why I had to. Mr. Wingrave was here.

At the past few dinners in fact he showed up. By Lord Julian's reaction, I assume it isn't common for him. He just wants to get under my skin, and I won't allow that.

Entering the great hall still amazes me. Though the bedrooms in the abbey - as well as lower class streets still use firelight, there are a few districts and places in Yonnam Abbey beginning to use electricity; I found this was the case in the great hall.

Just as I reach the bottom of the stairs I hear a voice call out, "Where do you think you're going so early?"

I grit my teeth and turn to see Mr. Wingrave leaning against the door to the sitting room. He smirks, "How long do you think you can avoid me for?"

I roll my eyes, "I'm tired, Mr. Wingrave."

Not everything is about you.

Though in this case, it definitely was about him, but that didn't matter.

"Don't you think it's a wonder that nobody has heard a single word about you almost becoming an upper class woman before?"

I sigh, "What are you getting at, Mr. Wingrave?"

"I see becoming a lady still doesn't suit you," He says snidely. "I'm saying that people might find it interesting- You lost your chances with me, but here you are suddenly with an upper class title and money that even outranks me. I think Lord Julian would be interested in knowing a gold digger wants to run the district alongside him."

Does he really think he has something to use against me?

"Why should Lord Julian believe such a story?"

"Because I still have that letter your dearest papa sent me."

He sent a letter?!

At that moment I never felt more angry at my father.

Why would he do such a thing?!

Not now-

I can't lose composure. Mr. Wingrave should be the least of my worries.

He could be bluffing... Right?

I huff as haughtily as I can, "If I were a gold digger, I wouldn't have had a problem with your cheating you son of a -"

"Easy now," Mr. Wingrave said, cutting me off. "I'm not here to bite your ear off, it's just a warning."

"A warning for what?" I ask, I notice that the door handle slowly turns by Mr. Wingrave's side. He doesn't seem to be aware.

"Well, put in a good word for me with Lord Julian, so that I might find myself with a- shall we say unfortunate death inheritance like you did. I'm sure you can find another dying lord or lady for that, right Audrey?"

Just then the door gets pulled open, and Mr. Wingrave falls back into the sitting room. All conversation goes quiet. I can't help but laugh out loud, which is foolish. It was far louder than I had expected. I pray nobody heard from the other room.

Dominique steps away from the now fallen Mr. Wingrave, smirking.

He stands, face red and turns fuming at Dominique, who merely puts his hands up.

"My sincerest apologies, Mr. Wingrave, I wasn't aware that anyone would be leaning against the door like that."

Mr. Wingrave looks at me one last time before huffing and rejoining his wife in the sitting room, while Dominique steps out and shuts the door behind them.

"Can I walk you to your room?" He asks.

I nod, and he hurries over to join me on the stairs. Dominique falls in step beside me, matching her slow pace as she is still adapting to the heels she wore.

"I overheard part of what Mr. Wingrave said to you."

I huff, "You already seem to know everyone's names, impressive." I say, trying to change the subject.

"Just... don't worry about him. He is a fool, and he wouldn't actually show that letter, even if he did have it."

Dominique holds up a letter to me, I gasp. It was my father's handwriting.

"How did you get that?"

He chuckles as we reach the top of the stairs. "The same way I found the letter you needed from Farah." He hands it to me. "Now, the tea party."

"The tea party?" I frown, not because of the subject at hand, but because of Dominique's tendency to change the subject often.

Dominique nods, "All of the ladies of the abbey are hosting one for others who are not attending the Prince's event at the capitol. Mrs. Dayholt is still here so she will be attending, along with a few others. You also should be going."

"Am I able to go?"

He shrugs, "It's happening in the gardens."

"In this cold?"

He laughs, "It's not that cold out. I believe It is outdoors for those anxious about the sickness, so I don't think anyone would stop you. That would be embarrassing for the hostess to have to kick you out."

"The hostess is Lady Vivienne, right?"

He nods.

Not very reassuring. I think to myself as I follow Dominique down the hall. "This is where we part ways," Dominique says as we reach my door.

How does he know where my room is?

He turns to Audrey, "Don't forget, tomorrow at noon is when the tea party will begin in the gardens."

I tilt my head at him. "Will I not see you again before it?"

He shakes his head, not meeting Audrey's gaze. He looks elsewhere. "I have some-business to attend to. So we probably won't cross paths for a while." He dips his head. "Goodnight, Ms. Hughes."

I almost laugh, "You can call me Audrey now." I call out as I watch him go back down the hallway. He stops, and turns around, taking backward steps as he smiles, "Alright,

Goodnight Audrey."

I feel sick as I turn to go into Farah's room. Every time I go near it, I'm reminded of her.

I wish I could have seen how she handled all of this.

As I begin to turn the doorknob to step in, I freeze as I hear voices inside.

Is there a couple using my room to -

It is only now that I realize that I am not by the right door. We had walked too far down the hall while Dominique and I had been talking, and had passed it by a long shot.

I hear as voices quickly go quiet from the other side of the door. I begin to back away.

"Are you sure?"

"I am... you've supported me far more than... do you really think I wouldn't stand beside you just because of..."

Was that -

Mrs. Dayholt and Lady Vivienne?!

I begin to take a step back when the door is pulled open. Vivienne steps out, holding the door behind her.

"What do you want?"

Though the hall light is dim, I can see that Vivienne's usual composure is gone. Her usual clean look is replaced by one of fear as a few hairs had fallen down from her perfect braid and a few beads of sweat drip from her brow. She looks irritated, and... afraid? Was she afraid of me finding her?

"I was tired and accidentally passed my room," I lied. "I should get to my own room now - Goodnight!"

I kick off my heels and grab them, hurrying down the hall before Vivienne can say anything in response. I push into my room and almost slam the door shut behind me.

It is only then that it clicks.

Oh my God!

12
PRIMARY SOURCE

"...Reports of more and more magic users dropping out of the academy due to loss of powers have been increasing dramatically. Not only this, but magic barriers are needing constant re-casts as they are now falling down within days. What could be causing the sudden loss of magic in four districts..."
- The Flaize Spells Paper, by S. S. Lilith

The next day is a late start, after tossing and turning all night wondering what to do with Vivienne and Emmett, I got just enough sleep to not be enough and be too much all at the same time. Paxton seems surprised when she sees me coming down the stairs dressed in a thick outdoor coat.

They didn't expect me to be ready to join everyone, to even be aware of anything different going on. But I knew.

The tea party would take place a little while after breakfast, which meant I would be arriving early. I open the front doors and step out into the cold late autumn air, a servant closes the door behind me and I let out a relieved sigh to be out of their watchful gaze. Looking around I realize, I have never been to the garden where this took place. It should be close, I guess as I begin walking down the road the gateway.

The fresh air was nice, even if it was chilly outside. The fresh air was nice, even if it was a little chilly outside. I even felt the pains in my chest alleviate more and more with each breath as I went further out of the building.

Dominique is right...

Whatever is causing this sickness is here, in the abbey itself.

As I continue down the road I notice a path breaking off of the road, I look down it to see where it leads to seeing it goes into a very lush and overgrown side of the abbey.

Surely this would lead to the garden the tea parties at, right?

I begin walking down the gravel stone pathway, feeling slightly less relaxed as the shade of nearby evergreens blocks the warmth of the sun, after a few minutes of walking the overgrowth breaks away to reveal a colorful land of growth.

I look ahead. It was a beautiful garden. Many types of flowers were being grown, from winter pansies to snapdragons. It was surprising seeing such beautiful blooms this late in the year. I know our garden has nothing that can handle this chill. In the center of the brightly colored growth atop perfectly round stepping stones sat a small garden table and chairs.

There were many servants running around setting things up for the upcoming tea party, putting out tablecloths, setting up trays and tea sets, and even putting cushions on the chairs and blankets out because of the cold. In the center of it all stood the tall and intimidating Lady Vivienne. She wore a warm-looking form-fitting dress with a mermaid skirt, it had a thick shawl with it placed over her shoulders, yet she still looks cold as she watches the servants work. Her watchful gaze even seems to scare the servants she is commanding around. As I step into the garden area
Vivienne's eyes immediately turn to me.

I don't stop and hesitate this time when I see her piercing gaze, I walk over and stop in front of her.

"Good Morning Lady Vivienne." I begin with a fake smile, "I am surprised to see you up so early, I thought you would be tired after last night."

The servants around keep working but seem interested in Vivienne's response, casting quick glances up from their work setting up.

"Yes, the dinner last night was very tiring indeed," She replies coolly, jaw tight as she grits her teeth at me.

"Do you mind stepping aside to speak with me in private?" I ask, "There are a few matters of my inheritance I need to discuss with you."

Vivienne seems taken aback by the boldness of the question, she frowns and glances at the servants once more before she nods.

Leading the way out of the main garden seating area, Vivienne hurries to stop beneath the thicker undergrowth where fewer of the flowers are. Turning towards me she crosses her arms, I stop a few feet away from her.

"What do you want?" She asks, her usually silvery and charismatic tone replaced by a gruff and irritated one. I can't help but smile.

This will be useful.

"I want you to help me get my title, and my inheritance. Everything that was supposed to be mine."

Her lip curls in disgust as she looks down at Audrey, "How exactly do you think I can do that? Shouldn't you be pestering Lord Julian and his mousy little wife?"

"You see, I have this hunch," I said as I step

closer, "You seem to carry yourself like you have some semblance of power here, you are a member of the board so I am sure you have some say in what goes on."

"And why do you think I would want you in power here? Everything dropped into your lap like that?"

"Wasn't everything dropped into yours?" I retort, Vivenne smirks.

"You know nothing of me, girl."

"Oh?" I say getting closer and closer to Vivienne, "How about this, how is Mrs. Dayholt? She usually is up early, but I have yet to see her after last night."

Vivienne's eyes go wide at this, making Audrey smirk.

"I'm sure her husband wouldn't like to hear of just how much she is enjoying herself when away from him."

"Hold your tongue!" She snaps, "You know nothing! Nothing at all of this situation, so if you dare contact that devil I'll-"

"You'll what?"

Vivenne stops, she seems frozen, just staring at Audrey for a moment before shoving past her, "Fine. I'll help you get your pathetic title and money, but after that, you're on your own. Then you'll truly see how out of your element you are."

She storms away, and I follow her back to the garden for the tea party.

It should be starting soon. I think to myself as I see the servants are all finished with set up.

I spot Mrs. Dayholt, who is the first to arrive, beside myself, Vivienne is already at her side. I watch as she leans in to whisper something to Mrs. Dayholts ear.

She cups her hand over her mouth and stares at Lady Vivienne, she looks as though she might cry.

I feel a pang in my chest at that, Mrs. Dayholt was one of the few here to be kind to me. Was this a poor maneuver?

She didn't deserve to be unhappy but...

I need to solve this, to deal with this sickness.

To be able to support my family before things get worse.

I look away from Mrs. Dayholt's teary blue eyes and Vivenne's cold stare. I have bigger problems to deal with right now.

Is that so wrong?

13
THE WEIGHT OF PAPER

"...a group of the King's men is being formed to check on the state of the border in the district of Yonnam. For the first time in centuries, there are considerations of sending a delegation across the border to Dragnior. While it will take a few months to form, the King is working hard to..."
- Official Statement from the King's Advisor

Things were going nowhere, even with blackmailing Vivienne. She was dragging her feet on doing anything to help her. I was restless in my room, it was midnight already, yet as I sat on the side of the bed in my nightgown, I could see the dark circles beneath my wide eyes in my mirror across the room.

I didn't want to admit it, or even have to acknowledge it, but the worst-case scenario was upon me. It was ever so light, but when I pulled my shirt down past my collarbone the beginnings of a branching pattern were ever so slightly visible. Coming from over my heart.

Is this because I am in the abbey now?

Is the source here making the process faster?

I stand up from my spot, fixing the shirt and looking away from my reflection.

Shouldn't more people be affected and not just me or...

Is there a way the board is keeping a majority of the upper class from falling ill?

I sigh, shaking my head. I have to find something, anything, to prove that there was something going on here. I was running out of time, for Mum, for Dominique, and now for myself.

I need to find a source or a hint at something wrong here.

Which means I am going to have to find Julian's office.

Sneaking around was nothing new to me, I've had to sneak in and out of my house early in the morning and late at night on occasions when I couldn't face my father, or when I had to work too late.

This was different. There was far more at stake if I was caught.

Barefoot, I walk through the halls, hoping, no - *Praying* everyone else is already in bed. It was an ungodly hour to be awake at this point, and with how early Lady Vivienne and Lord Julian were awake, it would be surprising to find they also didn't go to sleep until late.

Everyone had gone to bed after a long dinner of sharp remarks, sideways glances, and a dance of words to avoid being directly snooty. It was exhausting, and I even found myself desperately wishing to be back in my room. Even servants would be asleep after cleaning by this time of the night, yet I wasn't.

There were far more important things to do though. At least, that's what I keep telling myself as I reach the bottom of the stairs. The offices are all somewhere on the first level, each of the three members of the board had an office within the abbey as far as I am aware.

I have no idea where they are, or which would be which. I didn't even know where to start, I just know where they are not, as I already know where the front dining room, library, and sitting room are.

I glance around the great hall, it feels ominous. Without the loud and boisterous conversation or even the odd electric - powered lighting being off, it felt eerie. Even candles were not left about, and I hadn't even thought to bring a lantern with me, as I had become used to finding everywhere well lit.

It's so odd...

I had only recently learned more about the odd powered lighting in the abbey, apparently, most districts had already been constructing it to have more electric lighting throughout the cities, but in Yonnam only the abbey had it.

I'm guessing because it is newer and still being worked on they have to leave it off at night?

I shake my head, either way, this would make things a little more difficult.

Turning away from the library, I look to the hall that leads underneath the stairs. The hallway split into two directions.

I've seen Julian go right...

But am I looking for his, or Vivienne's?

Dominique did say he was snooping around the abbey as well, perhaps I should have waited and questioned him on it?

Dominique said he would be searching as well but - I haven't seen him at all.

Perhaps he is far better suited to this than I.

Speaking of...

I haven't seen him since he told me more about the tea party.

Turning down the hall, Audrey glances at each door. No lights could be seen except under one.

Wait -

Someone is still up.

Quietly, I sneak around the door, spotting one of the many large decorative statues, I stand beside it. If anyone left that room, I would have to hope they went back down the hall to the stairs, and not in my direction. Leaning against the statue, I try to slow my breathing so I can hear the talking.

"- There's talks of an envoy being sent to Yonnam, to inspect the district and the border -"

"Easy Lady Vivienne, it is just talk right now, besides - with the Prince's coming of age ceremonies no one of any real importance will be sent."

I recognize the second voice, the disgustingly silvery tone was all too familiar. It was Julian.

They're both here?

Whose office would this be?

And -

Is Dominique nearby?

While I stood by the statue, I felt as though I was being watched. Someone else was near, but in the darkness all I could see was what was near the door to the office.

"- more importantly, what are we going to do about Farah's *heir*? It was easy enough keeping an old woman away from the business - but her? She's getting through everything I throw her way - and fast - I'm not sure how much longer it will be before she starts getting involved in the business."

"That's not what's important here, Lord Julian." Hisses Vivienne. "She's easy. Just let her have some money to give to her own family."

"I'm surprised, Lady Vivienne. You've changed your tune, is there something to that?"

"Don't be ridiculous," She retorts, her voice cracking in the process. "Let her play pretend planner for the community and eventually we'll think of some scandal to ruin her name and reputation. Nobody will want her within the board and *viola*. Right now we need to focus on what's taking that mage so long to return!"

Mage?

It doesn't sound like they're talking about the barrier but -

What else could they need a mage for?

"Enough of this for tonight, I need some rest." Julian grumbles loudly.

"Tomorrow Belladonna will be visiting - I expect she wants to see me."

"And Priscilla?"

"She'll keep busy enough acting like she's doing the new Ms. Hughes work- It's no problem."

Suddenly the door opens, and I press myself against the wall. As she does she sees a small pair of glowing eyes watching her on the statue.

Is that a mouse?

While I couldn't fully make it out, I couldn't think of anything else it could be as it was very tiny.

I try to ignore it, it's too small to cause any commotion or problems, but even as I focus on Vivienne and Julian's footsteps I still feel keenly aware of its eyes upon me.

As soon as I can hear the echoes of heels and loafers on the stairs, I step around the statue and grab the doorknob. I twist it, wearily eyeing the mouse-sized creature, but to no avail.

The door doesn't open. Locked.

Did they lock it?

It makes sense, they probably had a lot to hide within the room, but *still.*

Audrey tries to recall how her father would unlock the front door after they had lost the house key. For a while, he would use mum's hairpins. He had shown Audrey how to do it as well, but that was many years ago.

I only have a few in my hair right now...

So only -

She picks them out of her braided hair, letting it fall down.

- *Seven chances.*

Before I can even hold a lockpick to the door, I feel something scurry over my foot. I jump away and look around.

Did the mouse run under the doorway?

Moment's later, a startled gasp can be heard from the other side of the door.

"Dominique?" I whisper.

Something clicks on the other side of the door.

The door opens with none other than Dominique himself standing on the other side.

"You were in there this whole time?!" He nods, "I was in the cabinet, but when I got out something startled me -" He chuckles. "Seems like it was good that had happened or I wouldn't have let you in."

I furrow a brow at him and nod, glancing around the office.

The walls were mostly hidden behind shelves and filing cabinets, a large desk sat in the center of the room, where many papers were spread about.

"What now?"

Dominique turns to the desk, and begins shuffling through pages.

"Here's hoping we find something."

I stare at him.

"This all seems - too easy," I said as I step closer to him. "How were you in here without them noticing you?"

"Easy, I was hiding in the cabinet. Now come look at these pages with me."

He begins rummaging through cabinets. I watch him for a moment.

I haven't seen him around for a while and now I find him here?

This is odd -

But right now I need to figure out the abbey.

I can worry about Dominique later.

Since he is looking through the cabinets, I sit at the desk and begin opening the drawers and skimming through various papers, books, pens and pencils, and many other writing supplies.

"I found something - it seems Julian was writing letters to a friend. Talking about the jobs he stole from Farah-"

I look over at Dominique. He had opened the cabinets and held a folder in his hands.

None of these cabinets look big enough -

Something is wrong.

I frown and begin trying to open the middle drawer of the desk while still watching

Dominique. I miss, and hit something beneath the desk.

What?

I get out of the chair and duck underneath the desk as I notice something on the bottom. Something attached to the drawer. Just as I do, I hear footsteps outside the door.

"Audrey, stay there!" A whisper echoes in the room.

Where is Dominique hiding?

Looking around the room from underneath the desk, I see nothing. Nowhere he could hide.

The door opens and someone comes into the room. The footsteps stop at the other side of the desk.

The sounds of paper crumpling and being rustled about can be heard atop the desk. Someone grumbles to themselves as they struggle to find something.

Is that Julian?!

The footsteps begin to come around the desk, I feel my heart beating faster and faster. It felt as though it could be heard throughout the room.

Please don't sit down.

There is no way I can explain myself hiding beneath his desk.

I could see his shoes stop right in front of

me.

Is he going to sit -

Suddenly, something bolts by his foot. Making Julian jump.

A voice comes from outside the room.

"Hurry up already, Julian. I don't have all night."

Julian sighs, "I told you, Lady Vivienne, I had the address right here." He grumbles. "Looks like we have lizards getting in as well. I'll need to have Mr. Smith set traps again."

Lizards?

The shoes disappear from Audrey's sight as he goes back around the desk.

"Now you go write that letter, I'll make sure I lock up this time."

The door closes, and Audrey hears the sound of it being locked from the other side.

I wait a long time, half an hour before I crawl out from under the desk. I say a half hour, but it was probably only a few minutes. It only felt like forever to sit under a desk.

"That was close, right Domini -"

Dominique was nowhere in sight. I sigh, "Are you still hiding?"

Audrey steps around the room opening every cabinet. Not a single one held the large redhead man. None could even hold him, they were all filled to the brim with folders and binders of various uses.

Dominique was not an overly large man, he was probably just a few inches over Audrey, but he was still too large to fit any of the cabinets.

How could he have hidden? Or get out of here for that matter?

I look around and realize I am completely alone now.

There's a lot Dominique is still hiding from me.

But I can't waste any time wondering right now.

Audrey looks back under the desk. A small chain dangled off of the underside. She pulls it, the bottom of the desk opens up and a small box falls out. A letterbox.

Jackpot.

I open the box to find letters, agreements, purchases, and more.

The envelopes are heavy, and have many papers shoved into each one.

Opening and unfolding them one by one I begin reading through the many words. Devouring each sentence furiously and faster than she had ever read in her life, in fear that Julian may return again.

What...

I drop the letters to the ground.

Holy magic?

Only mages of an extremely high ranking and certification can perform such -

There's no way what's inside these letters is true.

If it is -

Why does Julian need holy magic used here?

Did the magic fail - creating the sickness?

What was he trying to create?

I don't know enough on Holy Magic - but I do know the King is against its illegal usage by low-level mages, not to mention the dragonkin -

This could start a war.

14
RENEWAL

"...Reports of more and more magic users dropping out of the academy due to loss of powers have been increasing dramatically. Not only this, but magic barriers are needing constant re-casts as they are now falling down within days. What could be causing the sudden loss of magic in four districts all closest to the Dragnior border..."

-The Flaize Spells Paper, Article by S. S. Lilith

It's an odd feeling, having to watch at all sides as you sit at a table with predators. I watch how Vivienne and Julian interact in the morning, surprised I was able to get up at all after how late it was that I found my way back to my room. I don't only watch the pair of board members, but also Dominique, who sits across from me eating as though he had not disappeared the night before.

I still don't know if I should tell him about what I found. If I should even continue to trust him. He has hardly given me a reason to - and yet...

I feel like there is more to this.

How did he disappear last night?

After Audrey had barely avoided being

found by Julian, she had tried to look for Dominique but he was nowhere to be found.

Instead of searching the whole abbey, she had decided it would be better to go back to her room.

No matter -

I can't waste any time on that.

I need to quickly get into Farah's old position.

It's time I try something...

Taking in a deep breath, I speak up.

"I was thinking today I would assist Lady Priscilla in the tasks I will be taking over." I feel myself freeze up as I try not to flinch away from Julian's harsh gaze.

"I'll learn far better from doing it along with someone."

Priscilla smiles slightly, and opens her mouth to speak.

"Perhaps you should study a little while longer -" Julian interrupts. "Just to -"

"Why not? Lord Julian?" Vivienne adds. "Perhaps Lady Priscilla would enjoy the company while she works. It may take longer but she needs to learn eventually."

Perfect, they took the bait.

I knew they'd accept, being they want her distracted. I glance at Julian, how his face turns from annoyed to a disgustingly charismatic grin.

What a horrible man.

This makes me grateful for backing out of my own engagement. Would we have ended up like this?

If I had married Emmet, he would have kept on taking mistresses, wouldn't he?

I was lucky I found out, if Priscilla found out that would be bad for -

I think I have an idea for later.

Audrey smiles as she finishes her eating, a little surprised by her changed way of thinking since she had arrived at the abbey a little over a week prior.

Hopefully soon, I'll be able to send the money back to papa.

They should be able to last a little while longer.

But I shouldn't stretch it out too long.

Priscilla suddenly stands up to leave, as she does Julian begins putting his fork and napkin down. His eyes are on her like a hawk. Julian meant to stop her and warn her- to instruct her on what to say, what not to say. To make her even more of a puppet.

I can't let him intervene.

I quickly stand, "I'll come with you."

She dips her head as the two go out of the room, I ignore Dominique's raised brow and don't meet his gaze as I follow Priscilla.

As soon as the door shuts behind them Priscilla turns to me. “Thank you.”

“What for?”

“For - Coming out here with me. I’m afraid my husband would have given me an earful of orders had you not - Just - Thank you.” She continues across the hall.

“Wait here for a moment, I need to go get my things, then we will head out to the garden seating and-”

“Garden? Not your office?” I ask.

“I don’t have an office I’m afraid.” She says with a sigh. “And I... Prefer not to work in the library.” Moments later she
goes up the stairs, leaving Audrey waiting in the great hall for her.

Doesn’t have an office -

But Farah did.

So who’s using Farah’s office?

Did Julian take hers? Or did Vivienne?

Or perhaps someone else?

Most of the family is in the capital, for the event happening for the prince...

Though there were some upperclassmen from the higher end of the city who came to the abbey on occasion. *Could there be someone else causing problems?*

After waiting a few minutes, Priscilla returns with her arms full of papers and office things.

"Alright - Um - Follow me?" She says, though it comes out as more of a question than anything as she leads the way out the front door.

As I follow her down the road, I realize it is the first time in a while I had actually been outside. The fresh air was nice, even if it was chilly outside. The fresh air was nice, even if it was a little cold outside.

The cold air hurt to breathe in at first, but the fresh air was far less painful than the stifling feeling inside of the abbey.

"The gardens aren't too far, and nothing I have to do is too difficult."

I don't tell her I've already been to the gardens as I continue to follow her.

"Didn't you take on all of Farah - I mean, Dowager Davies' work?" I ask as I follow her onto a side pathway breaking off from the main road.

"I - Well..." She looks ahead. "Oh! That's where we will set up."

I look ahead. It was a beautiful garden. Many types of flowers were being grown, from winter pansies to snapdragons. It was surprising seeing such beautiful blooms this late in the year. I know our garden has nothing that can handle this chill. In the center of the brightly colored growth atop perfectly round stepping stones sat a small garden table and chairs.

Priscilla is quick to sit and begin placing the papers out on the obviously far too small table. I join her, choosing a seat across from her at the table since it is too cramped to be next to each other.

"What are we going to be working on?" I ask.

"Right now, Lord Halloway has asked that- well we just have to read over these pages and sign them."

Does she not call her own husband by his first name?

"What are these papers?" I take one off of the too-large stack and glance it over.

"Just... Different payments on things for here and the town." She looks up at me. "You don't really have to read them. Just sign it."

I furrow my brows at this. "So you just accept whatever Lord Halloway tells you to sign?"

Priscilla doesn't say anything, as she begins signing pages. Though her face is red as the brightly colored snapdragons that surround them.

I ought to keep most of these to question him later.

I glance up at Priscilla, she is becoming so focused on signing papers that she doesn't notice my stare.

Only glancing between the stack and the papers in front of her.

I hope I can get through more papers than her.

Time slips by as the pair go through papers. Though hours pass, the stack still had little more than a dent in it, even with Priscilla signing without reading it took too long.

I glance at the stack, it isn't even halfway done, and I have yet to find a single cost that was for anything to improve or help the town.

I look at Priscilla, who is only signing papers. Not reading a single one. Yet her eyes hardly focused as she signed the papers, she had slight dark circles beneath her eyes, and her movements were getting slow.

"Everything alright Lady Priscilla?"

She looks up, startled. "What- Oh, yes. I'm doing alright."

Just then, I can hear horseshoes clicking on the road. Turning away from Priscilla, I have to look through the flowers and brush to see a carriage being pulled down the road.

Who's coming here today - Mrs. Dayholt isn't leaving until tomorrow, so her carriage wouldn't be coming to -

It is then that I recall the conversation overheard between Julian and Vivienne.

It's her.

Should we start heading back, perhaps?

I look at the still working Priscilla.

She seems timid, tired...

I would want to know, I *did* want to know with Emmet, but Priscilla seems... Too soft for that.

I hope I'm making the right decision here.

"Mrs. Halloway, you seem quite tired. What do you say? We can head back and I will finish this all tonight in my room?"

Her eyes brighten slightly, "Really I -" She looks away. "No, I should finish these now for Mr. Halloway."

"I can tell him you did them all," I add. Priscilla looks down at the papers for a moment, by the look on her face, she was taking a moment to consider. After a long minute, she nods.

"Alright, just - take them straight to your room when we head back."

I smile as I take the stack of papers and stand to follow Priscilla out of the gardens and onto the main path.

This is either going to work extremely well to our favor, or completely against it.

I think to myself as I look ahead. Whoever was in the carriage was already in the house as the driver began taking it around to the servant's entrance.

I hope I made the right call on this.

As we reach the front door, I slowly realize nobody has noticed their arrival, not even the servants who usually open the door.

We must have just missed her then...

Perhaps this was for the best.

So I hurry to open the door for Priscilla. Priscilla freezes in the doorway, I peek around to see what made her stop.

"Lord Halloway?"

So I was right.

Up ahead in the great hall, I see Julian holding a rather small but well-dressed woman, he looks to the doorway, and his expression changes. He doesn't seem concerned, or even guilty.

Lord Halloway instead, shows anger. My stomach turns at this. *Surprised?*

Didn't you expect this?

I thought I would catch him by surprise but-

I didn't think he would get angry with her.

"Priscilla! What are you doing back already?" He tosses the woman's hand off of his arm and makes his way over to Priscilla, he begins to get uncomfortably close to her.

"Did you finish everything I asked of you? I think no -"

"We did, actually." I lie, stepping in front of her. "I thought Mrs. Halloway looked quite exhausted, so we worked hard to get it done so she could come in and rest."

"She looks quite fine to me," He growls as he glares at me. I feel sick to my core as he stares down at me, you wanted this to happen.

Now you need to deal with the consequences.

I look at Priscilla. She had makeup rubbing away, showing the dark circles that she had tried to hide beneath her eyes, she had run out of breath quite fast on the slow walk back, and there was deep emotional exhaustion seen within her eyes. Her exhaustion was to no one's surprise, at least for those who paid any real attention.

Without another word, Priscilla dips her head and quickly hurries up the stairs.

I turn to Lord Halloway. Clenching my fist at each side as I watch his pleased expression as his wife hurries away.

"I will be taking on all of my tasks starting tomorrow," I loudly state. "I have much to discuss with you on these... Payments being made." With a look at the woman who stands beside Julian, I almost feel pleased with her baffled expression. “And I would like to get some of my inheritance earnings sent home to my family.”

Without wasting another moment, I turn and make my way up the stairs to my room.

I do my best to control my expression, but feel my stomach turn with every step.

I had not held my tongue, I didn’t keep my thoughts to myself. It was relieving and yet -

I don’t know how I will be able to do anything more now, or if he might retaliate for this... but-

At least he looked afraid.

15
BINDINGS

"...Always bound between saying too much and too little, bound to never find rest, bound to a love who finds other lovers. I pity the soul bound to another who is not bound in return..."

- Poems by the Great Bryun F. Lumar, Founder of The Country of Flaize

Over the next few days, Audrey finds that both Dominique and Julian have suddenly become the most elusive creatures she had ever seen.

It had gotten to the point that Audrey would have better luck finding the rumored Dragonkin in the capital compared to being able to stop and speak with either of the men.

When I did see Julian he was either accompanied by his lover or Vivienne, and even she had seemed annoyed by being around him as much as she was.

There is only one other person I can speak with.

I'm not even sure she will have much to say to me if she speaks with me at all.

I would have to find a servant to help me,

but I was not going to ring a bell and get Mr. Smith or Mrs. Fink, both of which are the most likely to report to Julian.

I had to find Paxton.

I still didn't trust her after she had locked me away that one night, but I had no other choice. She was the lesser of the evils available to me at the moment.

I am sure she could be reporting as well but - Something tells me she won't unless asked.

As I make my way towards the servant hall entrance I find myself silently praying that no servants will ask too many questions. A servant spots her from the bottom of the stairs and hurries up to greet her.

"What can I do for you, Lady Hughes?"

I dip my head, face flush as I hear the title used with my name. "I am looking for my maid, Paxton. Could you find her for me?"

The young servant nods, "I'll go gether."

Audrey watches as they hurry back down the stairs and disappear into a room before she lets out a relieved sigh. *I would have had to face far more questions if it were Mr. Smith.*

I was lucky this time.

I can't keep relying on luck, I need to get a better understanding of the abbey.

Within a few minutes, Paxton appears and greets Audrey as she reaches the top of the stairway.

"How may I be of assistance, my Lady?" I lower my voice as I speak, noticing other servants walking about at the bottom of the staircase "I was meaning to return something to Mrs. Halloway - But I don't quite know where her room is."

"Would you like me to take it to her?" Paxton asks.

"No! I mean - No, I would like to discuss it with her as well."

Paxton simply nods, "Follow me."

I step aside as Ms. Paxton opens the door and leads the way out of the stairwell and back into the halls. She turns like she was going towards Audrey's room.

Does she understand what I asked or is she going to lock me away?

The maid passes by Audrey's room and stops at a room a few away from hers. She stops and turns to look at me. "This is her room, her maid was just in here so I do believe she is still awake." Paxton dips her head before disappearing back down the hall.

As I turn to the door, I take in a deep breath.

I can only hope I am making the right choices here.

Knocking on the door softly, I wait for an

answer. After a moment, I can scarcely hear a quiet 'come in' uttered from the other side. I open the door and step inside slowly. It felt as though I were in my own room, in fact it was rather plain and small.

Foreign objects and pictures of a different district were all that stood out from her vanity table, everything else was simple.

Priscilla almost blended with the room as she sits at the vanity table, scarcely moving as she looks at a picture.

"Lady Hallloway?"

Priscilla turns to face the door, her eyes grew wide.

"Lady Hughes!" She quickly sets down her pen, "I didn't expect you here - What can I do for you?"

As I step closer to Priscilla, I notice the puffiness around her eyes.

I shouldn't question her... not now.

Right now she needs someone who cares.

"I just wanted to check on you after yesterday," I begin, sitting on the footstool at the end of the bed.

"That's kind of you - and thank you again for sticking your neck out for me. I appreciated it." She smiles sadly. "Don't worry about me though. I am not sad about him being with that woman. I was aware of this for a while now. I just never thought he would bring her here."

I frown, "If you knew... Why are you still here?"

"I'm with Mr. Halloway because of an arranged marriage." She says as she turns in her chair to face me. "I've tried contacting my father on the matter of... getting out of this. Getting away from here, but this arrangement helped the academy grow..."

"Wait, you're in an arranged marriage to help the magic academy?"

Priscilla nods, "The agreement was to start sending more men from this district to the academy, where my father works, in exchange I would marry Julian. He needed a wife to be taken seriously as a board member, there was too much going around about him being a flirt - Well, none of that matters now. I just received a letter from my father... Mr. Fluor. I told him my suspicions of Mr. Halloway being unfaithful and, well my father blames me."

I stand and step over to Priscilla, resting my hand on her shoulder. "This is in no way your fault Lady Ha - Priscilla."

"How do you know?" She snaps, quickly her eyes widen. "Sorry - I -"

"I was engaged to be married to someone

my father wanted me to be as well." I said with a sigh, kneeling on the floor beside Priscilla. "I did not go through with it."

"I thought you and Mr. Madlocke are -"

"Oh!" I laugh, for the first time in a while. "No this is, well was before him. Someone, far different."

He is, isn't he? Audrey surprises herself by comparing the two. *Dominique may be hiding many things but... He doesn't seem corrupt like my fiance was.*

"Perhaps you shouldn't be thinking of everyone else, but instead make the choice on what is best for you."

Audrey suddenly feels startled by her words. *How am I the one to tell her this?*

These are words even I cannot follow.

Priscilla sighs, "I wish it were that simple. If I were to leave him I would be in - Anyways, thank you for telling me your story." She rubs her eyes. "I don't believe I have the same level of confidence as you, but thank you for coming here to console me. You're the only one who has tried." She looks back at her reflection. "We have dinner with more guests arriving tonight, from Fayehun, I can't miss it. So if you could give me some time alone..."

I dip my head to her, "Of course."

Turning away I begin to make my way to

the door to leave when Priscilla speaks up.

"Thank you again for coming here to check on me, I do appreciate it."

I step out of the room and close the door behind me softly. Sighing.

I hope Priscilla will be alright for dinner later...

This sounds important. Guests from Fayehun.

I find myself dreading every moment up to that dinner, and I had every right to be. It was as if everyone was beginning to be seated. I watch as Julian snatches the place cards up and swaps the seats. His face was red, and his eyes were not focused.

Has he been drinking?

That wasn't the worst part.

Julian swapped two name cards before most others had arrived in the room. I am seated the furthest from Priscilla, who was moved so Belladonna could sit beside Lord Halloway.

Dinners since Audrey's first at the house had been starting to go smoother, as talks of her had become a less popular topic as time had gone on. Though now, not being able to speak to Dominique alone and only seeing him at dinners was a problem. As I sit with a stranger on either side, I feel even more irritated when I spot Dominique had been sat across from me.

Audrey was surrounded by members of the family and guests she did not know.

"It's a bit odd, isn't it?" The man next to her says as he begins getting his food off the platter a servant held.

"What is?" I ask.

"Well," The man begins awkwardly. "They don't speak of it anymore, but I too am part of the family by unusual means."

I furrow a brow and stare at him, waiting for him to continue.

"Ah, I am sorry, I have yet to introduce myself. I am visiting from the Fayehun Port District, my name is Francis Bishop." Francis continues, he fiddles with his sleeve cuffs. "I was only welcomed into the family as I married Lady Glenis Tarlach."

I smile at this man's awkward attempt at being kind. "So what did you do before that?"

"I actually was a servant at the district hall. I would drive the carriage during events that the family held within the district."

Different from my case but -

That means it is not completely unheard of.

Someone in my class can *become upper class.*

"What I'm trying to say is, I find it funny we find ourselves seated together." He says with a chuckle. I nod as I begin cutting into the chicken on my plate.

A sudden roar of laughter comes from Julian, making me jump in my seat. I glance across the table, as everyone does.

Julian was drinking an awful lot, and had been drinking even before the dinner had begun.

Something has him on edge -

And it isn't just his wife finding him with his mistress.

No, he is being *very* open about his mistress now.

What stressed him out enough to make him so...

Sloppy?

I look at Lady Priscilla, who is staring intently down at her plate, she is teary-eyed and her cheeks are red. She was sitting as far to the side of her chair as she could to get away from the mistress that sat next to her and was so openly flirting with her husband.

If it isn't that because of that -

Is Julian afraid because I am making progress, or is it something else?

"Everyone, I'd like to propose a toast!" Julian cheers, holding up his glass. "To my lovely wife, Belladonna Manus!"

Others slowly and awkwardly raise their glasses, I look around, baffled. The only one not raising their glass is Lady Vivienne, who was too busy drinking it to hold it out. She downs her wine with a scowl on her face.

I look across the table at Dominique, he frowns, but says nothing as well.

I should stay silent. I'm doing so well -

At least, better now that -

I take one look at Priscilla and finds myself suddenly standing from my seat.

I lean onto the table, feeling my arms shake.

This is shameful!

"Shame on you for supporting this man openly being dishonest to his own wife," I call out.

I don't shout, and only speak loud enough to be sure all around me can hear. "I say we toast for Lady Priscilla Fluor, whom, despite her husband's ignorance and blatant disrespect, still carries herself in a respectable manner and does not lower herself to waste energy on such a man."

Julian falls back into his seat, startled by her speaking out, and everyone raises their glasses at the table. Everyone. I notice that Vivienne merely downs the

downs the remains of her drink at this. She

didn't look angry at Audrey in the slightest bit. No - her gaze was fixated upon Julian. Tonight her focus would be away from me, and I found great relief in this.

"You handled that very well," Francis says as I settle back into my seat. Her head was still spinning from her own outburst.

"I doubt Lord Halloway will bounce back from tonight quite so easily - but perhaps it will be easier for Lady Priscilla now."

I look over to Dominique, who looks both surprised and pleased as he grins and holds his glass up towards me.

I wish I could just speak with him.

He knows more than he is letting on...

Doesn't he?

Looking at Priscilla, she still looked quite displeased with her husband, but she had the slightest smile upon her face.

Hopefully, this means I will have gained an ally.

A *real* one.

Vivienne finally stands as everyone had been finished eating for quite some time.

"I believe we are ready to go through." Vivienne nods to the servants who open the doors to the sitting room. Servants pull out the chairs for the women and begin guiding everyone out. As Julian sluggishly gets up,

Vivienne pushes him back into his seat. "Not you -" She said quietly as almost everyone had already left the room. "You've done enough to embarrass yourself for one night -"

Have I done it?

It seems Vivienne may not associate with him as much in public if he continues to act like this.

Hopefully, this severs their partnership, even slightly.

I turn and quickly follow the group into the other room before Vivienne can turn her gaze upon me.

I need to speak with Dominique.

As she enters the sitting room she immediately spots Dominique standing by the bar with the man she had sat next to earlier. Francis Bishop. By the looks of it, they were already deep in a conversation. Sighing, I instead turn and go to Priscilla, who sits alone towards the side of the room.

"Are you alright, Lady Priscilla -"

"Please don't call me that," She says quickly. "Just Priscilla is fine right now."

I sigh, "Of course, *Priscilla*. Is there anything I can do for you?"

"What can be done, my husband is as dishonest as always and now knows that there are no limitations to it. None at all"

"I understand what you're going through, in a way." I sit in the chair next to her. "I've dealt with dishonesty in a man before-"

"Mr. Madlocke?" She asks. "Is he *also* disloyal?"

I shook my head, "No - this was, um, before Dominique. The engagement I mentioned earlier. I was engaged to a wealthier man as my family needed the money. I knew he was dishonest as well but when I found out the extent of it." I sigh. "I could have married him for his money, but his attitude? His personality and dishonesty would be around my brothers in their younger age. I didn't want them to become like him. So I broke it off."

Priscilla looks down, "You really think I should divorce him, don't you?"

"You don't?"

"I do, it's just - I can't."

"Because of your father?"

She shakes her head, "That... That is not the only reason, but it does play a part in this."

"He's holding something against you isn't he?" I lean in. "I know they're hiding something here, Vivienne and your husband. The question is - Are you in any danger?"

Priscilla looks up at her, suddenly looking more awake and aware than any time Audrey had seen before.

"Yes... I believe we all are."

16
UNABRIDGED

"...Though the Prince's coming of age ceremony has ended, more events are happening in the capital in spite of his sudden departure for unknown reasons. Where will the Prince go? Why is the King hosting more events without him?"

-Flaize Daily

That next day at breakfast, Audrey found herself to be quite tired after getting very little sleep the night before.

She still had yet to discuss anything with Dominique or Julian. She found herself dreading going into the dining hall to eat with the others that morning. When she entered the room, she was surprised to find only Vivienne and Priscilla sitting at the table.

"Where is Dominique," I ask cautiously as I slowly pull out my seat and begin to sit.

Vivienne narrows her eyes at me, "Your husband left earlier. Said he had some family business he had to hurry and attend to. Were you perhaps, unaware?"

"Ah," I pause before having to quickly summon a response. "I - did not realize just how early he had planned on leaving," I say as

I sit down beside Priscilla.

I grit my teeth, why did he not tell me anything?

"Julian wanted me to inform you that some money was sent to your family," Vivienne continues. "He won't be able to work with you today, so instead you'll be working with me. What was it you were questioning? Our investment choices? How we have worked hard to keep this place alive?"

I open my mouth to speak, but Vivienne suddenly stands. "I'll see you in my office in the afternoon, ask Lady Priscilla to show you the way."

With that Vivienne is led out of the room by one of the servants. Leaving Audrey and Priscilla alone at the table

I glance over at the servants who stand in the room. They weren't directly looking at either myself or Priscilla, but still I knew they were there to listen in on the two.

"Why don't we take a walk to the garden before you meet up with Lady Raithe," Priscilla asks quietly.

I nod and stand, following her out of the room with the eyes of the servants upon them as they leave out the front again.

"I wanted to thank you again for last night," Priscilla begins. "You stood up for me when everyone else was going to just sit idly and watch my embarrassment. I greatly appreciate this. I know you're trying to figure out what is going on at the abbey and... While I do not completely know - and I'm not sure how much I can help you. I want to try."

"I appreciate it but - How do I know I can trust you won't tell Julian or Vivienne?" Priscilla stops, making me turn to look at her.

"I've wanted out of this place since I was forced here by marrying Julian. If helping you could help me be free of him,
I'll do it."

The two continued walking to the gardens, nobody was around to hear them.

"Then I need to tell you, I found something - In Julian's office. Hidden letters. It seems Vivienne and Julian are hiding something somewhere in the abbey which is causing that sickness to spread in the area." I sigh. "I'm not quite sure what it is but - It's like a beacon. Failed holy magic or something of the sort attempted by lesser mages. I believe it is close to the border could be what's rousing the Dragonkin."

"I knew they were doing something with magic - Julian threatened me with it. I didn't know it was causing sickness -" She stops suddenly. "What if - Oh God, what if that is what happened to Farah?"

I stop to look at Priscilla, nodding. "I... Think that would be what took her." When Priscilla's eyes go wide I quickly continue, "It's just a theory - but the timing of their first letters to these mages and the time the sickness began are too close to be a coincidence."

"So what do you plan to say to Vivienne?" Priscilla asks.

I shake my head, "I don't know... If I am too direct - I'll have to work fast or even find a way out of here. If I'm not-"

"You won't be getting anything done?" I nod.

"Then..." Priscilla glances around. "Let's discuss a plan before you head inside..."

"So what makes you seem to think you understand what all we are doing here?" Vivienne asks as I sit down across from her in her office. "You've been here for barely a month, and suddenly you're demanding the position and the power. So tell me, *why* do you think you could command a meeting over this?"

I tap my shoe tip on the floor as I try to control my hands shaking in my lap. Julian may have been intimidating when angry, but Vivienne was a whole new level of intimidation.

"Because I inherit the position from Lady Davies. I also for one, know that you haven't had the barriers recast any time in the past year, maybe even more. You also have stopped funding the border patrols which are needed now more than ever."

"And how do you know this? Are you part of the border patrols? Are you a magic user by chance? I think no-"

"I haven't seen a mage cast the spell in years -"

"So you're blaming me for your own ignorance?" Vivienne snarls. "Because you happened to not see the mage work?" When I don't respond she continues, "As for the border patrols, we are still funding-"

"But you aren't," I stand up from my seat and look down upon Vivienne. "My *father* worked for the border patrols. They didn't have any money to pay anyone for the job, they couldn't afford it when people began to be injured. People believed that the barrier was the primary defense now, and even that we don't have."

"We do -"

"Then show me the papers. The receipts. Any signed agreements of a recent recast of the barrier."

"I don't have to show you anything, girl."

"But you do, as that is what should be my role in the abbey. I am aware Farah performed fewer of these tasks as she reached the end, but I intend to perform all tasks in my role. That includes being able to question your questionable purchases." I turn to leave.

"Where are you going?"

I heave in a breath quickly, not daring to turn back to face her. "I am going to give you a chance to fix the barrier." I say simply as I pull the door open. "Recast the barrier spell, then I'll consider only discussing the various odd purchases for around the abbey." I step out and shut the door behind me, ignoring anything else Vivienne had to say.

Quickly I walk down the hall, avoiding eye contact with any servants or upperclassmen I pass. I need to find what she's hiding here tonight.

I have very little time now, after that she'll be out for blood.

Why did Dominique have to leave?

He was helpful -

And I could use the help right now.

17
BOOKENDS

"Despite the humans and dragonkin signing a peace treaty centuries ago, tensions are still high between us as we interact with them very little. Even with the peace treaty, we don't know if we can expect them to uphold their end for as long as it has been. No dragonkin has crossed the border since the peace treaty, and no human has crossed into Dragnoir either..."

-A History in Flaize, Fifth Edition

That night I am within the halls of the abbey once more, nobody is awake or out of their rooms, not even Julian and Vivienne tonight. Even Dominique has yet to return.

This time I was on my own.

Even with everything going on and how little I trusted Dominique, I find myself wishing for the company I had momentarily had the last time I had snuck through the abbey.

I stop beside the office of Julian, there is no light on and the door is locked.

We did already look around in there, now the question is...

Where would an object of magical properties be hidden?

When it came to magic, I feel stupid searching for it.

Where could something like that even be?

What form will it even take?

I had only seen magic once before, and even then it was long ago. When the barrier was recast by a renowned magic user I watched as what looked like beams of light came from his palms and covered the city. It took a month for the barrier to turn transparent, but until it did, I would constantly leave the house to stare at it.

That was also when Farah was younger... so perhaps that is why the district had been kept better.

I continue down the hall to Vivenne's office, remembering how many doors I had counted to pass by before reaching her office.

Audrey recalls that long silent walk when a servant retrieved her for the meeting. It was farther down the hall of the first floor than Julian's and from outside seemed like a storage closet, with an unassuming door not as intricately designed as the rest. Audrey finds it ominous as she sees it along with the decorative doors in the dim lighting at night.

It's ironic, I would expect a woman like

Vivienne to have everything of hers be... Extravagant. Audrey thinks as she slowly opens the door, surprised to find it had been left unlocked.

This shouldn't be easy -

It's almost as though she expects this...

Should I turn back now?

I've already been able to map out most of the abbey from my walks while speaking to Priscilla, so perhaps I should check elsewhere first?

I stop as I hear servants out and about, I turn around, and down the hall there were two servants talking amongst themselves. They had yet to notice me in the darkness.

Why are they out?

I quickly open the door and push my way into Vivenne's office, shutting the door quietly behind me as I see a light filter underneath the doorway.

I take a few steps back and wait until they pass.

"Is there a reason why our work has been doubled?" One asks.

"Ms. Linton didn't tell you?" The other sighs, "Some servants are going to be out acting as patrolmen for the upcoming guests to see, so we have to pick up the slack since half of the servants will be gone."

Acting as patrolmen? I press my ear to the door, struggling to hear as they continue past and get further away.

"This is ridiculous," One sighs, making the other chuckle.

"We have a few days until the guest arrives."

"Who is the guest?"

"You really don't pay attention, it is the royal..."

The voices have become too far to hear now, I curse under my breath as I turn the lamp on in the room.

Acting as patrolmen?!

Is Vivienne going to fool royal guests into thinking this place is run well?

I look around her office.

She has to be hiding something.

The source of the sickness, whatever is causing problems with the dragonkin...
I have no doubt it is something within the abbey.

I have to find it tonight.

I've already seen Julian's office, and I've seen most other rooms in the abbey... perhaps it is too well hidden? What if I can't find it?

Audrey debates for a moment waiting until Dominique returns, but quickly shakes her head. *Have I required much assistance in all of these years? I can do this.*

Looking around the office, I find that nothing looks any different than it had earlier. Large shelves line the walls, a den desk stood in the center, and many paintings cover the wall behind the desk along with pinned bugs framed and hung around the room.

Audrey begins poking around, sifting through pages of paperwork for district policies and agreements, opening every filing cabinet, and glancing over every shelf. It was all too clean, too new in the office.

Is there a chance this was once Farah's office?

I shake my head, I'll have to figure that out later.

The whole time she can't help but feel as though eyes are upon her.

Surely what I am looking for is large right? Something that can drain magic from an area... It wouldn't be minuscule.

I look at the paintings, they all have eyes that feel like they are watching me. All portraits of various women. None of them are similar to the last, but there was something oddly similar about them all.

Strange... Are these women who married into the families here?

One painting is covered and leaning

against the wall nearby, I slowly creep over and pull the drape back a bit. It was Mrs. Dayholt, her round eyes and warm aura are beautifully painted, yet it was incomplete.

I look back to the other paintings, it felt like there is great importance in these paintings to Vivienne. Looking closer at each one, I notice how thin one canvas is. Stepping back I notice how oddly bulky it is as well in comparison to the others.

I grab the edges, ready to pull it off but as I lift I feel cold air come through.

A hidden door?

I pull it off of the wall to find it covered what once must have been a window, but had never been blocked off during expansions. It led to a hallway of another room. A room I had not seen or heard of.

Could this be it?

I turn around and grab an unused lantern off of the desk, I place it on the strange window frame for a moment. Taking a deep breath I look inside.

This has to be something.

I pull up my skirt as I climb up into the thick window frame, it was as wide as a desk and covered in dust and webs. I frown as I look down at the once untouched dust. It was as though nobody had been back here in a while. Was there another entrance? Or was it perhaps forgotten for so long? As I get out at the other side I find myself in a hallway, one end seems to end in nothing, but the other turns into a stairwell.

Slowly I head to the dark stairs, each old wooden step creaks as I place my foot onto it even with caution. The stairway wraps around and round, going on for what seems like forever until finally, I find its end. As I reach the bottom my stomach turns, as though my gut were twisting to get away from what lies ahead.

This must be it.

All that stands before her is a door.

Opening it, she is met by a horrible smell.

Audrey gasps at what she saw before her.

Along every wall was a transparent chain that covered every corner and crevice, the chains had many cracks within them, and a few links were almost invisible. It was as though it was trying to hold something in, and that something sat in the center of the room.

Is that -

A Dragonkin corpse?

In the center of the large room a stone-like figure laid across the ground, its wings were riddled with holes and tears across them, scales were strewn about the floor around it and those that still remain embedded in the creature were as dull as rusted silver. Its eyes stare blankly ahead, with the emptiness that came with being devoid of life.

How did they get a hold of this?

This isn't just misused holy magics -

They're using the magic of a dragon!

Those in the empire of Flaize knew very little of the Dragonkin, but this one thing was known - They had a stronger affinity with magic then human's had.

But to draw that energy out of one -

To combine it with cheap spells being poorly cast by low-level mages.

No wonder there are many setbacks to this.

But what was Vivienne trying to achieve with this?

A magic source of her own?

But she wouldn't be able to contain such energy - the energy of a dragon is too much for a human.

So why?

She is already in a good position of power-

But she wants more?

There was something oddly familiar about the dragon corpse. It felt as though she were looking at a person she knew when she looks at the rotting scales.

Was this even the work of Vivienne?

It was in her office, but this place looks untouched...

I can't stay here.

If this is the source I've been searching for, I need to get out of here before it affects me even more deeply than before.

I pull my shirt down to see the purple branching pattern on my chest has spread, more tendrils and roots were growing out from the source.

I can't stay here. If I do, I could die.

My lungs are screaming at me with every breath I take in near the dragon corpse.

Fresh air, I need to stay away from this place for a day.

I need to go home

18
THE PAGES WE REMOVE

"Though I longed to close the gap, To one day see the distance removed between the two of us, I now know of a secret abyss, So deep and divided, That even I cannot cross."
- Poems by the Great Bryun F. Lumar, Founder of The Country of Flaize

Walking through the streets as the sun rises now feels like a poor idea as my head is pounding and I feel regret for having not gone back to sleep. I clutch onto my bag as though it were the only thing keeping me going. It took me longer to leave the abbey after I decided to grab my things and go. Bringing money, new clothes, and a book with me had become a habit, but it was the first time I had since going to the abbey. I felt my chest ache a little less the further away I was from the abbey but I couldn't shake the horrible thoughts and doubts.

If I had fallen asleep within the abbey again, would I have died?

Hopefully, by staying away for a short period I can recover enough to return soon.

But do I have it in me to return home?

I know funding was sent back for them but...

Father will still blame me for not finding a way to bring them into the abbey.

I just need to see them one last time, in case something goes wrong. It will all be fine.

As I walk down the sidewalks of the streets it feels busier than usual. Servants from the abbey mix in with various people of the city on the sidewalks as the lower class people are curious as to what was going on. The streets themselves were still empty of horse carriages and riders, but I assume that will change within the next few days if someone from the capital was on their way here.

Nothing looks different, yet everything felt different. After being at the abbey for so long, when I finally reach the front of the house it feels foreign to me.

I haven't been gone for too long, yet...

Was it in such a poor state when I left?

The front garden was completely dead, though that could be because of the cold. The front door looks worn, and even the bricks of the small cottage look as though they were slowly giving up. The main thing that terrifies me is the boarded-up window.

What happened?

Cautiously, I step down the pathway to the door, pulling the handle the door pops open.

Papa still forgets to lock it, I see.

I hold onto the door for a moment, my heart racing.

Why do I feel so anxious?

With all I have done and faced so far -

Surely I can handle this?

Pushing my way in, I pull the door shut behind me as I look around.

The kitchen table is covered in old newspapers, dirty dishes filled the sink, and the floors were filthy with dirt being tracked in.

"Auddie?"

I turn to the hall, to see Fletcher and Remy. They hurry over and I lean down to pull them into a hug. I lean back and look them over. They look tired, more than any boy at their age should be. Their clothes were wrinkled as well, but most importantly...

Why were they still here?

"Why aren't you two at school?" I ask. "I paid for it up until the end of this semester."

The two exchange a glance quickly.

"Well..." Remy begins, glancing back down the hall. "Papa has been saying strange things."

"Papa forbids us from going back." Fletcher says angrily, "He says we need to stay home and wait until you come to take us with you to the abbey. Now that you're here, we can finally see Mum! We can all be together again! That's why you're here isn't it?"

I stare at the hope in my brother's eyes, they've been stuck here in this house the whole time I've been gone.

"Audrey, you're finally back I see."

I stand up from my knees to see papa standing at the hall entrance. Arms crossed, he frowns at me. His hair was a disaster, his clothing in an even worse state, and he held tightly to a newspaper.

"I've been following your story, I see you've moved on from us to a far better life, now being married, within the abbey, it must be nice." He tosses the newspaper away angrily, I quickly step in front of Fletcher and Remy, and I whisper to them, "You two need to leave, wait outside, I'll be out there soon."

The two of them hurry out the door, making papa begin stomping over, "Where are you running off too! I said no more schooling! Audrey is back now -"

"Papa!" I interrupt, "You can't stop them from going to school in the hope that I can take you with me." I step back from him, feeling my hands shake.

"So why did you come back? To remind yourself what you're free of?" He steps closer, looming over me, I back up.

“The abbey is dangerous, I can’t bring you with me yet -”

“But not too dangerous for you to live comfortably?” He screams, as he leans in I smell the strong scent of alcohol in his breath, causing me to cough.

“I should have known, after all we’ve done for you, after everything we gave up to bring you in - I told Amelia we never should have brought you in. All you and your kind ever bring is bad luck!”

Brought me in?

Rest of your kind?!

“What do you -”

Before I can say anything, he swings, I fall back to avoid it, landing on the ground. I am lucky he is drunk, but he still is ready to come at me. I roll away on the ground and struggle to spring back up to my feet, narrowly avoiding his attempt at stomping me while I was down. I take a few steps back to put distance between us.

“Papa, I’m doing everything I can -”

“You’re lying!” He shouts, knocking over chairs as he continues to come toward me.

I look at the door behind him, cursing myself for allowing him to get me cornered.

He has never been like this before -

Sad, but never aggressive. Something happened -

Something with -

Mum.

I shove past him and hurry down the hall, shoving my way into my parent's room. What lay before me was a horrendous sight.

Hundreds of empty bottles of magic potions and cures were tossed about the room, covering almost every surface. A woman lies on the bed, her eyes open and dull with her mouth hanging open and dried potion running down her cheek away from her mouth, as though someone had continued forcing her to drink it to cure her.

I fell down beside the bed, looking at the now lifeless form of my mother.

"Mum?" I cry out, pushing her arm, "Mum, please, please be ok. I'm doing everything I can to help, just hold on a little longer -"

"Don't you dare call my wife your mother again." Comes a raspy growl from the door. I turn to see papa standing with his lip curled in disgust. I hear the front door slam from down the hall, but papa doesn't seem to notice as he continues speaking.

"If you never would have left us, stopped

working to care for your mother, she would still be here." He scoffs, "You sent your pity money too late. I couldn't afford the cure until it was too late."

My fault?

My fault...

If it was that drastic, why didn't he do anything? Get a job instead of wasting away?

I knew that she was ill and left though. I remind myself. *Maybe it is my fault.*

I back up against the bed as papa begins to step closer, "We never should have brought you here, should have left you out in the woods to die like the rat you are."

A sob escapes my mouth, "Papa, what are you -"

"Stop calling me that!" He shouts, "You are not my child, nor Amelia's and you never will be! You're the furthest thing from us, you're a monster!"

Looking past him I see a shadow, *Remy and Fletcher?*

As he nears me I rush by him, trying to hurry out the door when my wrist is grabbed and he pulls me back. I turn back to face him as I struggle to pull his hand off of my wrist.

"Please, let me go!" I beg, looking at the face before me.

This isn't the man who raised me, not anymore.

He's gone.

Suddenly, there is someone else at my side, as I turn to see who had rushed in I'm met by a flash of red hair as someone passes me, the person rears back and clenches a fist before clocking papa straight to the jaw knocking him away.

My hand free I quickly step back to see Dominique standing over my father who now lay against the bed unconscious. It is only now that I feel the wet of tears falling down my cheeks.

Dominique turns to me, eyes wide with concern, "Are you ok, did he hit you?!" He steps closer to me to look me over but I step away, trembling.

"What did he mean, *took me in*?" I cry. "They weren't my parents? This whole time I was just the help of the house? Nothing more?!"

"Audrey," Dominique slowly steps towards me with his hands out. "Everything is alright now, ok? Nothing else is going to happen to you, I swear it."

Looking up at Dominique, it's the first time I feel like his words rang true. Even though I doubt it, I can tell he doesn't. Audrey steps towards him and he pulls her into a hug, holding onto her as she cries.

"I'm sorry I left you to deal with everything alone for so long, but I won't leave you to solve this alone anymore." He says softly. "We're in this together now, alright?"

I scarcely can focus on Dominique's words as my head spins, *I'm not their daughter, I never belonged here, where did I come from? Who are my parents really?*

What did he mean by my kind?

I shake my head before I can think of an answer, it was apparent - *obvious* even.
A patrol officer of the Dragnior border suddenly having a child? There was only one answer.

But I couldn't tell Dominique.

I pull away from the hug and begin to look back into the room at my parents- what once was my parents but Dominique blocks me.

"He isn't dead, just unconscious, we need to go help your brothers right now."

"Brothers?" I echo. "But they -"

"I know you still care about them, even now. Once we find somewhere safe for them we can talk."

Slowly I nod, Dominique leads the way back down the hall, and I cast one last quick glance into the bedroom before following him.

As I follow him outside, one thing

continues to ring in my head. My life was a lie, it is a lie. *Even Farah didn't know.*

Remy and Fletcher look afraid as they see me follow Dominique out with puffy red eyes and papa nowhere in sight. Fletcher more so than Remy, who just sighs.

"What's going on?" Fletcher asks, "Where is papa?"

"He is fine," I answer simply, "We need to get you two somewhere safe right now."

"Where? The abbey?" Remy asks, I glance at Dominique who looks at me for an answer.

I sigh, "We're going to Mr. Abbot at the library I work at. We'll see if you two can stay there for a little while."

I begin walking down the road making the three of them have to hurry to catch up. Dominique walks behind me with Fletcher at his side and Remy walks beside me.

"Hey, Auddie?" Remy says, I look down at him, all I can think as I look at his appearance, his likeness to papa is how did I not notice how different we look?

"Yes?"

He solemnly smiles up at her. "I'm glad to see you again. I missed you."

I feel my chest hurt from guilt as I look at my brother, he was so innocent, but part of me felt he knew. Even if he didn't,

Dominique was right. They are still my brothers. Perhaps not by blood, but they would always be my little brothers.

We continue down the familiar pathway that I had not taken in a long time. The path to my work, the path to the library. *What would Mr. Abbot say? Would he be angry too?* I feel myself grow exhausted. *I can't handle any more of this.*

"This is it," Dominique announces as we stop in front of the library. I took in a deep breath, my mind is still reeling and running amuck, yet as I look at my brothers I took a step forward.

"Wait here for a moment," I say to them. Dominique frowns, furrowing his brows.

"Are you sure?" He asks, "I can come with you if that's what you want."

I shake my head, "Just... wait a moment. I'll be ok."

After this, you can breathe. I tell myself as I left it, books stacked on the floors and shelves, the counter having more books out to catalog, but there was no man behind the counter.

"Hello?" I call out.

I hear shuffling from the other room, where Mr. Abbot's living area is. "We're open! I'll be there in a moment!"

I stand by the counter for a moment,

shaking as I wait until I hear his slow footsteps on the floorboards nearby.

Mr. Abbot appears from the doorway behind the counter, he stares at me for a moment.

"Audrey?" His eyes go wide, "It is you!" He hurries around the counter and stops in front of me, I can't help but flinch as I expect the worst. Instead Mr. Abbot pulls Audrey into a hug.

"I heard about you in the papers! You're in the abbey now!" He takes a step back to look at her, "I'm so glad to see you're moving up in the world."

I frown, "You aren't mad?"

He tilts his head, "Why would I be? Is something wrong?" He asks as he takes a closer look at my puffy red eyes.

I force a weak smile, and shake my head, "Nothing is wrong it's just, I'm sorry I didn't tell you." I sigh, "And I'm sorry I can't stay... I know I probably shouldn't, but I need to ask a favor of you."

He nods, "Of course, what is it you need?"

I motion to the door, "My brothers are outside and... I can't take them with me to the abbey. Home isn't safe for them right now either." I take in a deep breath and look down, unable to meet Mr. Abbot's gaze, "Mum passed away and papa is... grieving."

He frowns, "Audrey, I'm very sorry to hear about your mother... Of course your brothers can stay here, however long they need to." He chuckles, "If they're anything like you, they're never going to get bored while they're here."

I chuckle as I look around at the library, "Oh!" I reach into my bag, pulling out a few paper bills, "This is all I brought with me in case of anything, I'll pay you to watch them." I hand them to Mr. Abbot and his eyes go wide, "You don't need to bribe me to care for your brothers!" He says loudly, shocked by the amount in front of him.

"It's fine, you might need it with how things are going right now in Yonnam." I say, "Also, I know I don't need to pay you, I want to though."

Mr. Abbot slowly takes the money, "I won't spend a bit of it on myself, only on your brothers." He looks to the door, "Let them in, I'll find a good spot for them in the old guest room." As I begin to turn to open the door he continues, "Audrey?"

I turn back to face him.

"If anything happens at the abbey, I want you to remember there is always a place for you here, alright?"

My heart aches, yet still I feel a small hope

from those words.

"Thank you, Mr. Abbot."

I open the door as he shuffles back through the doorway, and sees Dominique sitting on the steps of the library besides Remy and Fletcher.

"Alright," I call out, "You can come in now."

They turn and spot me and Dominique stands, helping my brothers to their feet before following us all in.

Remy and Fletcher look around in awe,

"This is where you worked?!" Fletcher asks loudly as he rushes around to look at all of the books. Remy looks at Audrey.

"You have to go, don't you?"

Fletcher rushes back to stand beside Remy, "Do you?"

I sigh and nod, "I don't know how long it will be... but I will try to come back." I kneel down and pull the two into a hug.

"Mr. Abbot will keep you safe, alright?"

Fletcher and Remy hug her tight, after a moment pulling away so Audrey can stand the two of them glance at Dominique.

"Keep him safe," Fletcher says to Audrey, motioning towards Dominique, making him chuckle.

"Shouldn't *I* keep *her* safe?" He asks.

Both Remy and Fletcher shake their head, "Auddie is strong," Remy answers, "But please help her if she needs it."

Dominique smiles, "Of course."

At the sound of hooves on the pavement we turn to the door, I sigh.

"We need to go."

Remy sighs, "Please be safe Audrey." He says.

"I will be," I say, not fully confident in it but not wanting to make them nervous.

As I follow Dominique out the door I look back. "I love you two, take care of each other."

"We love you too."

19
BOOK MEND

"...And they were like fire, When their flames scorched the ground, the blaze like them was insatiable, As fire wants all it can reach, They would destroy the world, Before they let another hold it..."

-On Dragons, a poem by Bryun Lumar

Golden carriages are going through the abbey gates pulled by beautiful horses as I follow Dominique out of the library where I was leaving my brothers behind. I stand beside him as we wait for all of the carriages to pass.

"Where have you been?" I ask after a moment of silence.

He sighs, "I didn't mean to be gone for so long, but I needed to find out what was going on in the capital."

I turn to him, frowning, "How in the world did you get there and back?"

"I didn't go all the way to the capital, I went to the neighboring districts to find out more." He says as the last carriage passes. "I believe we have more time before the guests arrive."

"Wasn't that them?"

He shakes his head, "No, those would be the servants and help to arrive first. The guests shouldn't be here until tomorrow."

"Then... We need to find somewhere to talk." I say, glancing around the empty streets. "I believe I found the source."

Dominique looks down at me, eyes wide with surprise, "You surprise me, even I couldn't find anything." He steps down the front steps of the library and extends a hand to Audrey.

"There is only one place we can speak without being disturbed."

I take his hand after a moment, "Where?"

"Within Dragnior."

Walking within the forests of the bordering country Dragnior was something I could have never foreseen myself having to do with everything going on at the abbey. It was almost calming, if it weren't for the bordering country's forest. A pond with lily pads is softly lit by light filtering through the trees above.

After what transpired when I returned home though, I find myself looking deeper into the forests, where the branches grow so thick that no light is allowed through.

Was papa lying? He was angry... Should I be taking his words seriously? I think back to the expression on his face. I had seen him angry many times before, but this was different. *This was grim.* Every time I think about it I find myself trying to avoid thinking about mum. Her lifeless form.

That will be me soon if we can't figure this out.

You should have worked faster, have done better... So much death in so little time.

I look down at my reflection in the pond, my face looks unfamiliar now. I hadn't actually taken any time to look at myself in a long time.

This is you. After all of the death I caused, and things I have seen. I still look the same.

Right?

Shaking my head I turn to Dominique, he glances around the forests as he stops a few feet away from me, he frowns but his shoulders are relaxed. He doesn't seem tense.

"What did you find out while you were gone?" I ask.

He raises a brow at me before leaning on a nearby tree, "Well, to start, I found out a royal envoy being sent was not a rumor." Dominique sighs, "They're here to see the state of things in Yonnam, but I don't trust that they will be very useful."

"Are you against the King's chosen men?"

"That is the thing, you've seen the way the abbey here is run, right?" He asks. "People inherit titles, are raised on money and good lives - they don't know any different and do very little to change things. There are a few good ones within the leading roles of the districts, I will say that, but the bad outnumber the good by
by many."

"So you believe the king is like this?"

He nods, "The ruler of this country isn't chosen, it is inherited. Just like the roles surrounding it. I don't expect anything to get done with this envoy, not from the people I heard about being chosen for it."

I sigh and look down, "Then what are we supposed to do?"

"Did you find the source?" Dominique asks, I nod.

"It's very hidden, an old cellar that was boarded up. I found... A dragonkin."

Dominique's eyes flash as he stands straighter. "What?!"

"It... had these strange transparent chains around it that were breaking, and based on letters I found in Lord Jullian's office I believe many magics were used on it - including holy magic."

His mouth is left agape as he stares at me, this is the first time I see him truly shocked. "What... What are they doing with them?!"

I sigh, "It was dead... I don't know what they could be doing but, I think it may be some time of power source for someone."

"Who?" Dominique asks, more aggressively now. "Who do you think did it?"

"It was a hall attached to Lady Vivienne's office that led to it but -" I stop for a moment as Dominique begins pacing. "It may have been Farah's old office. I don't know who took her office over after she passed away."

"Do you think Farah would have done this?"

I shake my head, "I don't- but why would Lady Vivienne?"

He sighs, "I suppose that's what we need to find out. Who did it before we destroy it"

"We?" I ask, *he is coming back to the abbey with me at last?*

"I mean, only if you are up to it." He looks at me, letting out a deep breath. "You have done even more than I thought you would, and I'm sorry to say I left you alone for most of it. So if you want to leave it to me to return to the abbey, I would understand -"

"No!" I shout, Dominique flinches and I quickly hold my hands up. "I mean, I can't leave it now, not after all we've done to figure this out. This includes me as much as it includes you now."

I can't let their deaths go to waste. I owe it to them to fix this, I try to avoid thinking of the tightness in my chest, the lack of energy I have, and the thought of the aching pains I will have if I return to that place. *I need to see this through, even if it kills me.*

Dominique smiles, "You really are something else, Audrey Hughes." He glances around the woods once more before extending a hand towards me, "If you're ready then, let's begin making our way back."

I take his hand without hesitation now, walking in step with him as we make our way out of the forest.

Neither of them notice the eyes that open inside the pond as they walk away.

It felt as though we were walking forever, with Dominique having to slow his pace to stay beside me I feel pathetic as we slowly stroll down the road. After what felt like years had passed of walking the abbey comes into sight, in the dim light of the moon and the lanterns carried by servants by the entrance. Dominique grips onto my hand tighter, I cast a glance his way quickly. *What is wrong?*

I look ahead, there are two carriages that can be seen with guests getting out. I look at Dominique, brows furrowed in confusion.

"I thought we had until tomorro -"
I stop when I look at his face, his jaw is clenched and eyes wide as he watches someone.

"Dominique, what is it?" I ask.

"The guests... Not only is it the royal envoy here early, but also..." He stops walking. "It looks as though it is not only officials here to see the state of things. This is far too many people for that."

"What do you mean?" I ask.

He looks down at me, auburn eyes gleaming, "I believe they're planning for the war."

20
COMPLICATIONS

"... Prince Leon will be gone from the capital for an important trip, the King has announced it has to do with his coming of age ceremony, though there has not been anything like this with any other prince or princess when they turn twenty..."
- Flaize Daily

When I open my eyes, I feel as though I merely blinked and the night passed by.

Sitting up I quickly focus on my breathing and feel the urge to check my pulse. *I'm back in the abbey... Who knows how much time I have left to work within.*

It was a scary thing, having to consider how much time was left for one's self.

Like an hourglass, watching the sand fall piece by piece down until there wouldn't be a single grain remaining.

I push the covers off and sit on the edge of my bed for a moment before I hear a knock at my door.

"Come in," I half call, half wheeze out as I break out into a coughing fit. Slowly a small figure peeks into the room.

"Lady Audrey?"

I stand up off of my bed and open the door the rest of the way. I see Paxton standing there holding a pile of dresses folded over her arms.

"I am here to get you dressed and ready for today." As she steps past me into the room I follow her, feeling sick as I look at the corset dresses she lays out that I know will be too tight for me right now.

"What is happening today?" I ask.

Paxton looks over at me and I notice the deep bags beneath her eyes poorly covered by makeup. She half smiles.

"The royal envoy has arrived from the capital, we will be having breakfast together before there will be a meeting between them and the board."

Will I be allowed to go?

I think back and remember my last meetings with Lord Julian and Lady Vivienne. I had embarrassed him, and Lady Vivienne had been shoved into a corner. *I made a deal with her... recast the barrier spell would buy my silence, but did she?*

When I followed Dominique past the border there was no sense of a barrier being put up, it would take months for it to become invisible to the naked eye.

Will she trust me in the meeting? Or will she try

to keep me out of it?

"Where is this meeting going to take place?" I ask. Paxton merely shrugs, not even looking up at me. Paxton looks through the dresses, casting glances at me every now and then, I notice her hands are shaking as she does. I step towards her.

"Paxton, is that all?" I ask.

She raises a brow, "What do you mean, Lady Hughes?"

I sigh, "You have not called me lady until now, and you look exhausted. Is there something else going on?"

Paxton glances to the closed door for a moment before shaking her head.

I sigh, "Go find somewhere to rest for a while, I believe I can dress myself."

She looks up at me, eyes wide, "I couldn't ask that of you -"

"You aren't." I state bluntly, "I am asking it of *you*."

Paxton shuffles towards the door, dipping her head. She stops as she grabs the handle and looks back.

"Thank you," She whispers before opening the door and stepping out. I sigh.

I know the servants are being overworked now, but still. I wish she would trust me even a little more.

I listen as her footsteps grow distant, *is she not going down to the servant's area?* I sigh. *I wonder what she is up to now.*

Looking back at the dresses laid out I sigh.

Looks like I will have to be uncomfortable for today.

Moving the pile of dresses about I cannot find a single one I am willing to wear, every one of them will compress my chest and ability to breathe. With every breath feeling labored already in a loose nightgown, I know I would feel claustrophobic in any dress brought here by Paxton. I look over to the tall dresser, even though many new dresses had been brought in, many of Farah's dresses were still in there.

Opening the doors to the dresser, I immediately know which one to pull out, it was one Farah often wore to come to visit me. A loose-fit dress with sleeves that drape across and come together to be sewn into the skirt just under the bust. It was a sage green color and suited Audrey's softer appearance more than the brightly colored tight dresses lying on the bed.

I should look less intimidating at this event, perhaps that can help relax Lord Julian and Lady Vivienne about me going to this... meeting. And even if they still do...

Looking in the mirror nearby, I can't help but think of Farah as I look at myself. With my hair still braided from yesterday with a few loose strands falling down, with her clothes on I looked warm, kind, like less of a problem than I was. I didn't look like someone who had allowed the deaths of those closest to her. Which was exactly what I would need to look like for today.

This envoy will not find me to be intimidating at all, and will probably think *think Lord Julian and Lady Vivienne are making things up.*

Now the only question was, how do I ensure myself a place at this meeting?

Will Dominique have a plan? Or will he even be aware of this yet? Perhaps I can catch him in the hall -

As I hurry and step out of my room, I can already hear the loud boisterous conversations happening as people met in the great hall before breakfast.

Looking down the hall, I see many others leaving their rooms and going to the stairs, I stand outside my room watching for a moment. All of the people are wearing very extravagant clothing, beaded dresses of the current style, finely cut suits, and overall brightly colored outfits fill the hall. Looking at the great number of people I huff, So much for not having room. Seems as though making room quickly became a non-issue.

Would that have changed things for the better or made them worse? I ponder this as I suddenly hear footsteps behind me.

"Dominique?" I spin around to be met by a man not too much taller than myself. I quickly jump at this, and it takes me a moment to notice the armored knight behind him.

"I suppose you were expecting someone else?" He asks, his voice is sharp yet smooth. He seems calm here.

"Pardon me," I say quickly dipping my head before looking back up at him. The man before Audrey was only a tad taller than her, with sepia, reddish-brown skin, he had dark shorter curly hair very particularly styled, and he has a noticeably large nose. This man stood out, but not because of his appearance, but because of the way he carries himself.

"Are you by chance, part of the royal envoy visiting?" I ask, eyeing the guard behind this man. He chuckles, "I am a part of that, yes." He replies, "And you are?"

I quickly curtsy, *this could be my chance!*

"I am -"

"Lady Audrey!"

A booming voice echoes down the hall, I turn around to see Lady Vivienne standing atop the stairs. Her arms are crossed over her beaded cream dress.

"We are waiting for you downstairs, please do hurry." She says, waiting at the top of the stairs, her gaze no longer on me, but on the man who stood behind me.

I dip my head at him quickly, "Sorry again, but it seems I need to hurry off." I try to hide the bitterness in my voice.

Lady Vivienne's timing is nothing short of a coincidence. I begin to hurry down the hall I can hear the man call out.

"It was nice meeting you, Lady Audrey."

I smirk as I reach the end of the hall and stop in front of Lady Vivienne, she motions for me to follow her and we walk down the stairs side by side.

"Who was that?" I asked.

"Nobody important," she answers hurriedly, casting a quick glance back up the stairs.

I huff, "Someone not important on the royal envoy?"

Lady Vivienne glares at me frowning, and I laugh.

"Do you really think I am that far out of the loop, Vivienne?" I mutter. "I believe our agreement was if a barrier was put up, not if you sent out servants to watch the borders, right?"

We reach the bottom of the stairs as Lady Vivienne turns to me, I continue before she can speak.

"No need to look upset, I only think that if there is a meeting of any sort between the board and the envoy, I should be present, yes?" I step closer to her and lean in to whisper in her ear, her eyes go wide, "If that meeting does happen, and I am not there, there will be trouble." I stop and lean away quickly, stifling a cough before Lady Vivienne could notice.

I can't let her see that I am sick, if she figures that out and she is behind the source -

I back away, casting one last glance at her before I turn to go into the dining hall.

She would have me killed.

"Audrey!"

I jump at hearing my name called, spinning around I see two servants struggle to stop a man at the door. Mr. Wingrave. *Emmett.*

He storms over, shoving off the servant who grabs at his shoulder and pushing through the crowd gathered. I glance around, all eyes are on Emmett, and no one is looking at me. Yet.

I can't let him cause a scene for me, not now!

As I begin to step forward, I stop as I see someone else begin to intercept him.

Lord Julian steps forward from a group and grabs Emmett's shoulder roughly, digging his fingers into his arm. The people around them back away, though not everyone has noticed yet over the loud chatter. I watch as he leans in and whispers something to Emmett glancing over at me. Emmett pulls away and yells.

"She doesn't deserve to be here! I do!"

Now everyone has gone silent from previous conversations, now whispering amongst themselves, though all eyes are on Emmett.

I quickly step aside as though I were a part of the nearest group and not within range of Emmett or Lord Julian.

Lord Julian presses his fingers to his temple, "Mr. Wingrave, if you keep this up, I will have to ban you from entering this Abbey ever again."

Emmett steps back, eyes wide, "What, but Julian, you can't mean -"

"It's Lord Julian to you," He hisses, waving over the servants, "We're in the middle of something here so go home."

Emmett looks past Lord Julian, eyes scanning the crowd until they land upon me. His jaw clenches as he grinds his teeth. He says nothing more, just turning away shoving the servants aside as he makes his way back to the front door.

I let out a relieved sigh as I see Dominique making his way over.

His red hair tied up into a ponytail, and he wore his usual tailored suit, while everyone else watches Emmett leave, Dominique's eyes are focused on Audrey.

He stops beside me and leans in, "Is everything alright?"

I nod quickly, taking a step back.

"There is a meeting," I whisper, "Between the board and the envoy."

"That's excellent," Dominique said. "Depending on the outcome of that, then we can figure out our next move."

I see Lord Julian leading everyone into the dining hall.

"Looks like we are going through already." I say as I swiftly begin to follow.

I look back at Dominique to see he had yet to begin following, his focus had now turned elsewhere. I follow his gaze to see more people were still coming down the stairs, though not everyone seems to be going to the dining hall. Shaking my head I tap Dominique on the shoulder, turning his attention back to me.

"Come on, we need to go."

He nods and follows me into the dining hall, where I am fast to find my own seat, I look to the seat next to me, a place card sat on the plate, but it wasn't in the usual spot.

Has something been moved?

The seat is pulled out by a servant for the person who was to be seated.

"Interesting that we should be seated together, Lady Audrey."

I glance up to see who it was.

It was the man from the hall with his guard.

Looking back at the card, my eyes go wide.

Leon F. Lumar!

But why is he here without the King?

Someone has moved the cards. Someone wanted me to be here, next to him. Next to the prince of the country, the Prince of Flaize.

If something happens to him when we try to destroy the source -

A war would be unavoidable.

21
SPILLING INK

"...The smallest stone may change the course of the stream, just as one person can affect the fate of those around. We all hold a different kind of power, the question is how we use it..."
- Poems by the Great Bryun F. Lumar, Founder of The Country of Flaize

The prince sits down carefully next to me, casting a quick smile my way as we wait for everyone else to be seated. Fixing his blue tailored coat as he sits. I look away quickly, frowning as I feel the eyes of everyone burning into me. As though everyone knew, this was not was I was meant to be, at the prince's side.

Did Paxton move the cards? I think back to how she was acting after our conversation. If it was her, why would she do that? I highly doubt I'm lucky enough for her to change her tune for nothing, so why?

I look across the table at Lord Julian, he is looking at me with a frown, brows furrowed as he looks to the servant for answers. The servant nearest shrugs as they cast a glance between me and Lord Julian.

I look down at the table and realize the table has been extended to seat more people, and Dominique is now seated far down the table. He does a small wave at me with a smirk.

What am I expected to do here? I think to myself as I watch the last people be seated at the table. This was only breakfast, yet there were about twenty people at each side of the table. The servants begin bringing food around and allowing each person to get what they wanted from it.

This was more like the dinners, having servants serve instead of self-serve on the table against the wall, but with this number of people it was no surprise as to why.

"So what is it you do around here, Lady Audrey?" Prince Leon asks with a wide smile.

"I recently joined the board," I reply, voice cracking slightly as I stifle a cough. "The recently passed Dowager, Lady Farah Davies had me in her will to inherit her title and place within Yonnam Abbey." When I look around at the glares I quickly continue, "Your Highness." I add, making him chuckle.

"You can call me Prince Leon, I prefer that over constantly hearing your highness for myself and my father." He looks up to the servant and passes a few kind words to them as he gets his food from the platter.

I feel a little taken aback by his attitude. He looks and has the aura of many upper-class people I have met, but he still has joyful energy to him. I must look like all of the rest to him, since I have been here... *Have I become too much like one of them?* I shake my head and focus on getting food off of the platter a servant held down for me.

"So you only recently gained your place on the board?" He asks.

I glance around, I notice that eyes are on us, people seem annoyed... irritated at who sat next to the crown prince of the country. Does he not notice this? I think as I look back at his calm expression as he awaits an answer.

"Yes, I've only been here a little over a month, and haven't fully gained my position yet."

"Odd, what did you do before now?" He asks, his gaze unwavering.

He doesn't seem very... prince-y I think to myself. *I expected someone more... Holier than thou type of personality but... Prince Leon is more of a regular person than I originally thought.*

I feel inclined to look away every now and then, having a hard time maintaining eye contact with him. "I used to work at the local library in the upper-class end of the district."

"Upper class?" He looks down at his plate

now. “I believe your perspective on things will be very useful while I am here, Lady Audrey.”

Before I can say anything else, the man on the other side of the prince has gotten his attention, leaving me alone between conversations happening with others seated further away. I sit and eat my food, trying to look deep in thought rather than be left alone, which isn’t very far from the truth.

The prince seems kind... Which only makes this worse. If he were an off sort, it wouldn’t be as worrying keeping him out of the way but now...

He seems as though he is seeking to find out what is happening here, and it isn’t as simple as telling him.

If we are to destroy the source... We need to find a way to keep him from harm...

Should he be made aware of it? But it is a dragon! That could lead him to believe it links the dragonkin to here... Which still could lead to war.

I had not seen dragonkin, but I heard the tales, passed down from generation to generation.

Even with our advancements now, could we survive a war?

Knowing what I do now... if they are my people...

Will I be able to go against my own kind?

I frown and look back at my food, this is foolish. I don't even really know if that could be true. Papa was in a rage, his words carried weight.

Did they?

I barely even finish eating when I look around and realize everyone else has been finished for a while. Lord Julian even stands, and I sigh as I sit my fork down. Prince Leon casts a glance my way but says nothing as Lord Julian begins to speak.

"Alright everyone, we will be going through now, I have other matters to attend to, so follow Mr. Greene into the sitting area and socialize if you wish, and I will be taking my leave."

Lord Julian walks to the door we entered through, while the servant, Mr. Greene, guides the other guests into the sitting room. I sit there for a moment as the prince stands. He begins to walk away, following Lord Julian.

Is this the meeting?

I turn as I begin to get out of my seat when I see Prince Leon waiting, "Are you coming?" He asks warmly.

I quickly nod, "Yes, sorry... I was just deep in thought for a moment there." I quickly stand. "I'm coming."

Prince Leon smiles and begins walking after Lord Julian. I look back at the crowd as they go into the other room, Dominique stood aside and watched me.

He mouths something at me and I quickly turn and begin following the group going after Lord Julian. He leads the way into the great hall and to a door, I had never gone through. It was near the front entryway, and I had assumed it to be storage.

"We will be having the meeting in the waiting room, we have had it converted to be suitable to the number of people in the meeting..." Lord Julian trails off when he spots me, he frowns but says nothing as he sees me standing near the crown prince.

Leading the way into the room I glance around at how many people there are in this meeting. Lady Vivienne and Lord Julian were of course included, to nobody else's surprise. There was also the crown prince, myself, and around seven others joining. Which made me wonder why there were so many others. Are they here to inspect the city and the abbey itself? Or something else?

How many people will be put into danger if we attempt to destroy the source and something goes wrong?

I follow everyone into the room. It wasn't

overly large, but it wasn't small either. With two couches and four armchairs surrounding a coffee table on one side of the room and two desks and a small shelf of books on the other. For a waiting room, it seems rather comfortable. Everyone goes to the couches and chairs, and I follow, seating myself in an armchair closest to the fireplace, so as not to have anyone too close to me. Most others choose to stand, but Lady Vivienne and a few others sit. Lord Julian stands by the coffee table where there is no seat, waiting until everyone is comfortable before he begins to speak.

"So we all know why you're here, to discuss the rumors going around about the border and to ensure everything is running smoothly within the Yonnam District," he begins, voice booming. "Though I must admit, I am surprised and honored that the crown prince himself would visit for such a *trivial* matter such as this."

I frown at Lord Julian's toothy smile. *He is going to try to undermine the situation to seem like nothing.*

Prince Leon smiles, "No matter is too trivial for me to keep an eye on." He motions to the others around the room.

"Now that I am able to contribute more,

my father thought this could be a good challenge for me. Besides -" He grins an almost eerie smile, "I do not think anything involving the bordering dragonkin to be trivial."

"Are you nervous the rumors are true?" Lord Julian asks.

Prince Leon shakes his head, "I am unsure, but either way, it is better to be safe than sorry, yes?"

At least he is taking this seriously.

Lady Vivienne watches him for a long moment through narrowed eyes before speaking up. "What are your thoughts of dragonkin, *Prince Leon*?"

"Please refer to the crown prince as your highness when speaking to him," One of the envoy members says quickly. I look at the prince, he doesn't stop to correct them.

"The dragonkin are ruthless, they can hide within our crowds and they can use magic far better than we can. I don't hate them, but I am weary of any force that could be more powerful than my own."

I look at Prince Leon as he speaks, he flexes his hands as though he were trying to force himself to appear relaxed. As though he didn't mean his words.

Does he hate the Dragonkin? I feel my chest

ache, and am forced to heave in to take a breath, getting everyone's attention for a moment.

"Now, I'd like to ask a few questions, nothing too complicated," an envoy member says quickly, calling any and all attention off of myself. I feel slightly grateful for this, though Lady Vivienne's
eyes linger a second longer than I would like.

"Yes, Advisor Cabot, go on." Lord Julian replies, making the man, Mr. Cabot shift in his seat, pulling out a small pocket book with a pen and opening it before he begins to speak.

"It is about the border situation, how long has it been since the border has been recast?" He asks.

"It has not been too long," Lady Vivienne answers quickly. The man begins to ask another question but the prince holds up a hand to stop him.

"I'd like to hear Lady Audrey on that, considering she hasn't been on the board for too long."

The men of the envoy all exchange a glance, as though they were irritated that a woman be allowed to add on something like this. Lady Vivienne was never questioned because to be frank, she was quite intimidating, but me? I was nothing in comparison.

Before Lady Vivienne or Lord Julian can respond I hurriedly open my mouth to speak.

"It has been quite some time since I have seen the border be recast."

Lord Julian chuckles awkwardly at my eagerness to answer, "Well, you know there has been a shortage of magic users for a while so -"

"Then I will recast it myself while we are here," Prince Leon replies, my eyes go wide.

Can the crown prince use magic? With the shortage of magic users, I never would have thought he had any abilities...

"This means there will be less threat of dragon fire hitting any majorly populated areas within the district, should there be a war. Sadly, I cannot promise it can keep anything from crossing the border. We do not fully know what type of magic they possess." The prince says, motioning back to the advisor. "You can continue with your questions now."

Mr. Cabot nods quickly, "Yes, well. There is also the question of guards and patrolmen. Should anything be going wrong on the border -"

"We have men and women on patrol if that is what you are asking." Lady Vivienne retorts coldly.

I frown, looking around the room, a majority of the envoy seemed to care very little about what was transpiring in this meeting. Most aren't even focused on the people in the room as they gaze off into nothingness. This may not get us as far as I would like.

"The border patrol was only set up again very recently," I add, not meeting Lady Vivienne's glare.

"Is there a reason for this?" Prince Leon asks.

"It is -"

"It is because there has been little reason for it until now." Lord Julian interrupts me swiftly. I glare at him. Though this would be making me more enemies within the abbey, things needed to get done, and things won't change unless risks are taken.

"Is that so, Lord Julian? I thought it was due to lack of funding, at least, that is what my father was told when he lost his job as a patrolling officer of the borders to Dragnior -"

"Who allowed this foul-tongued woman in here!" One of the envoy members speaks up, face as red as a tomato, with veins almost popping out of his forehead. "All she has done is insult the dignity of everyone here, she hasn't even said anything useful -"

"Mr. Redhill I believe that Lady Audrey has only added useful information, and I should remind you she is also a member of the board here and is entitled to a say in the matter." Prince Leon cuts off his man quickly, "I believe her perspective will be very useful during our stay here, so I expect not another word on the subject." He turns to face Lord Julian while his man glares at the floor. "I would like Mr. Cabot to be allowed to go through financial documents and papers proving this, will that be made possible, Lord Julian? Lady Vivienne?" The crown prince asks the two, they exchange a quick glance before Lord Julian nods, "Of course, why would there be any problem?"

The prince smiles at this, "Then today I would like to be led through the abbey, and my men are allowed to go through the documents now if possible. Tomorrow we can visit the border itself and I will recast the border. Does this order of events work for every party involved?"

I nod quickly as everyone else nods or murmurs an agreement. *This means we have a chance! If they will all be going to the border... we - I just need to find a way to get everyone else out in case something goes wrong but...*

We may have a shot at destroying the source safely.

As soon as dinner was over, I didn't stay with the others in the sitting room. Instead, I hurried out into the great hall, telling anyone who would listen how tired I was and I was retiring early. Very little else had happened since the meeting, in fact, Lord Julian and Lady Vivienne were eerily silent about the matters of my outburst during the meeting with the royal envoy. I wait in the great hall for a moment, knowing Dominique would leave soon after so we could speak. It was odd, to know a person well enough to know their reactions and how to easily contact them. Dominique had left for a while, and yet it felt like everything fell back into place when he returned. I turn back to the sitting room door just as Dominique steps out, he rolls his eyes and sighs as he unties his long red hair from its ponytail, letting it fall over his shoulders.

"You seem tired," I say with a smirk, he stops beside me and scoffs.

"But of course, using this charm takes its toll after too much conversation."

I laugh at this, making Dominique smile. "Now, would you be interested in going for a stroll through the garden?"

I nod, "Let's go."

Dominique opens the front doors to the abbey, allowing Audrey through first before falling in step beside her. As soon as the door shuts, Audrey lets out a relieved sigh.

"Now, there are some important matters to discuss."

Dominique nods, "What happened at the meeting?"

"Not much, sadly, but I am glad to say the prince seems to be ready to take action."

"Action?" Dominique stops walking, making me stop a few steps ahead.

"Yes, what's wrong?"

"You don't mean... War do you?"

I frown, Dominique's oddly colored eyes were wide, and his shoulders were tense as he waited for my answer. *Is he that afraid of going to war? It doesn't seem as though that is all to it though...*

"I do not believe that the prince is that far yet, only I was saying that he was very receptive to what I had to say."

"Oh," Dominique relaxes slightly, as he

begins to walk in step next to me. "Then I am assuming all of the envoy members going through the abbey was of your doing then?"

I nod, "Tomorrow will be our chance!" I say excitedly, "We can find a way to destroy the source, and everything can go back to normal-" I stop at the end of my sentence, sighing.

What is normal going to be now?

Living in the abbey in fear? Alongside people in loveless marriages craving money? There would be no fear of a war anymore but... my life would never be the same as it had once been.

"What is it that you want to do once we finish this?" I ask as I look ahead. We were already nearing the gardens.

"I want to return home for a while I think." He says with a chuckle. "After everything here, I would enjoy some peace and quiet in my library." He looks at me. "Once this is all over, I want you to come with me."

"What?"

He pauses by the snapdragons blooming along the pathway, "I know, it might sound odd. I think you will need a breather from this place as well though, from District Yonnam in general."

I'm...

Dominique was not a bad man, far from it, as I look at him I could see a possibility of being happy going with him away from here, but that is a possibility I am not yet ready for... Nor should it be important with everything going on right now.

I sigh, looking down at the flowers, I hold one in my hand and press the petals, making it snap open. “I get it but... What about my brothers?”

“They can come too of course! I wouldn’t suggest you leave them behind.”

I glance over at Dominique, he seems sincere with his request.

“First,” I begin, making him stand straighter, “Let’s find a way to destroy this source and keep it as clean and safe as possible then... we can discuss this further. Alright?”

Dominique nods, a huge smile on his face. Does he not have many close to him if the idea of continuing to be near me makes him happy?

Suddenly Dominique freezes, I look at him quickly, “What’s wrong?”

He turns to look deeper into the gardens, “I do not believe we are alone.” He says quietly. “Stay here, I’m going to investigate.”

Before I can say anything Dominique has

already stormed off, disappearing deeper into the lush garden. I lean away from the flowers, I struggle to calm my labored breathing to listen for sounds of movement, when I hear a disgustingly familiar voice.

"Well, well, well, thought you could be kept safe with your man at your side did you?"

I spin around to see a bald man standing a few paces away, dressed in an outdated suit style that didn't fit him completely, with narrowed yellow eyes.

Emmett Wingrave standing at the garden entrance, flashing his teeth in a crooked smirk, he takes a step forward.

"You're nothing more than a scheming little brat if you think I'll let what happened earlier slide."

"What happened earlier? That was your own fault, not mine, Emmett."

Emmett shakes his head, "No, I told you that you had better get in a good word with Julian for me, but you didn't. This is your fault, just as everything in your wretched little life is!" He begins laughing, a sick maniacal laugh.

"Why... Why are you laughing?" I ask, backing up.

I had seen Emmett act odd, once he had a few drinks when we were engaged, but this...

This was a whole new level even for him.

As he begins to step closer, I notice moonlight reflecting off of metal. I spot the knife in his hand and immediately begin backing up further into the garden.

"Emmett, do you really think killing me will make this better for you?"

He laughs like a hyena, as he begins moving faster now. "You've been nothing but a pest to Julian these past few days, I am sure if I rid him of his problem... He will find a way to make me inherit everything you have!"

Suddenly, Emmett charges forward, I quickly turn and begin running further into the gardens. I can hear Emmett's laughing close behind as I take the various twists and turns of the paths trying to shake him off of my trail.

Come on! Where is Dominique when I need him?

Just in that moment, I see a flash of red through the trees up ahead, *Dominique!* I open my mouth to call out his name, I trip and fall onto the metal garden tables, I spin around to see Emmett was already upon me.

He holds the knife up towards me as I press myself up against the table.

"Anything left to say, my old *darling*?"

I don't even have time to think as I react, grabbing a chair next to me and swinging it at Emmett. I knock him to the ground. He falls to his side and the knife falls away from his hand. He reaches for it, scrambling to crawl close enough to get it but I stop my foot down on his hand as I see his goal. His cries are pathetic as I lean down and grab the knife. I quickly step away, holding the knife protectively in front of me as Emmett struggles to stand.

"Did you really think you could kill me? That I would *let* you kill me after everything I have lost to get this far?"

"Audrey?" Dominique yells from the other side of the garden seating area, but I don't hear him as I look down at Emmett's wide, fearful eyes.

"You don't have what it takes," He says with a cracking snicker. "I know you, Audrey, you are no killer."

"Are you sure about that, *Emmett?*"

Just then Emmett lunges at the knife in my hand, grasping for it desperately.

I do not know what snapped inside of me, but at that moment I felt something change as I thrust the blade forward with no attention as to its aim. For a moment my mind goes blank as a disgusting sputtering and gurgling sound comes from Emmett. The blade falls from my hands as I look down at the fear in his eyes as he collapses to the ground.

"I didn't want to have to do this... Emmett, I -"

"Audrey!"

I spin around to see Dominique standing a few steps away, his eyes wide.

"What happened?!" He rushes over, grabbing my shoulders and turning me away from the body I stood over.

"Emmett... He came here with that knife I just..."

"Defended yourself?" Dominique asks, I look up at him.

Was that what this was?

I hear a gurgling sound behind me, slowly, I begin to turn back to look at Emmett. Dominique grabs my shoulders and stops me.

"No! You cannot look at him."

Dominique quickly glances around. "I'll dispose of this myself... I brought you out here, this is my fault." He looks at me, and pulls my hands up to be lit by the moonlight. "You need to go clean up, fast." He says, "Go through the servant's entrance to wash the blood, all of the servants should still be attending to the envoy..."

I open my mouth to respond but no

words come out, Dominique removes his hands from me, taking a step around to block the sight of Emmett.

"You need to go, Audrey." He says.

I look at him, feeling blank.

"Go!" Dominique hurries me off, casting a quick glance back at Emmett. "Go now!"

I turn and begin hurrying back to the abbey, as I hurry I look down at my hands.

I... Killed him?

You were defending yourself! A small voice says. I shake my head as I try to look ahead, but I cannot stop looking at the crimson red that stained my hands.

Am I really going to bring chaos everywhere I go now?

Will I be able to bring order to Yonnam?

Or only more pain?

22
BURNING PAGES

"...A soul must be steeped in the dark before it can revel in the glory of the light..."
- Author Unknown

After seeing blood on one's hands it is almost impossible to forget the sight. Emmett's face moments before I had struck was lingering in my mind as I made my way down the stairs for the morning. Paxton had continuously asked me what was wrong all morning while I had gotten ready, but I could barely muster the energy to deny that there was anything. As I reach the bottom of the stairs I notice the envoy gathered along with Lord Julian, but Lady Vivienne was nowhere to be seen.

"Ah, Lady Audrey!" Prince Leon's face lights up when he spots me on the stairs, "We were just getting ready for our patrol through the city and chance to investigate the borders." He steps away from the group and stops at the bottom of the stairs, I pause a few steps away from him.

"I wanted to apologize for the attitude of my men yesterday, not all of them are used to the changes new times have been brought."

I nod, "It does not bother me in the slightest," I lie.

"Well, in any case," He continues, casting a glance back at the group behind him, "I would like to speak with you again, only you. I feel that you will have a more useful... perspective than the people who have been in the abbey since the start of the rumors."

Before I can say anything the crown prince has already turned away, "For now though, I can only take so many with me to the border, as to not cause a fuss, as I am sure you can understand."

I dip my head quickly, "Safe travels to you, Prince Leon."

The prince smiles and dips his head before retreating back to the group. My eyes follow him until I notice Lord Julian glaring my way. I quickly look away so as not to meet his gaze, and quickly hurry past the group into the dining hall for breakfast.

Only Lady Priscilla and Lady Vivienne were in the dining hall, both sitting at opposite ends of the table, since nobody else was around. I hurriedly go to sit closer to Lady Priscilla, but still put distance between us as I still feel as though my head is filled with fog.

Where is Dominique? Did he make it back in safely after...

After I killed Emmett?

I still could hardly believe my actions. Emmett has caused me a great deal of trouble but... I never thought I would have reacted like that. I didn't even give it thought, I just reacted.

Is that in the nature of dragonkin? I wonder. If papa was being honest about finding me... And if it really did mean I was one of... Them... would that explain my nature? Was this who I was to be now?

"Lady Audrey?"

I look over to Lady Priscilla, she has a concerned expression on her face.

"What is the matter?" She asks.

"Oh," I cast a glance at Lady Vivienne, who was watching through narrowed eyes. "I am only.. Tired, I did not get the best sleep last night."

"Is that why your husband has yet to be seen?" Lady Vivienne asks with a snicker.

I freeze, saying nothing, but my mind was a whirlwind of questions.

Was he caught? Does she know? How could she know? Perhaps he just slept in... Or it is taking him longer with the patrolmen... The patrolmen!

I had almost forgotten the servants were on patrol now that the envoy was in the district, what if he had been caught?

Caught cleaning up the mess I had caused.

Lady Vivienne gets up, tossing her napkin onto the table she storms out of the room, I look at Lady Priscilla who just sighs, “She is upset that Lord Julian didn’t want her to join the envoy on their route through town and... apparently the crown prince agreed that no women should be present for their safety.”

I nod and stare down at my plate, frowning.

“Lady Audrey?”

“Yes?!” I look up at Lady Priscilla quickly, a worried expression was worn on her face with her brows stitched together and lip pursed.

“Is everything all right?”

I shake my head, “Not really... in fact...” I stand from my seat and stop by where she sat, leaning down, “I need you out of the abbey today.”

“But why?” She asks quietly.

“Its... A matter of your safety. I’m going to try to deal with something but there is a chance it will go wrong.”

“What do you mean - Is there anything you need me to do?” She asks quickly.

I shake my head, “Just... stay at the library just outside of the abbey gates. My brothers are there with the owner, a man I trust very much."

Lady Priscilla nods, and before she can ask another question I hurry out of the room.

I may not have much time to prepare but... I need to do this on my own. I can't keep relying on the kindness of others - My parents for taking me in for so long, Farah for leaving me everything when she died, and now Dominique risking everything to help me when it could stop him from his goal.

I need to destroy that... abomination of magic.

It is up to me to destroy the source.

I can feel the pain in my chest growing as I descend down that dark staircase once more. An oil lamp in hand. I curse myself with every step. For allowing things to get this far, for not being able to defend those I loved, for allowing my life to crumble all around me. No more.

I won't let my world shatter any further.

Once I destroy the source of the sickness, everything will go back to normal.

I had been unable to find Dominique after last night, but I couldn't wait around any longer. I had to work while the envoy was still out of the house along with half of the servants working patrol.

Something could go wrong.

I stop at the bottom step and frown at the door in front of me.

What will this... Normal be? Am I to become one of the abbey members? To soon join in a loveless marriage like every other? To slowly be corrupted or become so exhausted with life that I do nothing?

Either way. I need to finish this, to avenge Farah, to avenge my mother -

But she was not your mother. This whole time...

I open the door and step into the room, the chains all around the room are even more transparent than before, but the dragonkin corpse remained. There was only one difference this time.

"Vivienne?!"

I step back into the doorway, horrified. Lady Vivienne stands up from her spot next to the dragonkin corpse.

"I knew you would be here- Sneaking about like a rat." She hisses, "Do you really think you're inconspicuous in your ventures? Lord Julian may be none the wiser, but I am not so easy to trick."

I step forward, "Vivienne, what is it you're trying to achieve here? This thing... is this what is causing trouble on the border?"

Vivienne scoffs, "I wouldn't expect you to understand, you're a human after all."

"Are you saying that you're -"

"Dragonkin?" Vivienne smirks, "Once I could make that claim, but now... I was stripped of my powers long ago. This-" She motions to the corpse beside her, "This is the only way I could find to get it back."

Vivienne kneels beside the corpse, laying a hand on it, she lets out a deep breath as scales slowly appear up her arm, but they stop halfway. "It has improved greatly over this last month." She says with a pleased grin.

"Why are you here?! You do realize what you're doing could cause a war with you - your... people?"

"I just need more time," She says looking back to the corpse, "Once enough energy has been drained from the district, I will have my powers back. I will be whole again."

"Energy drain? Then..."

This is her fault.

"Tell me one thing, Vivienne,"

"Why should I?" she retorts, taking a step towards me, a dark gleam in her eyes.

I don't shy away. "*Humor me.*"

Vivienne holds out her hand, a cerulean flame appears from her palm. "I will grant you one last question before I dispose of you,

Audrey."

"Farah, did she die because of this?" I pull the collar of my dress aside to reveal the sickly darkened tendrils that had grown even further, their coloring even darker and more branching than it had been on my mother. I couldn't even look at them anymore, and as Vivienne sees it her eyes go wide and she stumbles back.

"Farah... everyone else afflicted did not have anything like that." Vivienne sputters as she stares, "That can only mean... You are a dragonkin." Vivienne quickly regains composure, holding her tense hands forward with flames in either palm. "Who sent you? Xavier? Rowan? Quinn? Answer me!"

I stand paralyzed, unable to answer as I stare at Vivienne and the dragonkin corpse.

"Is that.. really what this means?" I ask. "All humans afflicted don't show as serious signs until longer periods of energy drain. Dragonkin carry more magic energy than that, those tendrils in that color, I've only seen it on myself."

"Vivienne, back down."

I spin around as I hear a deep voice behind me, A tall figure with red hair steps into the light.

"Dominique!"

Vivienne frowns, "What do you think you will accomplish by destroying my work?"

Dominique steps forward, "We will finally be free of this sickness you so selfishly caused."

"Wait!" Vivienne puts her hands up, the blue flames of magic have disappeared, "Don't! If you do anything to it... We could all die."

"That is a chance we will have to take," I say quickly, holding up my lantern high and throwing it onto the corpse, it immediately catches aflame, the dragonkin's scales weakened from decay and unnatural forms of magic make it extremely flammable.

"No! I was so close! I could almost turn back!" Vivienne lets out a screech as she jumps away from the quickly growing flames, her wild gaze quickly upon me. "Fool! Do you realize what you have done?!" The transparent chains on the walls begin to shatter like glass.

Dominique grabs my arm roughly, pulling me. "Come on! We need to get out!"

Turning away from Vivienne who watched her creation burn with terror, I rush up the stairs, the once cool air of the passageway now feeling stifling as my the markings on my chest begins to ache.

"Dominique," I huff. "The markings... Do yours -" We reach the top of the stairs and I stop.

"Wait - You're a dragonkin aren't you?" He turns back to me, eyes wide, "Audrey, now is not the time -"

Dominique is right, but that would mean...

"You're here to investigate for Dragnior aren't you?"

He glances back to the window leading into Vivienne's office, and steps toward me.

"You're right, I am dragonkin, but right now that is the least of your worries, we need to get out of here or none of this will matter!"

I feel my chest getting tight, smoke begins to filter up the stairwell as the fire continues to spread onto the wood of the stairs. Quickly I climb through the passage into the office, Dominique right behind me. The fire is right behind us as we reach the doorway, I don't look back as we run down the hallway into the great hall of the abbey.

"How is it spreading so fast?!" I yell at Dominique.

"It is a mixture of magics that should never have been used on one source- I'm surprised it isn't spreading faster!" As we pass by servants I quickly begin waving them out.

"Get out of the abbey! There is a fire!"

Most nearby servants begin running for the entrance as they see the flames coming from behind us, one young maid stares at me with wide eyes.

"Paxton she... she was looking for you!"

"Where is she?" I stop in front of the servant, placing my hands on their shoulders. "Where did you see her last?!"

"Going up to your room."

I look back at Dominique, his eyes go wide as he reaches for me.

"Audrey - wait!"

I dodge away from his grabbing hands and begin to rush up the stairs. Fire is already spreading up the side of the banister, so I hurry up the steps as fast as I can, kicking off my heels as I reach the top stairs. I run down the halls to my room, the fire was spreading even faster than any real flame should, almost on my heels the whole way down, I burst through the door to my room to find Paxton inside by a bundle of dresses. "My Lady! What is going on -" I rush into the room as the flames spread behind me, hurrying to the window.

"Paxton - we need to get out of here now!" I spin around as I hear crumbling, the door and wall around it have been burned through, and now flames were licking across the floor towards us. I turn to the window.

The fall might not kill us... I glance back at the flames. *I would rather take my luck with the fall than the flames.*

My chest aches with every movement, but still, I struggle to open the window. Paxton backs up towards me and the window, staring into the flames.

"Lady Audrey what - What is that?!"

I turn back around to see two large eyes appear in the fire, the amber and gold reflected the flames that lurch higher and higher as they consume everything around. A large four-legged creature steps out into the room, ducking to step inside and pulling down parts of the wall as it does.

A dragonkin. It's scales are unaffected by the flame, yet the creature still looks in pain as it flares up its wings and rushes towards them.

Did Vivienne get her form back?!

Grabbing Paxton's arm, I quickly step up into the windowsill.

"Jump!" I shout.

"Wait!"

I turn as a deep grumble comes from the dragonkin but it and the two of us quickly jump over the side of the window. I shut my eyes and brace for impact, when suddenly I feel something grab around my waist. I open my eyes, the large claws of a beast wrap around me, I look up to see the dragonkin; with its wings spread above me. Hearing a scream, I turn to see Paxton on the other hand of the creature.

If this was Vivienne we would be dead -

"Dominique?!" I call out, but the beast does not look down, it slowly descends to the ground, dropping us onto the grass as it crashes a few feet away.

"Dominique?!" I call out, but the beast does not look down, it slowly descends to the ground, dropping us onto the grass as it crashes a few feet away.

I look over to Paxton, but she was already up and running away from the abbey, away from the dragonkin. I turn back towards it.

"Dominique! What happened?!"

The large beast was sprawled out, chest rising and falling as it struggles to breath, it's wings sprawled out, scales shimmering from the flames of the abbey.

I hurry towards the dragonkin, falling to my knees by it's head.

"You saved us... me, but why?"

The large eye of the beast is fixated on me, and a low grumble comes from it.

"You may be different from me... But you don't deserve to die, Audrey."

As I look into the gold and black flecks of the eye, I put a hand onto the creature's cheek.

"Dominique..."

An unearthly screech comes from the abbey, and I look back to the flames. Gold and silver light come from the abbey, and something continues screaming. It was an otherworldly screech, much different from the sound that came from Dominique.

Vivienne?

The pain in my chest subsides, but a wave of nausea and agony washes over me. I feel my head growing faint as I push against Dominique.

"You need to go! Get out of here!"

Slowly he stands to his feet towering over me. He tucks his wings in before casting one last look at me.

"Stay safe, Audrey-"

"Lady Audrey!" Comes a cry from behind me.

I turn to many people rushing from the front of the abbey, the prince in the lead. His eyes turn cold as he sees the creature near me.

"Lady Audrey! To me!" He shouts, holding out his hand blue crystals form a spear in his hand and he rears back to throw it.

No!

I want to scream for them to stop, but I can't as I fall onto the grass around me. I look back to Dominique, he slowly backs away from me, looking between me and the prince before turning and running away. Each step makes the ground shake as he disappears into the forest.

As I watch him leave I feel relieved, sick, and guilty all at the same time, as I feel myself slipping from consciousness there is only one thing I can think as he leaves me.

Are the Dragonkin as evil as we once thought?

23
THE STORIES LEFT UNTOLD

"... You can take a wounded animal in, feed it, care for it, tend to it, and even train it, but in the end, it will always remain wild..."
- Author Unknown

Opening my eyes I feel my heartbeat begin to race as I remember what had happened before. *Dominique!*

I sit looking around, branches and thorns scratch me and I realize I was sitting within the undergrowth. The trees and grass around me feels familiar, but different. I was at the edge of the Dragnior Flaize border. Looking around, I felt comfortable for the first time in the forest. I could hear the screeches and shouts of rallying men nearby, and the forest floors rumble as something's movement shakes the earth beneath me.

Why am I here? What happened? Where is Dominique?!

Yet I didn't feel any fear in my heart, I only knew to wait. No matter how much I tried, I could not move a single muscle in my body.

What happened to Dominique? The Prince? Paxton?

Did I... Die?

All I could do was sit, still as a stone, watching what happened around me. Undergrowth rustles and the earth slowly stops shaking. The stillness should be comforting, but was the quite opposite. If I was dead, what is this? Where am I? I continue struggling, desperately trying to move, to scream, to yell, to call out but nothing happened. Suddenly everything I had done felt worthless, I did not even know if I had achieved in destroying the source. Was there a better future ahead for me if I had achieved my goal as planned?

Would there have been happiness for me in leaving with Dominique? Well, now I might never know. Apparently the afterlife has a cruel sense of humor.

Surely this is not the afterlife? I think as I look around, why would it be like this? This... Like this place?

This feels... familiar, but why?

I hear the screeching getting closer, and I see a warm firelight nearby from torches as a crowd rushes through the forest. All older men in the distance traverse the forest ground, but not one seems to have noticed me yet.

Perhaps one of them could know why I am here? What happened...

Someone emerges from the bushes nearby, a young man, with short black hair and a full beard wielding an axe. I look at the weapon in his hands and feel my heart freeze, but my body does not react, I only sit there, muscles relaxed staring at him.

"A beast!" He cries out, I stand slowly and realize I was his height.

Beast? Why is he...

I look down at my arms, my skin, everything that should be there was not. Instead, I see dark bronze scales, feet with horrible, crooked talons, and the end of a whip-like tail. I look back up at the man, he looks afraid, but curious. He was far younger than the others going through the woods, and less cautious.

He slowly steps towards me, and I take a step forward as well, making him jump away.

"Afraid?" I hear croaked from my own mouth, even though I did not speak it.

The man slowly nods, and I sit back down. I felt the sudden urge to not scare him, to be less intimidating so perhaps he might help me. I feel my scales and form shift as I look down. I watch as my form changes, morphs, transforms into something I know now I am not. I was turning human.

What is this?!

I look back up, the man's eyes are wide. "You are... just a child?" He shakes his head, "No! You are a beast." He steps towards me, with his axe raised, I put up my hands and shut my eyes tight, waiting for him to swing down, but the pain never hits. I look up to see the man's face closer.

He drops his weapon and begins to take off his coat, "Here..." He puts it onto my shoulders and steps back. "I can't hurt a child... even if you are that of a monster."

He extends a hand towards me, "Come with me, my wife, Amelia will know what to do."

I wrap the coat around myself, it was five sizes too large for me and I look down. *When did I get this small - and -*

"Who..." I feel my lips move but do not move them. "Who are you?"

"My name?" The man looks down at me, uncertain, "Connor Hughes."

Papa?! Then this is - A memory?

Slowly the world around me turns into black, trees fading into nothing until all I see is papa, and even that fades and I am left with nothing.

24
THE WORDS THAT REMAIN

"... Since the abbey burned down almost a week ago, the old town hall has become the new residing place of the board, it is confirmed that the prince has been in District Yonnam with the royal envoy. Who claims that he saw dragonkin at the site of the fire. Does this mean a war will begin soon? Or will the King try to reason with our neighboring country..."
- Flaize Daily

I open my eyes and sit up, gasping for breath. Looking around, I see nothing familiar. A simple wooden wardrobe, a desk, a door, a window, a mirror- all of it was blurry and hard to focus on. Looking down I realize I was in a small bed, I jump up and rush to the mirror and I quickly begin pulling at my shirt, I look at my reflection. The branching patterns in a disgustingly purple color that had spread across my chest were now a faded pale.

It's.... It's faded.

I spin to look to the window, *does that*

mean - the source was destroyed? Did we succeed?

Suddenly the door is pulled open, and a woman dressed in a puffy gray dress with white aprons steps inside and gasps at the sight of me, "You're finally awake!" she exclaims, and before I can say anything she is out of the room calling out for someone. Quickly I pull my blouse back up and look out the window.

Looking out, I see city buildings and busy streets filled with carriages and people on horseback alongside the many people walking down the sidewalks. "Lady Audrey!"

I look back to the door, the prince stands there, a relieved smile upon his face.

"We're lucky you pulled through!" He exclaims, taking a cautious step towards me. "Do you remember anything? Anything at all?"

I slowly step back, "I - I..."

What happened before I got here? We set fire to the source... and then...

It all comes flooding back to me, I look up at the prince.

"The abbey... what happened to it?" I ask.

He shakes his head, "It almost completely burned down, almost everyone made it out alive but..."

He looks up at me, "The Lady Vivienne,

along with your husband, died in the fire."

I stare at him for a moment, bewildered.

They don't know- Of course, they don't know! But Lady Vivienne....

"Did you find their bodies?" I ask quickly, crossing my arms tight against my chest.

He shakes his head, "The fire was... unlike any other I had seen." Prince Leon looks at me, "Do you happen to know what caused the fire?"

Slowly I nod, "This... will be difficult to explain but... I found something." I begin.

The prince's eyes went cold, "What kind of something?"

"Surely you sensed something wrong in the district?" I reason quickly, "Something off about the sickness? The rumors? Everything?" He nods, and I continue, "I found what I believed to be the source of this beneath the abbey. Holy magic mixed with many other things... and a dragonkin corpse."

"What... So you started the fire?"

I hang my head, "Yes, I did... but I believe it stopped the sickness." I pull my shirt aside to reveal the paled marks left behind. "I had the sickness until now, and I'm assuming others were miraculously cured as well."

The crown prince steps over to the window and looks out, "You *are* right about that, everyone in this district and others around have been miraculously recovering within this last week but... That dragonkin, what was it doing outside of the abbey?"

Dominique...

I begin to open my mouth but stop. I can't tell him. If I do... If I reveal how I knew Dominique and Vivienne were dragonkin...

He would know I am one too.

"I don't know what that *thing* was doing there," I reply.

The prince frowns, but says nothing as he steps away to the door, I hurry towards him.

"What now?" I ask quickly. He turns and looks at me over his shoulder.

"What do you mean? There is only one choice remaining." He says grimly. "A dragonkin corpse riddled with magic as you say was beneath the abbey, and one was on sight as the Yonnam Abbey burned to the ground. There is only one way this could go."

"War?" I ask, trembling.

He nods, "It is our only choice now. We cannot leave it long and allow them to cause more harm to the district." Prince Leon turns back to me and places a hand on my shoulder. "I will be leaving many of the members of the envoy here while I return to my father to speak with him. Lord Julian is...

Not suitable to ruling the board for this."

"What are you saying?"

"I am saying, that you Lady Audrey, are the only *good* board member left. I am leaving Yonnam in your charge and when I return," He removes his hand from my shoulder, "I expect you to assist me in making the charge on Dragnior."

I step back, eyes wide.

"Surely we will try to be diplomatic at first?" I say through heavy breaths.

He nods, "We will try of course, but I do not believe that it will go far." He dips his head, "Now I must leave you, Lady Audrey. My men will keep you informed and get you up to date on what is expected until I return. I am trusting you to rule as the Lady of the board, don't let me down."

With that, Prince Leon steps out of the room. Leaving me to my thoughts.

Isn't this what you wanted?

You gained your title of the inheritance, you destroyed the source, you even gained revenge on Emmett and avenged the ones you love! You have achieved it all!

No...

I push past the prince and hurry down the stairs, spotting the front door. I make a dash for it and push my way outside. I find myself in the middle of the town center, I look back to see the town hall cleaned up.

This is not what I wanted. All I wanted was to bring a better life to my family. Now it is up to me to fix this too...

Is this my life? Breaking things as I try to fix them?

I shake my head, *no, I will not fail again. I will fix this.*

For Farah, for mum, and for Dominique.

I would have to guide this war as best as I can, and never let my dragonkin blood be found out by either side.

PART THREE
FINAL EDITION

25
BEYOND THE BOOKS

"Knowledge can only carry one so far... Failure to use what you've learned makes the knowledge as good as dirt."
- Author

Snowflakes falling from the sky can be seen through a foggy window of the Yonnam District Town Hall, marking the earliest winter the district had ever seen. Inside, people are rushing to and fro as they hurriedly prepare for travel. Wearing thick bundled coats, many still shiver even indoors, as the building needed many repairs.

"Au - *Lady* Audrey."

I turn as I hear a begrudging voice, I sit down the blankets I was packing and turn to see Lord Julian glaring around with his nose upturned.

"Yes, Lord Julian?" I reply. He strides across the room towards me, getting in at least five other people's way before stopping by me.

"Would you finish packing the tents -"

"No, Lord Julian," I reply without skipping a beat. "I have just as much work as you do."

He rolls his eyes, "I highly doubt that."

"Just because you aren't used to working, doesn't mean you can pawn it off on others," I grumble. "Gosh, they really can't put you anywhere to work without you starting something, can they?"

He scoffs in response but says nothing as he turns back to get back to work. I sigh as I finish bundling the covers into their bags to keep them clean during travels. It has been two months- Two whole months since the source of magic had been destroyed. Two months since anything from Dragnoir has been seen or heard, and yet here we are, preparing to go across borders to negotiate with the Dragonkin. Negotiate, I can't help but laugh out loud, making others nearby stop and stare. Lord Julian and I are the only members of the board, so now we had to do all of the heavy liftings while still working with the crown prince, Leon, on any and all plans. Not that he would listen. He claimed it was only negotiations, but the attitude of everyone around it would only be a sign for the war to begin - no matter what the outcome.

All of this... packing feels pointless. Since it is the middle of winter, and we did not know how far into Dragnoir we would have to travel before we would be met by dragonkin, packing is required.

I wish Lady Priscilla didn't leave. I think with a sigh as I begin walking through the crowds of the king's men working. Lady Priscilla had left the abbey before the fire, so she was safe, but she went home. This surprised me, but I doubt I was anywhere near as surprised as she was. I just wish I was not left with Julian of all people to work alongside. It was a startling contrast to working with Dominique. While he was kind, warm, and witty at times, Julian is the exact opposite. Cold, lazy, and dull.

He had lost any charismatic charm he once had, replaced by a very broken man.

Yet sometimes Lord Julian has surprised me with his work. It makes me wonder what went so wrong in his life to make him this way.

Dominique... I can't help but think about him. *Was he injured? Did he also recover from the illness like everyone else?* I can only hope he made it back across the border safely.

As for Vivienne, I still didn't feel confident in the Prince's claim of her death. Did she get out and die from the smoke? Or were they able to identify her body?

I shake my head, focusing on what lies ahead was more important, and right now what lies ahead was crossing the border.

As I look ahead to see the entrance to the town hall, I hear an abrupt call from behind me.

"Lady Audrey!"

I spin around to see Prince Leon with a sharply dressed woman standing beside him. I glance her over as the pair stops by me.

"I wanted to check in and see if everything has been in order with you and Lord Julian." He says quickly.

I dip my head, "Yes, everything is going smoothly." I answer. The woman beside the crown prince furrows her brow and frowns.

"Where is it you were off to in such a hurry?" She asks.

I raise a brow at the prince as I look at the woman. She definitely looks like the soldiers that arrived recently... Who is she though?

Before I can ask, the prince quickly steps in, "Ah, I forgot to introduce to you my advisor, Odell Alborne. Her family has been working alongside ours for generations."

I dip my head to her, but she does not move, still awaiting an answer.

"I am going to check on my brothers, since you will be leaving soon I thought I'd -"

"You are aware you will also be accompanying the envoy, yes?" Advisor Odell retorts sharply. Someone calls for the prince nearby and he dips his head before backing off, leaving me alone with the intensity of Odell.

"You are aware you will also be accompanying the envoy, yes?" Advisor Odell retorts sharply. Someone calls for the prince nearby and he dips his head before backing off, leaving me alone with the intensity of Odell.

I look at the woman before me. She has her thick browns arched down as she glares at me through narrowed steely gray eyes, her arms crossed over her finely tailored suit which was one more in a masculine style. I stare at her for a moment before I finally respond.

"I was not made aware that I would be needed for the envoy, no," I answer bluntly, watching as Prince Leon disappears into another room.

She uncrosses her arms, relaxing slightly. "You and Julian are going to be traveling with us since you are the only board members left in this district. I am sure the crown prince would want any information you have regarding events up to this moment when we try to speak with the dragonkin leader."

I frown, though I am not completely used

to titles, it is odd how informal she spoke.

"How are we going to travel across the border in this much snow? We don't even have a map -"

"We have our plan set, Audrey, just worry about yourself being here when we set off. There is much more preparation to be done if we leave in a few days."

With that Odell Alborne turns away to speak with her men, no longer caring for anything else I had to say to her.

She is the advisor of the prince? I sigh.

This is going to be difficult, I watch as she prepares her men, pointing at the weapon containers and more as she directs. It seems she is already planning for a war. I begin heading back up the stairs to continue working when I hear a pitiful scoff nearby. I look ahead to see Lord Julian smirking at me.

"Think you could get away that easily?"

I grit my teeth as I pass him, "Let me guess, you already tried and failed, hm?"

Julian doesn't respond, striding up the stairs ahead of me with his hands held in clenched fists.

"I wish it were Vivienne and not you to survive." I hear him hiss under his breath as he rushes away.

Harsh words for such a small man.

I roll my eyes at his antics, even Fletcher and Remy were more mature than this sad excuse of a man. It was like dealing with a tantrum every time I saw him, and the most annoying thing of it all was the fact that I let him get under my skin.

Is this really what I have to work with? A small squadron of soldiers, servants, the advisor, and Julian of all people?

I look out the window as more snowflakes fall from the sky.

Farah, I wish by God that you could have been here to help me.

26
SCALE-BOUND

"They are a storm unlike any other, one that looks like a man but is much more, one that holds powers unlike any other. What makes this beast more than a man? What makes a man less than this beast? The answer, my dear child, cannot be revealed. As both are as savage as they believe the other to be."
- Myths and Stories, Author Unknown

ACROSS THE BORDER...

The moon was covered by clouds that night, making the dark shapes above difficult to discern from the black skies above them. The sound of winds cutting through winds creates a whistle in the air as a creature rushes its flight. It stares down into the forests below.
Will they listen? Should I even try?
It suddenly dives and disappears into the trees.
"You're late." Comes a silvery tone from another creature in the dark. A plume of flame comes from its breath as it lights a fire in the center of the clearing. Three dragonkin sat waiting for the newcomer.

Each is widely different from what it stood next to. One has no wings and scales like the bark of a tree. Another has no legs, but its wings fold into its back as it coils like a serpent. The last one is similar to the newcomer, with two wings but only two hind legs. A Drake, an Amphitere, and a Wyvern.

Three... There should be four.

"Where is Venniki?" The dragonkin hums as it reaches the others. "They should be here."

"Venniki didn't see a point, and quite honestly, I don't see one yet either." The legless dragonkin hisses at the newcomer, "Why did you call us here, Jorunmere?"

The forest green dragon dips its head, "Eirkeld, as polite as always I see."

"Let's move past any polite small talk," Eirkeld snarls through sharp fangs. "Kvenndra and Juritoft have been here even longer than I have." He says motioning towards the Drake and Wyvern respectively.

"I know you three are already aware of our... troubles at the border with the humans. Many in our territory are losing their link to magic." Jorunmere dips his head. "I would like to respectfully ask that you send warriors to aid if the humans are planning an attack."

"How do you think the humans are causing

this?" Kvenndra asks claws tapping onto the soft forest floor. "Do you have evidence?"

He shakes his head, "I've sent a few to investigate among the humans. Somehow close to the border they've made something that is draining not just magic, but energy from the air around it. Not everyone is affected but- something has to be done. I fear one of our own has turned on us."

"This fight is yours, and yours alone." Hisses Eirkeld. "This border is shared between your faction and the humans. This doesn't include us. Besides, why should we listen to you and not your king?"

"Humans don't know how to discern our factions, Eirkeld. To them, we are all just Dragonkin. Do you think they would stop after killing us? That they would not continue over our border with yours?"

"Jorunmere, I understand where you're coming from but -"

"But what?" He roars in response. "I've sent many dragonkin to investigate and none can find out how they are draining us of magic! At this rate, they can waltz beyond the border and slaughter us all -"

"This is only happening within, or near your borders, whatever it is must be coming from somewhere close." Kvenndra interrupts.

"Surely it isn't that far beyond the skills of your spies to find the source?"

"The source... It's suddenly gone."

"Then what is the problem here, Jorunmeer?" Eirkeld hisses. "It sounds as if it dealt with itself."

"That isn't the point, humans have harnessed magic beyond what we ever expected of them."

"Then you should not have agreed to that treaty centuries ago, we should have killed them all when we had the chance." Eirkeld snarls as he slithers towards Jorunmere. "*Your* Emperor decided upon that, not us!"

"You weren't even born then, Eirkeld! I will hear nothing from you on the matter." He turns to the Wyvern who had not spoken yet. "Juritoft? Will you help us?"

Glancing between the others, the Wyvern shuts its eyes after a moment.

"Jorunmere... I believe this will be up to you, and you alone. We are no longer under a single rule as it was in the days of old. If what you say is true, I need to prepare my own borders for such an attack."

Eirkeld smirks at this, scales rattling as they settle back down. "See? I told you this meeting was for naught." They turn their sour gaze back upon Jorunmere. "We're leaving, don't bother us again about the humans."

The three dragonkin turn away and disappear into the forest, leaving Jorunmere alone in the clearing with the dwindling flame. He looks down at it.

Even our fire is not lasting near the border... This magic - It must be of dragonkin, no man could create such a thing. So how? How were they doing this?

27
CUTTING CORNERS

"When we first arrived in these new lands, there would be many things we had to face. Many troubles and many battles to be fought, but none could have prepared me for the trials brought to us by the native dragonkin people."
- Bryun F. Lumar, Founder of Flaize

The day of leaving came far more quickly than anyone expected, and we are not at all prepared. Inside the old city hall, people ran to and fro. Like chickens with their heads cut off as last-minute preparations happen. With the unknown of what lies past the border, it wasn't too surprising to see so many people rushing around.

With horses pulling carriages of supplies, we only had enough for an extremely small group. A concerningly small one for the type of venture this would be. Since we couldn't get any more resources from the capital due to the weather, all we have is two horse-drawn carts of supplies, ten soldiers, and ten servants, along with Prince Leon, Advisor Odell, Lord Julian, and myself.

I stood outside by the entrance to the town

hall, watching the busy cobblestone streets as the small group prepared the carts with the last few things we needed.

Snowflakes continued to daintily fall from the sky, and even though I wore the thickest winter coat I had ever seen, the cold of this winter is far worse than anything I had experienced in my lifetime.

Could it be the amount of energy expelled back into the world from Vivienne's creation that did this? I ponder this as I watch Advisor Odell send multiple men back into the town hall, I furrow my brows at this.

Sending men back? Don't we need as many with us as possible during this?

I spot Prince Leon coming around from behind one of the carts and begin making my way towards him, as I do Advisor Odell watches me and intercepts as she sees my goal.

"Audrey, what is it I can assist you with?" She asks swiftly as the prince disappears along with two other soldiers he was working with. I clench my fist as I turn to the royal advisor. Titles are being used less and less during the anxieties with the dragonkin, the only ones that remain consistent in using them is the prince and Julian. The prince still did, because he is seemingly infatuated with positions and titles, while Julian just seems afraid of angering the prince. Advisor Lorene on the other hand, could care less.

"Advisor Odell," I say in as cheery a tone I can muster. "I was wondering why in the world we're sending men back to stay. Though this is a peaceful mission to speak with the Dragonkin don't we nee-"

"Peaceful?" The Advisor looks confused at my wording. "While we are going there to speak with them, I highly doubt the enemy is peaceful after causing this sickness and destroying the abbey."

"You think they did all of that?" I ask, astounded by the story she came up with. "Have you spoken to the prince?"

Advisor Odell nods, "Of course, the prince and I have spoken extensively on this subject alone since I arrived. What else do you think caused it? A dragonkin in its true form was seen escaping the abbey after all."

I sigh, seeing that Odell was stuck in her mindset. "Wouldn't that be all the more reason to bring more men?" I ask as I step aside for a servant to pass between us.

She shakes her head, "In this weather, we need to travel light, with as few people as possible." She places a hand on my shoulder. "Don't worry, a war will not start during the negotiation unless the dragonkin starts it, and I am only bringing along with us my best-trained men. We will be safe."

I furrow my brows at this. Her *best-trained men?*

I watch as she turns and walks away, *unless she was perhaps a general before becoming an advisor how would she truly know the extent of the men chosen?*

Perhaps this explains why she is so battle - *ready. If she was once a general, in what she was taught she would only know of the evil of dragonkin.*

I need to be able to keep this peaceful... A war wouldn't be anything we can handle. Besides, Fletcher and Remy are too young to -

"Don't think too hard, Lady Audrey, you might hurt yourself."

I sigh loudly as I hear Julian step out of the town hall. He is wearing a coat even thicker than mine, but he still shivers the moment he gets outside of the warm interior.

"What do you want, Julian?"

Julian scoffs at my informality, "It's Lord Julian to you, and I'm ready to get on the cart."

I laugh at him, making him frown, "And where exactly do you think you will fit?" I motion towards the carts. They were small and light, but filled to the brim with food, tents, and supplies. There was no room for anyone to fit with the supplies beyond perhaps one if they sat on the very edge of the cart. I watch as the smugness on Julian's face is replaced by one of dissatisfaction.

"Would you like to ask Advisor Odell to adjust so you have room?" I ask smugly, making him grit his teeth.

"No thank you, I'd rather do anything else than talk to that brute of a woman."

I chuckle, for once I agree with you, I think to myself. Something I would never admit out loud to Julian. He would become so much more smug and irritating if he found out we have common ground with anything.

I watch as he storms off. He really has changed from his usual cool and collected demeanor he had at the abbey. Though perhaps that was only because he knew Vivienne was working alongside him. That, and he still had Lady Priscilla to bully.

I am immediately pulled out of my thoughts as everyone begins to stop working and gather around Prince Leon, who stood on top of the cart on a few crates to speak.

"Gather around everyone! I have a few things to say before we leave!"

As I step forward to join everyone I notice a few of Odell's men whispering amongst themselves.

"Couldn't we do this inside? What's the point of prolonging our time in this cold?"

The other one nods, "It's like the prince hasn't been thinking strai -" They trail off, and I follow their line of sight to see Advisor Odell giving them an intense glare. They quickly nudge the man next to them and the pair goes silent. A chuckle at the sight of them, so anxious from the intense woman nearby.

I hate to admit it, but I'm impressed by her.

If only she weren't so... battle hungry.

I watch how she stares at Prince Leon, waiting for him to speak.

Will I be able to keep things peaceful during our time across the border?

I am shaken out of my thoughts as the small group goes silent for the crown prince's speech.

"I know we are going into enemy territory, and with such a small group I am sure you are all anxious." I look around to see none of his men are nodding, but the servants from the abbey - well, from Yonnam were nodding in agreement.

"Have no fear," the prince continues,

"We are going there with peaceful intentions."

I hear a few men scoff quietly at this, quickly coughing afterward to cover it as Advisor Odell begins making her way towards them.

They aren't wrong, so far this seems anything but peaceful.

I watch Prince Leon's expression, he seems cold, expressionless. *Does he believe we are just going for confirmation of war?*

I watch how his hand clenches over the hilt of his sword on his belt. *Is he eager for a battle?*

But why?

"If they strike, or deny negotiations, we will strike back in defense only. We will not be the ones to start this war, but we will be the ones to finish it!"

The soldiers and envoy members begin cheering at the end of his speech, rallying for a war. The smiles on their faces and hunger in their eyes told me these were not men for an envoy, but those hungry for battle. Men who had heard stories of the glory of war, but had never seen it themselves. I sigh as I look around and realize there were only young men with us here, no older men. No one with true battle experience. Just young boys whose thirst to prove themselves and go down in history.

Is this the best our country has to offer?

I no longer listen as the prince calls for us to leave, instead I look over and meet Julian's gaze. Even he looks afraid of those that surround him as the group pushes their way around him, eager to begin the journey across the border.

Will this be why we go to war?

28
ALLOWING THE PAST...

"The past is a weapon that harms the user. Only the one wielding it can decide to put it down, or continue to carry the burden."
- Author Unknown

I have crossed the border far more times than I ever thought I could. Even after the events of the abbey, I did not think that I would be here again. Especially not like this. The snowfall is getting worse, and the horses struggle to pull carriages of supplies through the snowy forest. This feels like a fool's mission, yet the prince, his advisor, and the soldiers all appear eager to move forward.

I can't help but glance around at the snowy border. It feels like yesterday I crossed with Dominique, how has so much changed in so little time?

I spot a small clearing nearby, I feel my chest ache as I recognize it.

Why did papa have to take me away that night? What made him do it?

If he hates dragonkin so much, why take one as a child?

Were they unable to have children early

on in their relationship? Or perhaps he was more compassionate when he was younger...
"Audrey!"

I am pulled away from my thoughts as I hear my name called, I turn to see Julian looking at me.

"What do you want?" I snap, annoyed to be interrupted while thinking, especially by him.

"I've been trying to talk to you for the past ten minutes," He retorts, as he falls in step beside me. We were towards the back of the group along with the servants of Yonnam. I frown at his behavior.

"Why would you want to talk to me?" I ask.

He rolls his eyes, "Don't take it to heart, but I am sick of hearing the blathering of these dogs."

I hated it. I hated agreeing with anything Julian had to say, but with our given circumstances, it was no surprise we would end up on the same page. Still, I scoff at him.

"I thought you'd get along well with dogs, given your track record." I say, grinning at his discomfort, he grits his teeth to stop them from chattering.

"You don't know the whole story - "

"I don't need to," I hiss through my own chattering teeth. "I know how you are. You are a disrespectful man, and Lady Priscilla deserves far better than you." I scoff, "I'm sure you're happy to finally be able to send her away."

"I didn't send her away, not like you're suggesting." He says bitterly.

I roll my eyes at this, "Are you claiming you did it for her safety? Come on, Julian, you know I'm smarter than that."

I wait a moment for him to respond, but Julian goes silent.

Does he really think his own intentions to be good? After every way, he humiliated Priscilla?

I sigh at his silence, finding it to be equally as annoying as when he spoke.

"How long until we see a dragonkin?" I hear a servant nearby ask. "Are we planning on walking straight into their cities or...?"

A soldier near her replies, "We will most likely be intercepted soon, there is still a peace treaty in place so we should be allowed to be taken to their cities... or whatever type of place they have here."

"You don't think they'll have a city?"
The soldier shrugs, and I stop listening.
I've never thought about that much...

What are dragonkin cities like? Are they anything like our structures or... They are probably bigger.

Are all dragonkin large? I wonder as I think back to Dominique's form. It wasn't like the stories I had been told, he was fairly small if he could fit inside the building but then again, they could have a variety much like humans.

Would my dragonkin form be like his?

I try to imagine what I would look like transforming, I've only ever seen sketches of dragonkin from old history books, and none looked like Dominique. Who even knows if I can transform.

Isn't that the main factor that would make me dragonkin?

I sigh, even if I remember being found on the border as I was, what if I couldn't transform anymore?

That could be a good thing, depending on how this goes...

I notice a servant staring at me, I glance over at them and look at their face for a moment before recognizing her.

"Paxton!" I call out, she hurries over to my side smiling.

"I was wondering if you would notice me," She says cheerily.

"I'm sorry, it's just... well you know."

She nods, and I frown.

"Why are you here?"

She falls in step beside me, making Julian

roll his eyes. "Well, I was one of the servants who volunteered to join."

I look at her, eyes wide, "You volunteered? But... Why?"

"After what happened to the abbey, well... I wanted to see what the dragonkin were like. Understand why it happened."

I look at the confidence in Paxton's eyes. She truly believed that the dragonkin as a whole caused the fire.

"You've shown a lot of kindness to me since coming to the abbey. When I learned you were going as well that really helped me commit. I want to be able to help you now, especially after -"

"There's nothing you need to repay me for," I say quickly, stopping her from apologizing. "But I am glad to have you here." I lied.

She smiles at this, and as another servant calls her she dips her head and hurries off. Julian chuckles.

"Once lower class, always lower class I suppose."

I sigh, "At least I still have people who are happy to see me, for more than what they can take from me."

I watch Paxton as she eagerly talks to the other servants. She came here because of me.

Did I really have that much of an effect on her?

Looking at the path ahead through the forest I feel exhausted. This is a lot for her to commit to...

If anything happens to her now, it's on me.

Julian stops as talk ahead gets suddenly loud, I glance back at him.

"What, are you afraid of noise now?"

He glares at me but doesn't respond as it gets louder. I shake my head and walk around the side of the carriage to see ahead better, as I do I feel my stomach turn.

A deep guttural growl can be heard from ahead, coming from a large figure.

"You've crossed into Hylligard territory, explain yourselves!"

Julian steps around the cart beside me and I see him tense up.

"That's... That's..."

"A dragonkin?"

The dragonkin up ahead had to duck down to face the front of the envoy, its legs taller than the trees and spread wings seem to take up the sky.

Prince Leon wants a war with this?!

This dragonkin was almost twice the size of Dominique's dragon form. What if this was what is regular for the race? What if Dominique was small for his people?

We would stand no chance.

Prince Leon and Advisor Odell do not cower in the face of the dragonkin before them, which can be counted as confidence or as cockiness, but either way the dragonkin looks vaguely impressed as he waits for an answer.

"We are here to speak with your king over the transgressions of your people."

"Transgressions?!" The large dragonkin's round pupils turn to slits as they glare at the prince. I notice Prince Leon is shaking slightly.

He can't start off this aggressive! I begin walking toward the creature slowly, still hypnotized by the sheer mass of it.

We don't stand a chance against this single dragonkin!

I begin hurry forward, ignoring Julian trying to stop me as I stop beside Prince Leon.

"We only wish to speak to your ruler, there was an accident in one of our districts we need to discuss with them."

The dragonkin seems to relax slightly, leaning back to look at me, its pupils slowly turning round again. They stare for a moment before narrowing their eyes at me.

"I will only allow four of your kind into our territory further."

He keeps saying territory... are the dragonkin divided amongst themselves?

Prince Leon grits his teeth, “How can we trust that only four will be safe?”

The dragonkin doesn’t look away from me, “There is still a treaty in place, yes? Or were you not aware of this, human?”

Prince Leon glares at me when he realizes the dragonkin would not give him attention. He rests his hand on his blade.

“Fine, four will go with you.” He waves his hand to me. “Bring the Lord Julian, you will be coming as well.” He says with a glance my way.

“And me, young master?” Odell asks.

He doesn’t look her way, “Of course you will be coming with me.”

The dragonkin nods, “Fine.”

I look back to where Julian stood and wave him over, he quickly shakes his head, and I hear a deep laugh behind me.

“Afraid are we? Good.”

I chuckle a bit to myself as Julian begrudgingly listens and slowly walks towards the beast.

“Is this form too much for you all? Perhaps something more... familiar, yes?”

People around gasp as the dragonkin slowly morphs, scales shift and wings shrink until a woman stands before us.

She was still taller than everyone here standing at almost seven feet tall, she was incredibly well muscled as well, she did not wear clothes, rather she still had scales worn as though they were armor. She has incredibly strong features, and long messy gray hair. Is she older? If she was, she carried it well.

How old could she be? Dragonkin do age differently than us - That means I would as well...

I spin as I hear a thud behind me, seeing Julian on the ground unconscious.

I can't help but to laugh out loud as everyone around stares in awe at the dragonkin.

"Someone had better carry him, because I will not wait." The dragonkin woman says as she laughs and begins leading the way deeper into Hylligard territory. I begin to follow, when Prince Leon puts out an arm to stop me. He glares deep into my eyes, "Never embarrass me in front of the enemy like this again, understand?"

"They are not the enemy!" I say angrily, making Prince Leon sigh.

"You're right," He says, "Not yet."

"Why-"

Why are you so war-hungry? I want to ask

this, but I know if I continue to speak he will force me to stay behind, so I dip my head and clench a fist behind my back.

"Anything else?" He asks.

I shake my head slowly.

"Good." He says as he turns to the dragonkin. "Get Lord Julian up fast so we can follow."

It feels as though hours pass of following the dragonkin woman through the snowy forest and leaving the cart and men behind. It was more than likely feeling long due to the chilly silence, which was colder than the winter air. The dragonkin woman kept casting glances back at us while leading the way, Prince Leon and Advisor Odell both seem annoyed with my earlier outburst, and Julian looks as though he has seen a ghost. All of which added up to a very silent and tense group to trek through the woods with.

"We're almost there," the dragonkin woman says suddenly, making everyone perk up slightly.

"Can we trust it," Prince Leon whispers to his advisor, Odell shrugs.

"Only time will tell, young master."

I want to say of course we can trust her but even I cannot mean that. I want to trust her, but at this point in time, Advisor Odell was right. Only time could tell if she was worthy of trust.

"We are lucky it could recall the peace treaty," Prince Leon comments. I notice the dragonkin woman glare back at him, but if she heard she doesn't say anything. Merely shaking her head and continuing to lead us through the woods.

Suddenly the trees break away to show something unexpected. A massive ravine which tore deep into the earth. We stop by the edge of it.

"This doesn't make sense," Advisor Odell quickly pulls a map out of her bag, "Our maps don't show a ravine here -"

"Of course it wouldn't, that map is ancient!" The dragonkin woman scoffs. "Welcome to Hylligard."

29
...TO AFFECT THE FUTURE

"Ever since the prince left the capital to speak with the dragonkin over the latest rumors involving them, the king has yet to make any statements regarding the situation. What is going on with the royal family? Where is our king during this harsh winter, when we need his guidance the most?"
- Flaize Daily

"This is... Impressive!" Julian exclaims as he looks down into the ravine. I nod in agreement as I look at the structures within the ravine. The dragons within look far smaller than the form that the woman next to us could take. Perhaps she is meant to patrol?

Looking at the structures, I find myself surprised to see many stone bridges have been built on stilts that disappear into the darkness of the bottom of the ravine.

"Why are there bridges?" I ask, the dragonkin woman turns to me.

"Well, not every dragonkin can fly of course!" She lets out a hearty laugh. I feel my face flush at her laughter as I watch her walk to the nearest bridge. It led to a wide stone platform that many dragonkin sat upon. When nobody follows her she stops and turns around, arms crossed.

"Come, we need to go directly to Hraikon."

Prince Leon turns to follow, "Is this the king of all dragonkin?"

"He is the ruler of this territory, yes." She answers simply before continuing across the wide stone bridge. Prince Leon and Advisor Odell exchange a glance before following. I begin to follow when I glance back and see Julian was still hypnotized by the city in the ravine.

I glance at the others before walking back to him, I nudge him, making him jump.

"Come on, we need to follow." I say quickly. Julian falls in step beside me as we hurry to catch up and cross the bridge.

"I never imagined the dragonkin had such structures!" Julian exclaims as he continues to look around in awe.

"What did you expect? A mud hut?" I ask with a sigh.

Julian scoffs, "Of course not. I just... never thought about the subject much."

I raise a brow as I look at Julian. His usual cool and snake-like demeanor was replaced by one of child-like awe at his surroundings. It was very unsettling to see.

I try to stick closer to the dragonkin woman we follow as we pass through the center clearing. Many shapes and sizes of dragonkin watch us as we pass. Some snarl and growl at us, others watch in awe, while some just don't care about our presence.

I found myself amazed by the variation in each dragonkin's dragonic form. Some had four legs and two wings, others had two legs and wings as front legs, most interestingly were the amount of dragonkin without wings, or even without legs and wings. It was dizzying to take in the amount of differences from dragon to dragon.

Scale color, size, and shape. The variety in horns and those with odd horn-like growths on their lower jaw, not to mention the variety in size.

I feel myself growing excited as we continue deeper into Hylligard. The buildings built by the bridges are fairly large with huge openings, and at the end of the bridge, I can look ahead to see more rooms were built into the sides of the ravine. Tunnels.

This is amazing! Dragonkin are so much more complex than we ever knew! Nothing I've ever read about could have prepared me for this!

I pause for a moment looking back as the others follow the woman into a tunnel. *Why is it that we know so little? Even though there is a peace treaty... Why has there never really been peace between us?*

"Audrey!"

I hurry after the others and enter the tunnel.

It was very open, feeling as large as the great hall in the Yonnam Abbey. There were large stone barrels that held
firewood and burned with strong flames which lit the tunnels as we continue in deeper. The walls were very well cut out, with stone pillars and detailed carvings in the walls. The floors were covered in woven rugs, and surprisingly books were almost everywhere. While many look familiar to the type of books back at the library in Yonnam, some books were far larger than others. I watch as two very small dragonkin run through the tunnels past us, not even noticing us. From their size and attitude I assume they were children.

They would be like Fletcher and Remy...

I can't help but feel guilty for not checking on my brothers in a while, but I haven't been able to get away to visit the library. I can only hope papa hasn't caused any trouble for them...

As we continue down the tunnels it suddenly opens up into a large room. The walls are covered in paintings, and where one would expect a large throne of some sort there is just a raised ledge, upon it sat the strangest looking dragonkin that I'd ever seen.

They have two heads?

The dragonkin that led us here slowly shifts back into its dragonic form, only it is smaller than before. She dips her head to the two headed dragon.

"King Hraikon, these humans needed to speak with you, in peace over the recent events across the border."

"So you are aware of what happened at the abbey." Prince Leon states boldly. The two headed dragon ahead raises a wing, and almost every dragonkin in the room leaves except for the one that led us and two others. I look to the two left behind, one is staring directly at me, its nostrils flaring.

The dragonkin, Lord Hraikon, looks over us with his four narrowed eyes. I look at him, he looks familiar, disturbingly so. Which was not something I felt familiar with when it came to dragonkin. I knew I had never seen a dragonkin with two heads before, yet something about him gave me a sense of deja vu.

Prince Leon dips his head, "I am Prince Leon, son of King Sterling, ruler of Flaize. I am here to speak with you over the transgressions your people have done against my own."

"It has been some time since man has come across the borders to speak." He says slowly as his eyes stop upon me, I meet his gaze.

"We are here because of the magical disturbance in Yonnam. We've been tracking it for some time within the capital, but only recently did the situation grow worse." Prince Leon begins.

I glance at him.

Tracking for some time? Is he bluffing or...

Was the capital aware of the sickness for some time and did nothing during the Prince's ceremony season?

I clench a fist, I can't say anything here. I think to myself as I look at the dragonkin surrounding us.

"Tell me, why do you think this... energy disturbance was us?" King Hraikon asks.
"Many of my people have been suffering from the energy drain caused from across

your border. I think I should be asking you for this source."

"They're just looking for a reason to fight us," hisses a small skinny dragon near the edge of the room. "Pinning blame on us for their own failed experiments, we should -"

"Aslumnirr! Silence!" The other dragonkin interrupts her. Making them glare across the room.

"The source was a hidden dragonkin corpse riddled with magic hidden in the basements of the Yonnam Abbey!" Prince Leon loudly continued. "When the abbey went up in flames, a dragonkin was seen escaping the building. They crossed the border shortly afterwards before my men and I could do anything."

"I see why you would jump to such a conclusion," Jorunmeer says with a sigh. King Hraikon nods, "Have you ever considered that it is an outlier? A dragonkin working alone?"

Prince Leon looks momentarily taken aback, as if he had never planned for such an answer. Advisor Odell steps forward.

"It is easy to make such a claim, but why would there be one of your people working alone against the people? During the Prince's coming of age season as well. The timing is nothing short of coincidental."

Aslumnirr growls, "Coming of age ceremony? That's your excuse for coming here to accuse us of transgressions against your kind?"

King Hraikon nods to this, silencing Jorunmeer from adding anything with the raise of a hand, then looks back to Prince Leon.

"What is it you came here to achieve? For us to admit to a crime we did not commit?"

Prince Leon grits his teeth, "To make someone pay!"

I look over at the prince, he is trembling.

"Many of my people died while I was within the district because of a single one of your people. The question is whether you will bring them forward or not. If you don't..."

"Then what? You'll kill the king here?" Aslumnirr asks.

King Hraikon's pupils become slits at this. "Do you really think you could?" They stand up to their full height, still not reaching the ceiling of the large cavernous room. Glaring down at the crown prince with both heads.

"King Hraikon!" Jorunmeer interrupts, making the king settle back down onto the stone ground. "This isn't worth a war over, you know this -"

"It is!" hisses Aslumnirr.

"Stop!" I yell suddenly, surprising everyone in the room. I step forward despite Advisor Odell's glare. "This is not worth a war. The dragonkin we saw..." I look back at Prince Leon.

I can't have him know that this dragonkin wasn't bad if so... He will learn that I am also dragonkin.

I take in a deep breath before turning back to King Hraikon. I dip my head toward him before speaking.

"We do not know that the dragonkin waswhat caused the source," I say quickly. "If it's a third party, is there a chance you sent your own people across the border to investigate?"

Jorunmeer's eyes go wide and King Hraikon laughs, "There was only one dragonkin foolish enough to want to investigate the magic disturbance when it began, and that was my son, Doruquinn."

I look at Hraikon, That's why he felt familiar! He reminds me of Dominique's dragonkin form... That means...

"Is he here?" I ask. "So we can question him ourselves?" If Dominique is here, we can fix this quickly! I imagine seeing him walking into this cave with us, and us quickly crafting a story as to what caused the source. The third-party, Vivienne.

Jorunmeer shakes his head, “We haven’t seen him in many seasons.”

Seasons? How long has he been in Flaize? I feel my heart drop, If Dominique isn’t here?

Then... Did he survive escaping? Did he... No! Surely he lived. Perhaps he is out there somewhere... injured, but surely alive. Right?

“How convenient,” Prince Leon remarks snidely with a glance at Advisor Odell. “That the one dragonkin to be held responsible isn’t available. It seems your people never change. Still lying snakes as told in history for centuries.”

“King Hraikon you must listen to me,” Aslumnirr pleads, “We must be readying for war! I’ve been saying it since the energy drain, they’re just hunting for a reason to slaughter us all! Just as before!”

“No, that isn’t it at all!” I yell.

“If it is a war you wish for, know that it is a war you will get.” King Hraikon solemnly says as he looks down at Prince Leon.

“I should have known your kind is not to be trusted. In the name of those who died, I declare war on the dragonkin of this territory.” Prince Leon states boldly.
“In one month’s time we will be at your borders for a war.”

Jorunmeer looks to the king, "King Hraikon! You cannot allow this-"

"Jorunmeer, don't be a fool!" Aslumnirr hisses as the older dragonkin. "You think your age has become wisdom, I think you've become naive in your elderly years. We need to fight to survive!"

Prince Leon smiles at their struggling, he turns to lead the way out, "We must fight a divided house, this will not be difficult for our people."

The dragonkin who guided us here begins to follow us out, I glance back to see Jorunmeer still staring at me.

I mouth a few words at him.

"I will find Dominique."

His eyes go wide, and he begins to step forward until King Hraikon and Aslumnirr continue arguing. He casts me one desperate look before turning to speak with the others.

"What was that?" Julian asks quietly, looking around wearily.

"I am apologizing for our prince's eagerness for war." I whisper back.

Julian sighs, "I hate to say it but I agree with you."

I turn to him, eyes wide, "You agree with me?!"

He smirks, "I said I hate to admit it,

alright?" Julian sighs. "You might find me a fool, but even I'm smarter than wishing for war."

I frown and look at Prince Leon leading the way out.

"If only all of us could think like that." They haven't seen Dominique in seasons... has he not returned since setting out to investigate the districts?

I sigh, finding him may prove to be more difficult than I imagined.

That is if he is still out there.

No! He has to be! I can't give up and believe he died, if he escaped the fire, perhaps he played it safe and hid nearby?

I'll have to look into that when we return to Yonnam...

Now I only had one chance left, find Dominique, and pray to God that Prince Leon would recognize his dragon form and call off the war.

If I couldn't do that, then everything I have done to this point has been for nothing.

My world would shatter if this war were to happen.

30
BETWEEN THE LINES

"The school of magic is close to closing down during this winter, as there have not been enough students with magic capabilities joining the university. Could this be the end of magic for humans?"

- The Flaize Spells Paper, Article by S. S. Lilith

It didn't take long before the cart came into sight, and we all traveled back together in a pack. The soldiers reacted too eagerly at hearing there would be a war, which I found both shocking, and not. They saw a dragonkin, a single one was terrifying. Why - How are they so eager to fight?

When we finally returned to the town center, Prince Leon already had people readying a carriage with a few men to take the news back to the king, to call in reinforcements.

I feel my feet aching beneath me as we step off the snow onto freshly shoveled brick streets. As soon as everyone gets in a hurry to work and prepare for what is coming, I begin to try to step away.

I need to get to Fletcher and Remy... and Mr. Abbot at the library.

If war will happen, they will be calling for those in Yonnam to prepare for war...

And it will be fast. I clench my jaw and grind my teeth as I glance back to ensure nobody is watching me.

Why did the prince have to give a month?! Is he really so eager to prove himself?

This isn't the right way to do that. Making your people go to war for your own pride -

"Audrey! We need assistance!" Advisor Odell calls out to me, I turn back and sigh. Lord Julian laughs out loud at me and immediately regrets it as Odell's attention is turned to him as she begins to command him around as well.

I look back to the streets one last time before sighing and turning back to help the others.

I need to find a way to get away and hide my brothers and Mr. Abbot.

Before soldiers begin collecting every man and boy to train.

The rest of the week is wasted by trying to stop Prince Leon in the city hall, but every time I am deflected by his advisor, Odell.

She was like a shield for him, keeping me far enough away that I could never question his decisions. *Is Odell also hungry for war? Does she hate the dragonkin as much as everyone else seems to?*

Should I confront her then? Since I can't catch Prince Leon?

I clench my fists and drop the crates I carried. Hearing the metal clanging inside, I recognize they are weapons.

I sigh, *a week already gone.* I can't keep doing this. I had to do something. I grab my bag and sling it over my shoulder.

I storm past Julian who was sitting on the top of the staircase leading to the entrance, he lazily looks over his shoulder and furrows a brow.

"What's wrong with you?" He calls out, but I don't respond. I have no more extra time to mess around with. I continue walking down the hall, knowing I will find
Odell somewhere commanding her men and the servants, and I am right. She stood in the center of the hall, pointing about and directing servants as to where to set up weapons containers. I stop right next to her.

"Advisor Odell," I loudly say. She turns, eyes narrowed when she sees me. "I need to speak with you."

"Then speak," She replies bluntly, already looking away from me.

I shake my head, struggling to keep my

cool. “Somewhere alone.”

She sighs, and looks back to the men and women working. “Fine, but I only have a moment to spare, less than that even.”

I lead the way to a room that is still devoid of people, its use yet to be decided. I step inside and Advisor Odell steps in behind me.

I turn to her, she watches me through narrowed eyes and her lips are tightly pursed.

“Why is it that you and Prince Leon are so eager for a war?” I ask, making her chuckle.

“A blunt one are we?” Odell says as she crosses her arms and leans against the wall. “You were at the meeting with the dragonkin leader, you saw how it went. Who are you to question the prince -”

“I’m not a heretic, but I am also no sheep.” I retort, making her raise a brow. “You saw that meeting as well, don’t tell me you’re foolish enough to believe the meeting didn’t turn sour because of our attitude.”

“You heard that scrawny dragonkin, they were ready for a fight.”

I shake my head, “That wasn’t the leader, and this isn’t my question. Tell me, why are you so war-hungry Odell?”

Advisor Odell looks taken aback, I do not wait for her to answer.

"If this is all to allow the prince to prove himself, recognize that countless loves will be lost to make the prince feel good about himself, and for you to feel right in your thirst for battle. Trust me when I say, this is a people that are not wanting a fight, but they will give us one if we strike them. I've seen the danger of dragonkin firsthand, it is a war we will not win."

I step around her to leave and she doesn't stop me.

As I begin to walk back down the hall I spot Prince Leon.

"Your majesty!" I call out to him, gaining me his attention as his gaze turns upon me.

"Yes, Lady Audrey?"

"I wanted to speak with you," I say as I stop in front of him. "You don't have to go forward with this war, I can -"

He shakes his head, "No Audrey, I have to now. My father believes that by gaining this land to the north we can finally grow as we need, not to mention finally take care of the meddling dragonkin."

"Meddling? What?"

"They caused countless deaths in the district, with that magic failure - it drained the life out of many innocents, not to mention the fire -"

"But what if I could prove it wasn't them? That it was a third party?" I ask. The prince laughs, "There is just one problem, you couldn't." When he sees my expression he continues. "This war is my destiny. There is no changing it now."

I take a step back from him, eyes wide, but he is no longer looking at me.

"We have men being rounded up for training from Yonnam, so don't worry. We will be ready to face this."

They are rounding up men? That means -

I need to go help Fletcher and Remy to escape now, then I will begin my search for Dominique.

I hurry down the stairs past Julian, who gets up and begins following me.

"Where are you going now?" He scoffs, and I roll my eyes.

"Why do you care?"

I open the front door and step out, not caring about the cold. Julian still follows me.

"I'll take any reason to get away from Advisor Odell's commanding nature, thank you."

I sigh, I don't have the energy to stop him.

I hurry down the streets, with Julian miraculously keeping up with my pace.

He is huffing as though he was out of breath but still matches my pace.

"Why such a hurry?" He asks. I don't even answer, just shaking my head.

It isn't long before the familiar sight of the Heirloom Library comes into view.

Only the sign is completely covered in snow. As we reach the front I look at the porch. There were tracks going in and out.

Am I already too late? I wonder as I step up to the door and knock.

"Why are we at a dump like the - Wait, is this the library you worked at before the inheritance?" Julian asks as he looks at the sign. "Shoddy sign, isn't it?"

When I hear no answer, I open the door and step inside. Books were everywhere, and dirty footprints covered the floor. I feel my heart race in a hurry through the rooms yelling, calling out.

Hunting for any sign of my brothers and Mr. Abbot.

"There's nobody here?" Julian mutters to himself as I stop and lean against the counter. "Were you the only one running this place?"

I shake my head, "No... They were taken."

"What?"

I feel anger rise in my chest at Julian's constant talking, I grab him by the collar of his shirt and hold it in my clenched fists.

"They're gone! I'm too late, they have already taken my brothers and friend!"

Mr. Abbot is far too old, and the boys are too young - I can't let them go to the battlefield. I need to stop this before it gets that far. I need to cross the border again.

I must speak with King Hraikon and Jorunmeer alone.

I slowly put Julian down, and hear him gasp.

"Your... your arms?!"

I look down at my arms, my sleeves have slid back, and where my skin should be were many tiny speckled scales.

Dragon scales.

31
BEHIND THE COVER

"Do not always believe what you see, for we all show the image we desire others to perceive."
- Author Unknown

"Audrey?!" Julian pulls my hands off of his neck. "What in God's name is -"

"Wait! Calm down!" I interrupt him, holding my hands up. I look at my arms, the scales are slowly melding back into normal pale skin, I shiver as I watch it happen.

"You're... You're... Dragonkin!" Julian exclaims as he watches the scales disappear.

"I... I know." I say after a minute.
Julian begins to back away towards the door, as soon as I notice I bolt behind him and press myself against the exit.

"Julian, you cannot tell a soul." I quickly say. "If you do-"

"If I don't, what will happen?! Are you working with them?!" He exclaims wildly.

"What? No!" I feel myself tense up at Julian's accusatory words. "You know that I grew up in Yonnam, if you really did spend weeks looking into me before allowing me into the abbey then you should know that."

"Then what -"

"Hush!" I interrupt yet again. We both stare at each other in silence as loud metal footsteps can be heard outside.

"Soldiers," I whisper. "They're looking for men to take to training camps."

I can't just let Julian go, not now. Surely he would tell the prince almost immediately... and I need to stop this war before it affects Fletcher and Remy any more than it already has.

Julian's face goes pale, "Surely I would be fine -"

I shake my head, "No Julian, they would take you too." I heave in a deep breath as I prepare for what comes next.

"You need to come with me." I say with a sigh

"Excuse me?"

I slowly step forward from the door. "If you leave right now you will be sent to train before you can even speak with Prince Leon or Advisor Odell. If you come with me... We can try to stop it."

Julian scoffs, "How do you plan on doing that?"

"By finding Dominique."

"Your dead husband?" He snorts, "I didn't expect you to run to any man for help, especially not a dead one."

I laugh, I forgot that he thinks Dominique is my husband. I shake my head, "He is not dead."

Julian strides away from me, letting out an anxious laugh, "You really have lost it now."

"The dragonkin seen escaping the abbey," I continue, ignoring his remark. "That was Dominique. He was helping Priscilla and I to escape the fire."

When he hears Priscilla's name I notice his whole aggressive demeanor falter slightly as he stops pacing, he looks to the ground.

Is he feeling guilty since the fire?

Then again... They were both forced together after being caught in a scandal... They both probably struggled with that. I grit my teeth. *No, Julian is cruel. Don't try to rationalize his behavior.*

"Then... Did he start the fire?" He asks, his normal demeanor returned.

I nod my head, "I did."

"Why did you not get Priscilla out first?"
I can't help but snort at his sudden caring attitude, "Who are you to suddenly care about her?"

Julian clenches his jaw, "Just because I didn't love Priscilla as my wife, does not mean I didn't care about her."

"What do you mean? By taking lovers you think that was caring for her?"

"She should have left me, she was supposed to. It was the only way for her to leave without tarnishing her name."

"Then you are an even bigger fool than I thought, she couldn't leave you. Her father wouldn't let her."

Julian's eyes go wide, he looks back up at me. "What do you -"

"Priscilla and I were working together, she told me about her letters to her father when I tried to convince her to leave... She didn't. I had no time left to convince her, I had to destroy the source."

Julian sighs, "Then I know who did it." He says solemnly, he looks up at me.

"Vivienne did."

He nods, leaning against the counter he lets out an exhausted breath. "I knew she was using magic users for something... and I'm going to assume this is the 'magical disturbance' the prince spoke of during the meeting?"

I nod, making Julian hang his head.

"That doesn't explain much, like why you have scales on your arms."

"Had scales." I correct him, "And... I only recently found out about this myself."

Julian curls his lip in disgust, “So if we find Dominique you think we can convince the prince to call off the war?”

I nod, making Julian laugh out loud, when I say nothing he slowly trails off.

didn’t. I had no time left to convince her, I had to destroy the source.”

Julian sighs, “Then I know who did it.” He says solemnly, he looks up at me.

“Vivienne did.”

He nods, leaning against the counter he lets out an exhausted breath. “I knew she was using magic users for something... and I’m going to assume this is the ‘magical disturbance’ the prince spoke of during the meeting?”

I nod, making Julian hang his head.

“That doesn’t explain much, like why you have scales on your arms.”

“Had scales.” I correct him, “And... I only recently found out about this myself.”

Julian curls his lip in disgust, “So if we find Dominique you think we can convince the prince to call off the war?”

I nod, making Julian laugh out loud, when I say nothing he slowly trails off.

“You are kidding right?” When I say nothing he continues, “How are you the woman who managed to achieve so much, yet this is the best solution you can come up with? Do you really think the war-hungry little prince will call off the war at the word of a dragonkin? Two at that!" He says motioning towards me.

I roll my eyes, "I'd like to see you do better."

He pauses for a moment, looking around as though something in the room might spark an idea. As I hear more loud footsteps on the streets outside I step away from the door. I feel sick with every footstep.

Were Fletcher and Remy scared when they heard the soldiers?

Did they try to hide?

"We need to get out of here before we are found." I say quickly, "We don't have any time to waste."

"Where do you plan to go?" He asks, slowly following me towards the back door.

"Back across the border, we are looking for Dominique."

Julian hisses through gritted teeth, "I already said that was a bad idea -"

"You did, but you also haven't given me anything else to work with." I hiss back at him as I step out the back door. "Now I need you to shut up and put your hood up while we hurry to the border."

He begins to open his mouth to respond but shuts it as we step out onto the snowy street. Julian begins shivering as he pulls his hood up over his head, messing up his slick hair he frowns. I smile as I begin to lead the way. Slightly happy to see him uncomfortable.

I hate that I have to work with Julian of all people now, I think even Vivienne would be better to work with than him. At least she *is clever.*

As we hurry down the streets I notice more and more soldiers rushing through the streets. Did more troops arrive from the capital?

Then why are they forcing Yonnam men to train within a month? Why take young boys if there are trained men?

What is the thought process here?

Do they just want more able bodies to use as shields for soldiers?

"How do you expect to find him?" Julian whispers as he walks in pace beside me. I shrug.

"We look for him, perhaps he is hidden somewhere along the border." "And if another dragonkin finds us? Then what?"

"Then... We reason with them?" I say after a moment. "In fact, we should speak with them.

Julian sighs, "The sun is already setting, are you sure about crossing the border at night?"

I nod, "We don't have any more time to lose, not with the fast deadline Prince Leon so cleverly set up for us."

He nods at that, and then goes silent. When we finally near the edge of the Yonnam city there are a few young women hurrying through the streets to light the candle posts, I notice that the soldiers walking the streets look confused at this. Pointing and laughing at the woman, I scoff.

I'm guessing ours is one of the only districts so far behind.

If we had better lights, would Fletcher and Remy have felt less anxious about coming home from school alone?

I turn to Julian, "Is there a reason the board has failed to upgrade lighting throughout the district? Or really do anything to interact with the district?"

"You've really got your priorities for conversation backward." Julian looks away, "Does that really matter right now?"

"Yes."

Julian rolls his eyes, "Vivienne was in charge of that." I furrow my brows at this.

"So you did nothing?"

"Nothing with the district directly," He grumbles. "I only did as was expected of my life."

"Again, nothing?"

Julian spins to face me, "Stop questioning me! As if you would understand any struggles of the upper class!" He snaps.

"Of course I wouldn't! While I fight to survive your fight with petty problems such as picking the right dishes and cheating on your wife!"

Julian looks ahead, jaw clenched. "Let's just get across the border."

"Finally, something we can agree on." I retort sharply.

We continue walking in silence, and as we near the border I notice servants are still patrolling along the border.

"Ugh," I groan as I grab Julian's arm to stop him from continuing, he stops and glares at me.

"What now?"

"Don't tell me you didn't see the patrol?"

He raises a brow and looks ahead, "So?"

"So?!"

"It's only servants from the abbey, they will let us pass if I command it."

I shake my head, "Not anymore Julian, I wouldn't try it." I look past him at the servants patrolling.

Perhaps there will be a gap between where they meet that we can take advantage of? I think to myself as I watch two servants pass each other and continue along the treeline.

"What's staring going to achieve?" Julian asks after a few moments of silence. I ignore him and continue watching them until I notice a familiar face.

"Paxton!" I call out, hurrying forward as soon as I see my own lady's maid. She holds up her lantern as I get close to her, Julian slowly and wearily trailing behind me.

"Lady Audrey! and - Lord Julian?" She looks confused as she sees his face. "What are you two doing here, together no less."

I lean in to Paxton, "We need to cross the border Paxton." Her eyes go wide as I whisper to her.

"Go back?! But why?"

"We need to stop this war Paxton, you saw that dragonkin before. Do you think we stand a chance against something like that?"

She slowly shakes her head, "No... I don't. But still, have you spoken to Prince Leon? Or Advisor Odell?"

I shake my head, "They're too battle-hungry to convince quite yet. The dragonkin were not eager for battle until they challenged them at the meeting." Paxton frowns at this.

"Are you sure about this?" She asks, casting glances between Julian and me. I nod.

"It's better than waiting around for a pointless war," I say quickly. "We just need you to let us pass."

She sighs, glancing around for a moment, "Fine, but... take this." Paxton holds out the lantern to me, I take it quickly.

"I'll return to the town hall to get another, while I am gone hurry across."

I smile, "Thank you Paxton, I will not forget your kindness."

She dips her head, "Nor will I forget yours, my lady."

Julian scoffs and begins to storm past us both into the forest, I nod to Paxton once more before following him.

"What's wrong with you?" I ask as she turns and begins to walk away. He shakes his head.

"Nothing, as always, it's nothing." He snaps.

"Hey! What are you two doing!"

We both spin around as a servant calls out to us.

"That worked," Julian snorts. I grab his arm and begin pulling him forward as I notice Paxton hurrying to intercept the servant.

"Come on! We need to go!" I keep pulling Julian, forcing him to keep in stride with me as I pick up the pace. He pulls his arm away.

"What do you think I am? A child?!"

I stop a few feet ahead and turn to him, "With the way you're acting, yes I do!"

"If you have a problem just spit it out!" He shouts. "I'm tired of your attitude! I'm tired of being forced to work with those beneath me!" Julian continues shouting and yelling, I put my hands up.

"Julian, you need to quiet down-"

"You're just like Rowan!" He shouts last, at this his eyes go wide and he clenches his jaw shut.

I furrow my brows, "Who the hell is Rowan?" I yell back, feeling my skin prick as I yell. I pull up my sleeve and look down at my arms.

Scales again?!

Before he can respond a voice can be heard nearby.

"I knew I was right, I could recognize your aggravating tone anywhere, Lord Julian."

We both turn and look deeper into the pitch black forest, I hold up my lantern but still can't see who, or what spoke.

Julian looks sick to his stomach, "Who... Where did that come from?"

"I don't know but... Why did it sound like -"

I step forward holding up the lantern, the light revealing a large scarred dragonkin face.

"Hello, Audrey dearest." It hisses through

finely pointed teeth. I drop the lantern into the snow as I hear its silvery voice.

"Vivienne?!"

32
A QUERY

"...One of the things I loved about being around Vivienne was her passion for life. All forms of it. From painting those she cared for to preserve the smallest of insects that died in her garden. Despite all of the deaths in her time, she still had an appreciation for life..."
- A Eulogy for Vivienne, by Esme Dayholt

"Good to see I am still remembered," Vivienne laughs as she looks at us. "And I see that you are learning more about yourself." Quickly, I pull my sleeve down over the scales. I feel my stomach turn as I look at her. She is dragonkin, but her dragonic form looks... Wrong. I might not have seen many dragonkin until recently, but I can tell it is a twisted version of her form.
Scales peel and twist in all wrong directions, and many pale ivory scales meld into patches of human-looking skin, she has four legs and two wings folded back but the wings look far too small to allow flight, yet her eyes look normal.

Large uniquely shaped dragonkin eyes in a golden amber color. This is indeed the very same Vivienne we knew.

Julian looks at me with wide eyes, "She's dragonkin too!?"

I cannot tear my eyes away from her as I hold my lantern up to her face, "Yes... That's why she created the magical disturbance. To get this back."

"Get this back?" Julian puts his hands on his head, "I've been working with a dragonkin woman this whole time?!"

Vivienne lets out a hearty laugh, "Ironic to see the pair of you together." She says, eyes glittering from the firelight. I step towards her.

"How did you escape the fire? I thought you couldn't transform?"

She dips her head, "I could not. Well, not completely. This is not how my dragonic form once looked, but for now, it will do."

"What now? Now that you have your form back, what did you plan for now?"

Vivienne hisses, "I had plans before you forced my hand. Now the humans think I am dead, and now I have to re-plan everything." She looks at me, licking her lips. "Perhaps I should take revenge, and kill you here and now."

I hold my head high, despite feeling my stomach turn at her words. "That would achieve nothing, killing me won't put everything back together."

She snorts, "No, but it would make me feel better about it."

"Why... Why did you create the source? Is this why you wanted so many mages to use in the abbey?" Julian asks, slowly stepping towards her as well. "Is this why the mages never came out of your office? Gone forever? I covered up so much for you, and this is what you were doing?"

"Easy to do when all you wanted was to have fun with women," Vivienne snidely remarks. "You really became your brother, in spite of your pathetic attempts to become your own person."

Julian steps forward with his hands clenched into a fist, "You know nothing of what you speak."

Vivienne rears back as he steps closer. I quickly step between the two.

"This isn't what's important right now!" I shout, glaring back and forth between them. I look at her, "Vivienne, there is a war on the horizon because of what we did. The crown prince saw Dominique in his dragonic form escaping the abbey and now he has declared war against your people."

"I think you mean our people, little

dragon." She rolls her eyes and settles down onto the snow, "Besides, what do you think I can do about that?"

I sigh, "To start, could you help us speak with King Hraikon?"

"So, you've met the king of Hylligard, interesting. He cast me out many, many moons ago. He will not eagerly welcome me back."

"Wait... You were banished?" I ask. "Why?"

"He didn't like that I took human lovers over my lifetime, I wanted to be able to come and go, visiting them and staying for a time before returning to my own life. You've met one of them as well."
She chuckles, "Perhaps all of them, you've at least seen."

"The paintings in your office... That's what that was?"

She nods, and Julian snorts, making Vivienne glare at him.

"Ironic that you would judge me for such actions when you are not so different from myself." He comments snidely.

"At least I don't cheat on the partner I am currently with," she sneers back. I sigh.

"Stop with the pitiful bickering you two." I look at Vivienne. "We're going to Hylligard territory again. We have no more time to waste, you're either with us or against us."

"Why such a rush?" Vivienne replies as she stands, swaying her tail around like a whip. I think of my brothers, they are probably in a training camp now. Are they ok? Have they been hurt in training - or worse?

"We only have a month until the dragonkin meet us on the border to fight." Julian snaps, "I am not going to fight and die for the prince's foolish wants." He begins to storm past Vivienne and myself off into the darkness. I glance at her one last time before I follow him with the lantern.

Vivienne slowly lets out a sigh, "Fine, but you are going in the wrong direction." Julian stops and turns to face us, face flush.

I stop and look back, "Fine what?"

"I'll come with you."

Julian begins laughing, I glance back at him. He is hunched over holding his gut as he continues laughing.

Has he finally snapped? I huff, took him long enough.

"What made you change your mind? Is life boring now that you've achieved your goals, hm?" Julian asks after a moment.

"I will not allow a war when Esme still exists in this world." She says solemnly. "I do not know if she thinks I am dead or living, but after everything I have put her through to help me gain my form back, I will not allow a war between our peoples."

I open my mouth but no words come out, I was far too surprised to speak.

Did Esme Dayholt motivate her to gain back her form?

Did she know of the consequences?

"Who cares, come with us or not." Julian remarks as he continues into the woods, slowly I nod.

"Let's go then."

The sun was rising by the time we reached the ravine. There are far less dragonkin out at this early hour, and looking into the ravine felt far different in the early morning light. It feels odd to be here with Julian and Vivienne, but I know at this point I had no other choice for who I kept in my company.

Vivienne sucks in a breath as she looks out over the ravine. "I never thought I would see this place again..."

Julian snorts, "Neither did I, and I was just here a week ago."

As soon as I step a single foot onto the

bridge, a roar echoes throughout the ravine. Looking ahead I see three large shapes from the king's tunnel, and all around dragons are coming out of tunnels and buildings all around.

The scrawny dragon, Aslumnirr lands in front of us on the bridge while many others gather around.

"What are you doing here?!"

I dip my hand and hold up my hands, "We are not here to fight, we came back to reason with King Hraikon."

"Reason with him?" The dragonkin spits by my foot. "How dare you return after last time! You should throw yourself off the cliff before I can tear into you!"

I clench my fists, there was no time for this, Fletcher and Remy were in danger if I didn't succeed. I step towards the dragonkin.

"Get out of the way." I hiss, making them flinch in surprise.

I back up as King Hraikon and Jorunmeer step forward to stand beside Aslumnirr, I glance at Julian and Vivienne.

The two look just as afraid as I feel as they look at the many dragonkin surrounding us in the air and on the ground. Vivienne presses herself to the ground, staring up at the dragonkin anxiously with her tail swaying behind in tight-knit motions.

The two-headed dragonkin, King Hraikon leans down to face me, "Why have you returned human? Didn't your prince already speak the truth?"

I shake my head, "He doesn't understand what happened at the abbey, I was there but he wasn't."

"Then why speak to me instead of him? And why bring this back to us?"

"Vivienne is the cause of the magical disturbance, she was trying to regain her dragonic form and -"

King Hraikon lets out a deep growl, making Julian shiver. "Maybe we shouldn't have come here." He whispers.

"That was taken from her for a reason," the king growls. "A symbol of her banishment."

Vivienne dips her head lower, I shake my head to the king.

"And what was that reason? Because she was close with humans? Because she could love?"

"Yes!" King Hraikon hisses, "There may have been peace, but the humans and dragons must be divided."

"Tell me why," I demand, not breaking away from King Hraikon's gaze.

"I don't need to!" He bellows back, "Vivior - Vivienne as you call her - needs to pay for daring to return here!"

King Hraikon rears back and raises his arm, slashing at Vivienne. As he does I raise an arm to stop him, shutting my eyes as I do. I feel my arm clash with his talons which tear into my skin, followed by gasps and cries from the many dragonkin around.

I look up my arm, where my arm should be. It was a whole dragonkin arm that stopped the king's blow. I scream and hold my arm out and slowly it shifts and shrinks back into my normal pale skin.

"She's dragonkin!" Aslumnirr gasps, "She's a dragonkin on the human side!"

King Hraikon leans back, one head turns to face his advisor while the other continues to watch me.

Julian leans in to whisper to me, "Why reveal it now?!"

"I didn't mean to!"

"You mean you can't control it?!"

Jorunmeer steps forward, turning back to face King Hraikon, "My king, let's just give them a chance to speak. If they give a compelling case we may be able to come to a peaceful compromise -"

"They came at us first!" Aslumnirr hisses into the king's ears, "Why should we give them a chance?"

"I will not accept a pointless war and allow my brothers to die for the stubbornness of two leaders." I shout, out, gaining the attention of the dragonkin king once more. "You will listen to us."

King Hraikon growls before he spins around on the bridge, tail thrashing about. "Follow me, we will hear you out for a moment only."

Jorunmeer lets out a relieved sigh, glaring at Aslumnirr before following the king. The rest of the dragonkin make way for the king and we follow. Vivienne slinks low to the ground as she follows, I furrow my brow at her sudden meek nature.

"Vivienne, stand up. You have nothing to be guilty of here." I whisper sharply, she shakes her head.

"You of all people should be joyous to see me like this."

I shake my head, "Well, I hate to admit it, but I'm not. Now stand up, we need to be confident in our choices."

Julian sighs, "I hope you have a better idea than I do on what to say once we get in there."

"Me too."

We reach the mouth of the tunnel and Julian gives me an exasperated look as we follow the dragonkin inside.

As we stop in the large cave opening King Hraikon turns to face us. His two heads swaying about as he looks at us.

"Now tell me, who are you? Who are your parents? And what territory are you from?"

I shake my head, "My name is Audrey Hughes, I was taken in by a border patrolman and his wife so I do not know anything of my dragonkin heritage."

He narrows his eyes, "Then why did you protect Viv- Vivienne? She is the source of the magic disturbance, which means she is at the center of all of this. Why spare her?"

I dip my head, "I say this with respect, but I don't believe she is the problem."

Vivienne sits up and stares at me, eyes wide. Julian nudges me.

"What do you mean? This is her fault!"

"It isn't" I say louder this time for all the dragonkin throughout the tunnels. "There was a time when I would have agreed, when I would have pointed at her without question."

Vivienne anxiously looks between me and the dragonkin king, "If this is meant to help -"

"Hush!" I quickly interrupt her before continuing. "The problem here is far deeper. The problem is the rift between the dragonkin and the humans. If there was no rift - if Vivienne did not lose her dragonic form none of this would have happened."

"So you condone her actions?" Jorunmeer asks, his voice strained with confusion.

"Of course not," I reply as I turn to face him. "I lost many people to the sickness caused by her creation. Yet still, she is not the root of this problem."

"So are you here to yet again accuse us of being wrong?!" Aslumnirr hisses, rising up to stand next to King Hraikon.

"I am saying both sides are at fault, but a war is not worth it." I say quickly. "If I can find Dominique, your son, will you call off your side?"

"Dominique - You mean Doruquinn?!" King Hraikon leans forward now, intrigued. "You know of my son?"

"Yes! I was working with him to uncover the magic disturbance Vivienne created, we were separated after the fire that destroyed it and the ruling house of our district."

"I've - seen him," Vivienne adds, "In the woods... We traveled together for some time, before splitting up."

"Do you know where he went?" I ask her, she quickly shakes her head.

"I do not, but I'm sure we can track him down based on where we last spoke."

I can't help but feel aggravated that she had kept this information until now, but I keep silent as the dragonkin king begins to respond.

King Hraikon leans back for a moment, shaking his head. "Doruquinn is next in line to rule this territory, perhaps... If you can find him, we can consider calling off our side from the war."

Dominique was next in line to rule?

It shouldn't be surprising, I tell myself, *Dominique was very private during our time working together.* Still, I feel upset about this. Finding out just how much about himself he hid.

"I will find him," I promise. "After I do, I believe I can convince the prince to call off our own side as well."

Aslumnirr laughs a silvery grating laugh, "So you came here without the approval of your prince? Priceless."

"I will convince him," I lie through grittedteeth, meeting the gaze of Aslumnirr unflinching, she looks away first.

I feel Julian tense up next to me, he knew how bold my lie was, but he says nothing of it. Staying silent as he wearily eyes the many dragonkin that surround us.

"Then it is a deal. I promise this to you,

Audrey, the dragonkin of the humans, if you find my son and bring him back I will agree to speak with your King of a firmer peace than one we had before."

Vivienne sits up, "Does that mean I would be pardoned?"

"I'll consider it," He hisses, eyes narrowing as he looks at Vivienne's sickly form. Disgust apparent in the expression upon both of his faces. "Now leave."

As we turn to leave I dip my head one last time to the king, "Thank you."

He dips his heads in return despite the anger it causes from Aslumnirr. As I turn and follow the others out I hear an argument breaks out between the three.

"Are you sure we can handle this?" Julian asks as we cross the bridge back across the ravine.

"I don't know we have much of a choice in the matter."

Vivienne dips her head, "There is one thing we will have to fix."

I look at her, and she grins.

"If I am to be pardoned and this is to work well for all of us, you will need to fully shift."

33
Hidden in Ashes

"Training camps have been set up in the neighboring districts of Yonnam, with young men from the three districts being required to be taken there for service to the king and country. Is there a war on the horizon?"
- Flaize Daily

Dominique

It has been many moons since the burning of the Yonnam Abbey, since the source of all energy drain has been destroyed. Many days and nights since my goal had finally been achieved, yet I feel further from satisfaction than I ever expected I'd be. Sitting in a small gully by a frozen river, I feel my scales ache from the quick and unexpected shift, and from my encounter with Vivienne.

I'm glad she finally decided to leave me alone, I think begrudgingly. *Still, the company was better than nothing. Even after we fought.*

The shifting process is taking longer than usual.

Looking at my wings and body, I could tell I was able to shrink down slowly, but I was too afraid to try to shift back into my human form.

I destroyed the sickness, I prevented my death.

So why do I feel as though I achieved nothing? Why do I feel lost?

I couldn't have done it alone. I think begrudgingly. Audrey did most of the work in the end.

And you left her alone.

Shaking my head, I slowly tighten my wings to my sides to shelter from the cold. I didn't expect a human to be so calm about working alongside a dragonkin - Well, she wasn't human after all but she was raised as one.

Raised with the same disdain and hate for our people.

So why do I keep thinking about her? She was useful, that's all. I tell myself, yet the thought doesn't have the effect it was supposed to. She was more than that. Audrey was kind, she allowed me into her life.

With her help, is there a chance that we *could improve the relations between dragonkin and humans?*

In order to do that, I would have to return to Flaize. To return to Yonnam.

I slowly stand up, feeling my skin crawl as I slowly shift back into my human form. I don't stand and wait as I shift. I begin walking back towards the human territories.

I need to find Audrey, it's time we worked together.

No more secrets.

Hours pass before I finally reach the border, it is already deep into the night when the Yonnam district city comes into view. The city is brightened by firelight as the lanterns have been recently lit.

Peering out from the trees, I am surprised to find a patrol group is in order.

Ironic, is it not?

The border patrol only gets reinstated after everything we went through.

As soon as they pass, I creep out from where I hid and hurry into the dark alleys behind the streets. The bitter cold air made it hard to smell anything, even in the dirty back streets of the city. I find myself picking up the pace, hurrying to get back to the abbey, to find even the slightest hint as to what had happened in the aftermath.

Audrey surely made it away - Right?

Thinking back on that night, I remember leaving her outside of the building, other's were on their way as I flew off. I didn't want to leave her there, but there might not have been enough time to shift.

There was not enough time to shift, right?

I clench my teeth, *I should not have left her there. Even if I was found out as dragonkin, at least I would have ensured her safety.*

Besides, there is a very high chance I was seen fleeing the abbey. If I was... I'm afraid to know what conclusions the prince came to.

As I reach the middle of the town, I am surprised to see the once avoided part of the city was now the most lively. The city hall once abandoned with the rise of the aristocracy now seems to be the center of any semblance of rule.

I peer out from the alleys to see the town hall. The many windows once boarded up now have light filtering through the foggy glass. The front doors are almost never closed with soldiers going in and out, and even servants can be seen hurrying around. I frown at this sight, *everything seems so... Different, and not in a good way.*

Is Audrey in there?

Would she be?

I shake my head. There is one place I needed to check first. I continue down the alleys towards the upper-class end of the district. Yet there was not much of a difference between the two sides of the district anymore, everywhere felt of the aftermath of the sickness. The slow pain of a recovery is still underway.

Did everyone here manage to recover? I wonder, recalling my own markings disappearing after the fire. *Did we destroy it in time to make a difference?*

I have yet to see any normal people in the streets, just soldiers and servants, but it is late into the night. *Surely people would be out as they once were in the morning?*

This winter is harsh. Did Vivienne's project have an effect on the weather as well?

It doesn't take much longer for me to reach the abbey gates. The evergreens that once blocked any view of the abbey now were burned and offered coverage for the once great building. Nothing was left. Just a large pile of ashen rubble stood in its place.

I shake my head at the sight, but can't help but feel relieved. *Nothing good came of this place,* I remind myself. *At least I was able to meet Audrey because of it. At least now I know that there is a chance for peace.*

I turn to look at the old library, the place Audrey and I left her brothers. *Even if she is not there, I wanted to ensure the safety of her brothers. Fletcher and Remy.*

They were kind and curious young boys. I have a feeling that they too would think much like their elder sister.

That they would accept the ideas of peace between dragonkin and mankind. As I begin walking towards the building I hear papers crumple beneath my feet. Looking down I move my foot aside to see fliers. I lean down and pick one up. Crumpling it after quickly scanning it over.

Training camps?

That means...

We are *at war.*

As I look up to the library once more I hear footsteps coming towards me, looking over I see many soldiers in the streets facing me.

"Dominique Madlocke," Comes a clear mocking voice from behind the soldiers. The person who spoke steps out into my line of sight.

"You're supposed to be a *dead man.*"

34
REBOUND

"Very little is known on how Dragonkin are able to transform, but those who were miraculously able to see it and live claim that it seems magic in nature. Has the race perhaps mastered an ancient magic? Or is this a natural ability that seems like magic to us?"
- A History in Magic: Creatures of Magic

"Why would Audrey transforming lead us to win this war? Won't they no longer listen when they see her shifting?" Julian asks once we are far enough from the ravine. "Wouldn't a dragonkin fighting other dragonkin look bad for everyone?"

Vivienne rolls her eyes at this "There are myths and legends about such a battle." She mutters, "But the real reason is, if she cannot shift, we will not find her husband in time. I can't keep carrying both of you." Vivienne looks at me, "Now, is there a reason you didn't tell King Hraikon that you two are married?"

I laugh, "Well, because we aren't."

Julian and Vivienne exchange a surprised glance.

"Then why did you claim that you were?" Vivienne asks. "What did that achieve?"

I shrug, "It allowed me to have an edge against you in the abbey, and gave me an ally."

Julian groans, "Really? That's it?"

I nod, making Vivienne chuckle. "Looking back I feel it should have been apparent, clever choice, girl."

"That isn't as important right now," I say quickly, feeling my face flush at Vivienne's praise. "What is this about a legend?"

Vivienne snorts, "Old dragons who wished for better peace between our kind and the humans made up stories and tales of all sorts. The most popular one was of dragonkin meeting dragonkin on the battlefield. One fighting for the dragon kind the other for humans."

I shake my head, "That's ridiculous, I won't be fighting anyone, and I definitely will not be doing it for only one side."

Julian scoffs, but I ignore him as I continue speaking with Vivienne.

"So how do I shift, more than just small portions and the worst times?" I ask looking up at Vivienne. "Are you even able to shift back right now?"

She nods, "I can, but right now I prefer to

stay in my dragonic form after so long spent as a human."

I frown, "Then how are you going to teach me?" I ask, making her grin an awful fine-toothed smile.

"Who said I was teaching? This is a trial by fire," she says, lurching forward she grasps me in her claws before spreading her wings and lurching upwards. Cold air bites at my skin as we rush up into the air far higher than I ever imagined she could go.

"Transform or die, girl, and don't forget to fly" She hisses at me before letting me go and falling back to the ground, as I begin to fall I look down and I feel my stomach lurch.

I can't transform this quickly! What is she thinking?!

I shut my eyes as I wait for impact, feeling my jacket break away as my back stretches and grows.

"She isn't going to fully transform!" I hear Julian scream.

Vivienne hisses, "Shut up!"

As I hit the trees I feel an odd feeling on my back, I fall through the branches and land on the ground. My whole body aches and feels bitterly cold as I sit up, groaning.

"Did you really sprout wings just to use them to glide?"

I sit up and look at the movement behind me, I gasp as I see two large wings sprouting from my back.

"*Wings*?!"

"Why so surprised? *Most* dragonkin have wings."

I look at her, eyes wide. "You mean there was a chance I wouldn't have wings?"

She shrugs, I quickly stand to my feet. Spinning around to look at the wings on my back that tore through my coat.

"Now can you pull them in on your own?"

"How do I do that?" I ask.

Julian tilts his head, "Didn't you do it before?"

"Not intentionally!"

Vivienne frowns, "You really are struggling with this, you aren't just making it up are you?"

I scowl at her, "Why would I make this up?!"

She watches me for a moment, before sighing, "Fine. Teaching it is. Just... you have to focus on it. Imagine your human form, focus your muscles in that area and think about how it is supposed to feel. That's how I mimic a human form."

I slowly flex my shoulder blades, thinking about how my back was supposed to feel.

Slowly I feel as the wings meld back into my body and scales turn into skin. It was a gross feeling, one that nothing could prepare me for. I pull off my coat and sigh.

"You could have given me a warning about my coat." I sigh, tossing the coat aside to Julian who begrudgingly catches it.

"If I had, you would have been made aware of my plans. Now try to grow the wings back, I believe we can work with that."

I roll my eyes, Vivienne really doesn't make the best mentor, but it's better than nothing.

I focus all of my energy into my back yet again, as I do I feel a gripping pain in my chest. I held my hand over where the markings still were from the sickness.

"I thought I had healed..." I say quietly.

Vivienne sighs.

"My creation was draining energy from you, we will have to be patient with your progress getting it back." She leans down towards us. "We don't have time to wait, we can move fast with just me so... climb on."

Julian looks up at her, "Wait really?"

I look at her, she is a smaller dragonkin than most, but she is still very big compared to us. *Still, it is surprising that she would extend the offer.*

That goes to show how much she is willing to do to be pardoned...

As I climb up onto her back and sit between her wings I look back to Julian as he struggles to climb up.

"Vivienne, after you are pardoned were you wanting to return to Dragnoir?"

As Julian climbs up she stays silent, and once he gets settled she stands up to her full height.

"I do not yet know, but I would like to have the choice." She holds her head up. "I hope you two can hold on tight because I plan on moving fast."

I feel Vivienne's body tense under me before she bolts across the forest floor. I lean forward and hold on with my legs on either side of her, Julian grabs onto my arm and I curl my lip in disgust.

This is... amazing! I think as we weave through the trees fast, *we were covering ground at an almost alarming rate at speeds I never thought imaginable.*

"I should be able to catch his scent, but still keep an eye out for tracks." She calls back to us.

"Alright!" Julian shouts, his voice cracking as he does.

I can't help but grin as I watch trees fly past

us, Vivienne even seems a little happier as she rushes through the snow over hills and ledges throughout the woods.

Surely we will be able to find him like this. And now that I can understand shifting... Once my energy is back, perhaps I can watch from the sky?

Hours pass of hunting, and not a single trace of Dominique can be found this far into Dragnoir. Julian finally calmed down after a while, but Vivienne was getting more tense.

"Come on!" She growls as we stop in a clearing. "I need to find him! Where could he be!"

"We all need to find him, Vivienne." I add, "I hold up the lantern as the sky begins getting dark, allowing Julian and I to see. "We should find him soon."

"Are you sure he didn't go deeper into Flaize?" Julian asks.

Vivienne hisses at this, "If he did, I am going to find him and hurt him for making us hunt this long."

I squint as I try to hold my lantern out to allow further sight into the woods. The sun had already set long ago and it was almost midnight by now, so seeing into the forest is difficult.

"Perhaps we should continue working on your transformation, I'm tired of running -"

"Shh!"

I jump off of Vivienne's back and begin hurrying through the woods, ignoring the shouts of confusion behind me. I hold out the lanterns and continue forward. I stop as I reach my goal, looking down I grit my teeth.

"Do you think this is his?" I ask as Vivienne and Julian stop behind me.

Looking down into a gully with a stream running through it, a small stack of burnt wood sits along the edge with a makeshift cloth tent. Without hesitation, I jump into the gully and slowly walk towards the mess of a camp.

"Vivienne, do you smell anything? Anything that could prove this is Dominique?"

"I hate being used as a dog." After a moment of sniffing the air, Vivienne growls. "It's too cold, I can't really distinguish a scent if it's old."

I continue looking near the camp, Surely there is something right? Julian hops into the gully as well, followed by much grumbling as he trips to his knees.

"Stupid rocks!" He curses as he stands,

brushing off his legs. He leans down and picks one up.

"Julian, that is no rock!" Vivienne hisses, making me turn from where I am searching. I hurry over to him and grab the thing out of his hand as soon as I see it.

"Red scales! This has to be him!" I shout with glee. "This means he is alive!"

"But injured," Vivienne adds, nodding towards the snow down the stream. "From the looks of it a few more scales lead that way."

I turn to look back down the stream, "Isn't that..."

"The way back to Flaize?" Vivienne guesses. "Maybe he had to heal before he could go back."

"Perhaps he started going back to Yonnam after we left?" Julian suggests.

I immediately begin rushing down the stream, making the others have to hurry to keep up.

"Audrey, you can't just keep going off without us -" Vivienne hisses.

"Why not?" I snap, "I'm the only one doing this for more than myself, why should I trust you two to help me save everyone?"

Julian frowns and looks away, and Vivienne hisses, "You have your goals just as anyone else, your problem is you think you can achieve them on your own."

"I can though -"

"You had Dominique before," She reminds me. "I know this is the least desirable group, trust me I'd sooner want to kill you than work with you, but these are the cards we've been dealt. We must play them."

I roll my eyes and continue down the stream, "Thanks, you are very reassuring. At least Julian is smart enough to not argue this."

I cast a glance back at Julian, half tempted to ask why he is suddenly so timid until I see the look on his face. I turn ahead, choosing to stay silent instead of antagonizing.

Why can't I do this alone? Why is this the group I am forced to work with?

I shake my head quickly, feeling guilt tearing at my chest.

Did I think like this before? Or did that night with Emmett mess with my head?

Perhaps this will be my curse for that. I scoff to myself.

It may be my own to bear, but I will not let it affect anyone else. I will solve this myself, I can *solve this myself. No matter what they say.*

We just need to find Dominique.

Before anyone else does.

35
DEDICATIONS

"War has been declared against the Dragonkin of Dragnoir."
- Official Statement from the King's Advisor

"Vivienne, we will need you to shift back into your human form now," I say as the building of Yonnam becomes apparent through the trees. The sun is just rising as we near the border, and it is only now that I think of the many problems that could arise with showing up with a very disfigured-looking dragonkin.

Julian nods, "Are you able to, is the question."

I glance at him, it was the first time he had spoken in hours. Though I find it annoying to admit, his silence is almost more annoying than his chattering.

"Who are you to question my abilities?" Vivienne snorts. "I will be able to shift... When I need to."

I spin to look at her, "So you mean you can't shift?"

Vivienne begins stepping back into the woods, "I can, I know I can, but I will not unless absolutely necessary. This is not at all necessary."

Looking at Vivienne, I notice how shifty she is being. Continuously casting glances down at her talons and tapping them as though making sure they were still there. I sigh.

"Are you afraid you won't be able to turn back into a dragon if you turn human again?"

Vivienne curls her nose in disgust but doesn't deny it. Julian snorts.

"We don't have time for this," He grumbles, "Just shift and come with us." She shakes her head, "I did not do all of this work just to shift back and lose it so easily - No. It is not time, and I am not ready to shift back yet."

I sigh, "That's... almost understandable." I say after a moment. "Just, stay safe and out of sight here."

She dips her head, "Of course, I will be waiting here at the border." Turning to go deeper into the woods, she casts one glance back.

"I'm sorry I can't do any more for you." Julian gruffly sighs and continues walking towards Yonnam, I look at Vivienne, taken aback by her apology. I dip my head toward her.

"Don't worry, I will find Dominique, for all

our sake."

She sighs, "You can't just do this alone, I tried that once and you see me now. Remember this."

Without another word Vivienne slinks away deeper into the forest, leaving me alone to hurry and catch up with Julian.

There is an important difference between her and I.

At least I am not working for myself. I tell myself as I hurry to reach Julian beyond the treeline where he is standing still.

"What's wrong?" I ask as I stop next to him.

He frowns looking ahead, "The other day, weren't the streets filled with soldiers?" He asks, raising a brow at me.

I nod, "You're right..." I continue forward onto the roads. "Come on, we need to look around."

As we walk through the streets the city feels like a ghost town. Nobody is out on the streets yet eyes could be seen peeking out of windows. Children, young women, mothers, and the elderly all watched from the safety of the indoors as we walk through the streets searching for any sign as to what had happened while we were gone.

"What do you think happened?" Julian asks quietly. I shrug.

"I'm not sure..." I trail off as I begin to hear the sounds of shouting and yelling ahead.

I exchange a glance with Julian before I start rushing towards the sounds, him hurrying to catch up after a moment.

As we pass by my old house I try not to turn and look, but can't help but cast a glance it's way. The snapdragons are still blooming in spite of the cold, the brightly colored petals the only bright thing on the cold and dreary street. Through the window I half expect to see papa peering out. Waiting for me, but he is not there.

He has probably been taken to the training camps as well.

If Julian notices how I look at the house, he doesn't say anything as we hurry towards the loud clamor at the heart of Yonnam.

As we near the center of the city, deep growls and guttural hissing can be heard. I feel my heart drop as I recognize the sounds as dragonkin.

"Why... Why do I hear a dragonkin?" I ask aloud, slowing down as we near it.

Could it be -

Dominique?

But why would he be here in his dragonkin form?!

Why not stay here as a person instead?!

I almost feel like laughing, *why am I at all surprised or confused? I didn't know him, not truly, no matter how much I wish I did.*

None of that matters right now, right now all that should matter to me is stopping this war and saving my brothers.

As I feel this sudden surge of emotions as we stop near the center of the town I can feel as my body slowly shifts. My back and arms itch as I feel scales forming from my skin.

"Maybe we should stay back," Julian mutters as we get closer and the loud noises can be identified as soldiers screaming and shouting. "This might not be safe, we should make a plan -"

I look at him, "You can stay here if you want, I'm going to see what is wrong."

"Your... Your eyes!" He whispers, "Audrey, you're shifting!"

I ignore him, turning back to the streets, "I am going forward. I will help Dominique, and I will save my brothers. If you want to stay back and cower you can do that alone."

Julian snarls, "Fine, get yourself killed if that's what you want." He turns away, and I don't stop to see what he is doing.

I turn back to the streets and continue on.

The town hall is only a street away.

By God, I hope nothing terrible has happened.

I turn the corner and I am met with a shocking sight.

Soldiers are circling something, screaming and shouting with glee and taunting their catch.

In the center of the city, there is a dragon chained down to the earth.

It wasn't just any dragon.

It is *Dominique.*

I begin shoving my way through the soldiers, who growl or yell at me in anger as I get in their way.

As I reach the center of the masses I struggle to push my way through anymore.

"Dominique!" I scream out over the soldiers. "Dominique! I'm here!"

As I shove my way through, I see the large dragonkin head firmly pressed to the ground.

It is indeed Dominique, I recognize the fire red scales from the night at the abbey. Its large eyes focus on me immediately, and I feel my stomach flip as I see the pain behind them.

"Dominique, I -"

Suddenly I am shoved aside by one of the soldiers, the last thing I see is the dragonkin rear up before my head hits the stone and the world goes black.

When I open my eyes the town center is empty, there is nobody around anymore. Slowly I sit up on the cold cobblestone street.

I look around, everything is blurry and looks.... *Off.* Like everything is where it should be but moved wrong.

I slowly stand to my feet, looking down I brush off my skirt.

What happened? We just arrived back in Yonnam...

Did Julian ditch me?

I look around and realize that people are appearing.

Wait -

Everyone's faces are blurry, yet as I look closer at a specific one I recognize their strong features.

Dominique!

I open my mouth to call out, but no words come out. I furrow my brows as I stare at him.

Is this another memory? But... That's not possible.

This is in the present, right?

"Why didn't you help me?" Dominique asks. "Why did you stand there?"

My eyes go wide as I watch his expression change to anger. I grit my teeth as I remember.

They caught him, he was chained down. Why is

he here?

I take a step back, and as I do more people's faces become visible.

"Why did you let me die?" My mother cries, reaching out for me with fingers hooked like claws. Grabbing desperately. Vivienne steps forward, "You can't even transform, how do you think you can fix everything like this?" She snarls.

Julian scoffs as women hang off of his arms, "She doesn't belong in this position. Does she think she can make a change? She's lower class!"

I turn to run when I see one face I never thought I'd see again.

"Farah?!" I finally manage to croak out.

She steps forward as I glance around, all of the other shapes and structures around disappear.

"This is just a bad dream!" I shout to myself as I look around, everything is just darkness now. "This isn't real, it can't be!"

"Audrey," Farah calls out to me. I cast a glance back at her. She smiles solemnly at me, "I'm not here to hurt you."

I look at her face. She looks better. Not sick anymore.

Is this a memory? A nightmare? Or could it actually be...

"I wanted to apologize for all I've left to you," Farah says quietly. "I did not mean to leave you for a much longer time, I thought I would have fixed everything myself."

I frown after she speaks, her words sound familiar. Much like my own earlier. Slowly I step toward her.

"How are you... Is this you? Are you Farah? Or just a memory of you?"

She smiles, "Does that really matter right now?"

I stare at her face for a long moment.

How long has it been since I've seen her face bright?

No bags under her eyes, her voice unstrained?

I slowly reach out for her as I feel tears slipping down my cheek and pull her into a hug.

"I'm so sorry Farah," I cry into her shoulder. "I'm sorry I didn't recognize sooner what was going on, I'm sorry I couldn't help you, and I'm sorry-"

"Shh," Farah pats my back as she holds me in a comforting hug. "You don't need to apologize. Nothing was your fault, it was my own for not asking anyone around me for help."

She leans back to look at me, and I sob looking at her face. "I need you to know this going forward, don't make the mistakes I made. You are going to need to rely on the help of others to reach your goals."

I snort through my tears, "Have you seen who I'm left with? Farah, I have to work with Vivienne and Julian, they hate each other and me."

She laughs, "I know they might not seem like the best to work with, but there was a time when the two of them and I worked well together. I am sure you can bring out that side in them once again." She sighs and pulls her arms away. I frown as she does.

"What's wrong?"

"I can't stay any longer, know that I am proud of everything that you've done," She says, cupping a hand on my cheek. "You can handle this, but only if you are willing to ask for help."

Farah slowly fades into black before I can say anything else and I fall to the ground bawling.

Farah still believes in me, despite everything.

Slowly the world around me turns to white, and I rub my tears away, trying to stifle a sob.

I need to find Julian, we need to free Dominique.

Together.

36
ARCHIVE

"Sometimes there is more wisdom in the man who has seen less than the man who has seen the world. For the man who sees the world forgets the smaller things, while the man who has seen less sees the whole image through the smaller things in life."
- Poems by the Great Bryun F. Lumar, Founder of The Country of Flaize

"You're finally awake." A solemn voice echoes throughout a small room. Slowly I open my eyes, my head pounding as I slowly sit up on a cushy surface. I look over to see Advisor Odell. I clench my jaw as I feel pulsing in my head as I sit up. I look around, we were in a small office, I was in a small bed shoved into the corner of the room, and Advisor Odell sat in a chair beside the desk. She watches me with her lips pursed and arms crossed.

"My men brought you here after you passed out." She says after a long moment. "You've been quite the showstopper over this past month. First, you speak ill to me and even the crown prince, then you disappear for days.

When you do return, you make quite the reappearance. First, we catch a dragon, then you appear calling out your dead husband's name." She leans forward in her seat, "I want answers."

I smirk, "I'm surprised, I thought you only needed more reasons for war, not actual information."

She sighs and uncrosses her arms, "I was only recently made aware of how little you were interrogated despite being our main witness of what happened in the abbey."

"So? It didn't matter before, why do you care now?" I look around. "Why is it you here and not the prince?"

"That doesn't matter," She says quickly. "I just need to know, why did you call out for Dominique?"

I hold my mouth shut for a moment, debating whether or not to tell her. I let out a deep breath.

I can't keep sitting on a pile of secrets. I look at her with dismay. As much as she is the last person I would want to tell, it looks as though this is my only choice in the matter.

"I think you know why I called for him," I reply, watching her gaze.

"Your... Husband is dragonkin?"

I nod, "And it's because of him and I that

the sickness was eradicated. From what I hear you were tracking it and did nothing, too busy celebrating the prince turning a special age, I suppose?"

Advisor Odell clenches a fist, "I had no control over that, we may have been aware of the sickness spreading but nothing could be done until after the ceremonies."

"Why? What is a ruler without his people?" I challenge, "Do you really believe he has any right to come here and cause us more problems after not assisting us before?"

She doesn't respond to that, instead, she stands and takes a step toward me. "If you claim that you and your husband did nothing wrong, then who caused the disturbance? Was it a dragonkin under Hraikon?"

"Why does that matter?"

She leans on the edge of my bed, looking down on me. "Because it makes the difference on whether or not this war has a purpose!"

I scoff, "Even if I do answer, will you believe me."

"We will see, now tell me."

Slowly I sit up and stand up to her, meeting her gaze with narrowed eyes.

"Like I said before, it is a third party."
She grinds her teeth, "Then what is the source of the problem? The roots to this tree?"

"The tensions between our people and the dragonkin." I say. "If it weren't for that, none of this would have happened."

I feel my confidence falter for a moment, *it means even Farah would still have many years left with me before passing due to old age.*

"You believe this?"

I nod quickly.

She steps back from me, shaking her head. "I will speak with the prince myself,
his opinion is the final one."

I curl my nose at her words, "Is that really what you think after all of this?"

Advisor Odell doesn't respond, instead, she strides across the room and opens the door.

"You can leave, I won't say anything." She scoffs, "Not that anyone will notice. You've been out for days."

"Say anything?" I ask, "Was I considered a prisoner?"

With that Advisor Odell leaves the room, and leaves me alone.

Wait... I was out for days... that means -

The deadline is tomorrow.

I held a hand on my head, it was still throbbing, but I didn't have the time to worry about it.

I hurry to the door and peek out, there didn't seem to be anyone around. I slowly step out and try to act natural as I walk down the creaky floored halls.

"Where are you going?"

I spin around, inhaling sharply as my head stings from the quick movement.

Julian stood leaning against the doorway, scowling as he looks at me.

"'What are you doing?' is the better question," I say through gritted teeth as I hold my head.

He sighs, "After you collapsed I came here."

I scoff, opening my mouth to make a sharp comment but stop. Recalling what he said last time.

Farah said I can't do this alone...

"Why is it you compared me to a Rowan before?" I ask, making him stiffen up, his eyes wide. Quickly he shakes it off, looking away.

"Why are you asking about that right now?! There are more important things at stake -"

I nod, "You're right." I turn to walk down the hall. "I'm sorry for my harshness earlier, I should have listened to you. We should have made a plan."

Julian looks taken aback, he doesn't say anything so I begin to walk away. As I reach the stairs of the town hall, I hear his footsteps behind me.

"What are you doing?" He says, I glance back. "If you're sorry then you should be listening to my plan now."

I smile at his confidence, *he must have had a good plan up his sleeve.*

"I thought you had a good plan up your sleeve," I groan as I stand beside Julian. We stood outside the old patrolman building which was now a schoolhouse, nearby in the clearing before the forest where many soldiers surrounded the chained-down dragonkin. Dominique.

"This is a good idea," he snaps back. "It will work!"

I shake my head, "If it doesn't work, it will make things way worse!" I look up to the tower of old patrol building. "Will the spotlight even work? It's magic based, it could be broken."

An old construction of magic, before electricity use of crystals was common for basic spells. Used as a conductor of magic. It was often used on patrol towers before barrier spells were used. Though the chances of it still being operational were slim to none. *Why did I even think for a second that Julian could have a good idea?*

Better yet why am I still here doing it?

Julian smirks, "I'll go get it on, you can bet on that."

I furrow my brows, "Why are you so confident?" I ask, making him look down.

"I used to study magic, I wanted to go to the academy to serve as a magic user... Rowan - well. My family believed I didn't have it in me. So I only studied crystal magic."

I look at him, is that why he became such an awful person?

"You were right about what you said earlier, that Vivienne and I were only working for ourselves. That made me think a lot... I'm going to make sure this goes down right, I still need to ask someone for forgiveness." He laughs, "If she will even listen to me."

"Hey," I grab his arm, "we're going to solve this, not any one of us alone. Alright?"

He looks at me with a furrowed brow, then laughs. "I could swear you sounded like Farah just then. Alright Audrey, we will do this together."

Before I can say anything in response he nods toward the soldiers.

"Alright, I'm going in."

Julian sneaks around the corner of the building and out of sight. I sit there, baffled as

I wait for the signal.

Perhaps Farah was right about them... Maybe they were once better people.

I watch the soldiers as I wait for Julian to get into position, I could count ten of them. Though two were currently sleeping while the others circled him, cursing and spitting insults at him. One of the older soldiers watches them, a disgusted expression on his face, he calls something out to them that I cannot hear and the others immediately turn on him. Shouting in anger back and forth. I sigh.

This division is pointless. The dragonkin has done nothing wrong, and if we aren't careful we won't be able to have peace between our peoples...

A few moments pass before a loud explosive sound comes from the guard tower. I step away from the building looking up. Immediately a ray of light shoots from the tower and into the forests. Lighting up the snow-covered trees.

"What are you doing?!" One of the soldiers screams up at him, making the sleeping soldiers wake. Julian peers out beside the light source.

"I saw movement in the woods! It could be an ambush!"

The men all look back and forth between

each other and the forests, eyes wide.

"What are you waiting for? Hurry and check it out!" Julian shouts as they stand there. After a moment they all scurry into the forests, I peek around the corner as I hear Julian cheer. One soldier remained by the Dominique. He steps close to his face, I slowly begin to step out from my hiding spot. Creeping close as I hear him begin to speak.

"You can understand me can't you?"

I stop a few feet away from them, the man has yet to notice me. Dominique's eyes land on me and I quickly hold a finger in front of my lips. He quickly looks back at the soldier as he continues to speak.

"Don't take what they say to heart, the young ones are fired up to fight for their country, they don't know how foolish this really is."

I slowly take a step forward, watching the back of the man for any movement to show he has heard me.

How am I going to knock him out? Maybe if I hit him right...

I slowly stand up, clenching a fist as I get ready to hit him. Dominique's eyes go wide.

Suddenly the man lets out a roaring laugh, making me freeze up.

"I had already planned on freeing him

once those fools got bored, I'm surprised to see someone else had the same idea."

The old soldier turns around to face me, I hear Julian behind me calling out for me to run, but I stand my ground.

"Now why do you want to free him?" He asks, and I glance behind him at Dominique.

"Because he has saved my life."

The man looks vaguely surprised by this answer but smiles nonetheless. He steps aside, tossing keys my way.

"These keys unlock all ten locks holding the chains to the weights. I'm going to go after the others." He dips his head at me and smiles. "Good luck ma'am."

I smile as I watch him leave, *perhaps there really will be a chance for peace after this all... If there are more people out there like him.*

Immediately I get to work on unlocking Dominique's chains, as Julian rushes over, stopping next to me out of breath.

"I don't know how much longer that will distract them," He says, wearily eyeing Dominique. "How did you even get caught?"

"I was seen shifting back to human - I tried to turn back to my dragonic form to protect myself but they were already prepared for that," Dominique growls as I begin unlocking each chain. "Why are you here?" He hisses at

Julian, making him back up a little.

"Haven't you heard? I'm a full convert, might even become a priest next." He huffs as he takes a few paces back from Dominique.

"Why can't you shift now?" I ask, he shakes his head.

"I can't shift with these chains on me... I don't know how but the prince was able to enchant it to prevent magic."

As I unlock the last chain, the hook of the lock doesn't move. It was stuck in place.

I grit my teeth, "It's stuck."

Julian begins pacing, "Of course it is!"

"Once we get this off, we need you to return to King Hraikon," I say quickly, casting glances to where the soldiers disappeared to. "He is waiting for you. Once you get there, we will have met the deal with the dragonkin end."

Dominique's eyes widened, "You made a deal with my father?"

I nod, continuing to struggle with the lock, "Vivienne will be within the country as well - You'll probably meet her along the way." I look up at him. "I need to know one thing."

He nods, and I take a deep breath, "Why did you first come to Flaize? King Hraikon says you've been gone since before the sickness started."

"I am sure you are now aware I am next in line to rule the Hylligard territory alone, yes?"

I nod, and Julian begins nervously pacing as we speak.

"I am leading in the faction of dragonkin who wish to open borders with your people. That is why I came here, that is why the rumors of dragonkin began."

He sighs, "After many situations like Vivienne's, I wanted to learn how to avoid something like this eventually happening..."

Julian frowns, "So you were trying to prevent this early on?"

Dominique nods at this, I cast a quick look at Julian. He looks conflicted at this.

"Julian, we have a problem," I say as I begin yanking at the lock as hard as I can.

He scoffs, "And we already have at least ten, what's your point?"

The shouting of soldiers is getting louder, I raise a brow as Julian notices this and groans. I continue to pull at the lock.

There is only one way I can do this -

"This might hurt," I warn. I focus all of my energy into my hand and watch as my fingers turn into talons and scales form out of my skin, I slash at the chains, but they don't break. I continue slashing and clawing at them until finally, they break away, my talons also catch Dominique in the process and he winces.

I wave him off, "You need to go!" I yell out, trying to get my hand to turn back.

He shakes his head, "What about you?" He glances at Julian as he says this, making him scoff.

"I'll be fine, just go!"

Dominique dips his head down to my level, "If anything goes wrong, meet me in Hylligard territory, I can ensure your safety there."

I shake my head, "I will not run, from anything. Not now."

Dominique chuckles, "Of course not." He dips his head to Julian before raising his wings and beating them down, slowly lifting up into the air before flying over the forests and disappearing into the dark night sky.

Shouting and yelling can be heard from the woods, and the soldiers' voices get louder and louder as they begin hurrying back.

"We need to go," Julian says as he begins backing away from the woods, casting glances between the darkness of the forests and where I stood. I look down at the chains for a moment, as I held them I couldn't shift. As soon as I drop them I am able to turn my hand back.

How can he enchant such a thing...
Is there really such powerful magic capabilities in the royal line? Is this why Prince Leon is so confident? I turn and begin running alongside Julian through the streets.

Even so, that doesn't give us enough of an edge.

"The deadline is tomorrow," Julian says between breaths. "Do you think we will be able to convince Prince Leon before then?"

I shake my head, "I don't know."

We do not get very far down the street before many figures come into view. Stopping, I feel my heart flip as I recognize Prince Leon with many soldiers behind him.

He stands to the front, his gaze unwavering as he glares at us.

"*What* have you done?"

37
AS IT IS DECREED

"...Since the abbey burned down, much has changed within Yonnam. Most contact with those inside is seemingly cut off while the prince and the Flaize army reside there, we can only hope for the best in these coming weeks for better news ahead..."
- Flaize Daily

As I stare at Prince Leon with Julian at my side, I realize Advisor Odell is at his side, her expression unchanging as I meet her gaze.

"We saw the dragonkin flying away," Prince Leon states grimly. "Your husband."

I suck in a breath and open my mouth to speak. Before I can get a word out, Julian steps forward.

"Yes, we freed the dragonkin," He retorts, stepping closer to the crown prince.

"Why are you helping a monster, Lord Julian? You are a Halloway. Why turn against your people now?" The prince scoffs, "I always knew your family was meant for ruin after your brother, Rowan fled the country."

I look at Julian, he is frozen in place.

Clearly taken aback.

Rowan... That name... he mentioned it before.

I step forward feeling fueled with rage now more than ever.

"He is not helping a monster, and he did not turn against his people. Julian is smart enough to see that this war would achieve nothing."

"Are you questioning my motives, girl?" Prince Leon hisses through clenched teeth.

"Yes I am. You weren't even in the abbey during the sickness, it is not you who stopped it from spreading. You only came here for the aftermath despite being aware of the district's struggles. So tell me, why do you think this war is worth it?"

Prince Leon doesn't meet my gaze any longer, turning away as he continues to speak. "No, you do not make the important decisions, you will not one day rule. This is all up to me, and my reasons are just."

Advisor Odell narrows her eyes at the prince's words but says nothing as he continues.

"It would take a miracle for the dragonkin to show up tomorrow and not fight. We can't have anyone go soft on the battlefield." The prince turns away. "You will be on the battlefield with me tomorrow, and you will fight as I command it." As he begins to walk away his last words echo in my mind.

"Dominique is only a dragonkin. He will fall as one in the end, and it will be you who kills him."

The prince turns away from me, looking to Advisor Odell, "The battle is only hours away now. The men from the training camps will meet us on the borders." He casts one last glance at us. "I want these two armored and ready to fight."

Advisor Odell frowns but says nothing against it as the prince continues on, leading the soldiers past us to walk along the border. I watch them for a moment, slowly joining the soldiers with Julian at my side.

Where are we going - The clearing!

I recognize that the destination is the clearing at the eastern edge of the border, where trees are sparse and mostly farmland stands.

I look at Julian, he sighs and hangs his head.

"We cut it too close," he says solemnly, "It looks like they will meet on the battlefield after all."

"No," I say as I begin marching after the others. "*We* cannot let all of our work go to waste."

Julian shakes his head before beginning to follow me.

"Never thought you'd end up being right, Rowan, perhaps I am a fool after all." He mutters to himself.

38
THE BEGINNING AND THE END

"There is no victory in war, no joy in battle, and no excitement in returning home. How can we expect such things? When war leaves those behind that we fought to save. In war not only do we lose our loved ones, but we lose ourselves."
- Bryun F. Lumar

Snow is falling down from the sky as the sun hits the horizon. In the fields of the Dragnior Flaize border, thousands of soldiers are gathered. The term soldiers is used loosely as many were boys forced from their homes to train in service of their king and country. Scared children along with war-hungry men. Julian scoffs at the sight as I try to look among the faces for a sign of any familiarity.

"Look at these fools," Julian says, hands shaking at his sides. "They think this will be easy."

I shake my head, "The ones here who have seen the dragonkin will know our chances, the others have no idea."

He clenches his jaw, "I'm not ready to

die." Julian whispers.

"You won't," I say back. "I won't allow that to happen."

"Ironic, I never thought I'd hear that from you."

I chuckle anxiously, "And I never thought I'd be the one to say it to you."

"Do you think Priscilla would forgive me?"

I turn to look at Julian, surprised at his sudden question. "Forgive you?"

"If I die here, would you tell her I'm sorry?"

I widen my eyes at him,

Julian has changed so much in so little time.

I shake my head at his request, "No, you will tell her yourself when this is all over. You owe her that much."

The trees ahead shake, making everyone around tense up and ready themselves. No command comes forth from the prince, yet.

The two-headed dragonkin steps out from the trees. King Hraikon, moments later his advisor, Jorunmeer, steps out from the trees. King Hraikon, moments later his advisor, Jorunmeer, steps out into the light. Followed by Dominique and Vivienne.

The prince steps forward as King Hraikon does, scoffing at the dragonkin leader.

"Is this all you bring with you to fight? Do you really think you stand a chance?"

"We are not here to fight," King Hraikon says, dipping his head. "You met your end of the bargain, so now we wish to speak."

"Speak?!" Prince Leon laughs. "After everything your people have done to ours."

The dragonkin king shakes his head, "Our faction as a whole has done nothing to you."

With this King Hraikon turns to Vivienne, she steps forward and dips her head. Slowly she shifts, skins melding into her body until she is back into a familiar form. Her human self.

"The events of the abbey were of my own doing," Vivienne yells out for all to hear. "My actions were mine, and mine alone."

With this I step forward, "She speaks the truth, I was there in the abbey, and I started the fire to destroy her creation." I turn to the prince as he glares at me and I dip my head. "This war is the creation of misunderstandings and a false pretense of peace before the sickness. Is this really worth fighting for?"

The prince doesn't meet my gaze, instead turning to the dragonkin. He looks conflicted.

Yes! Perhaps he will now see reason -

"No!"

All of the dragonkin spin around as the trees behind them shake, Prince Leon pulls out his sword and the soldiers follow in suit. Holding position. Battle ready. Awaiting the command.

A scrawny dragonkin breaks through the treeline, rearing up on its hind legs and flaring its wings out as it roars.

"This war is our destiny! It is time the dragonkin no longer hides and cowers at the sight of humans. It's time that we stop shifting into such a puny form to stay safe near the borders. It's time for blood to be shed."

"Aslumnirr -" Jorunmeer growls, "This is not right -"

I step forward, "I will not allow the bloodshed of so many innocent lives based on the few that are war hungry." I cry out. I turn to Prince Leon, "If they will not fight us, why should we fight them?"

He shakes his head, "It seems as though there will always be some willing to fight."

I step forward, placing a hand on my chest, "Then I will be the one to fight."

Julian grabs my arm, "What are you doing?! You don't know how to fight!"

I shake him off, "I will fight you," I motion to Aslumnirr, "If you cannot win, there will be no battle."

Aslumnirr scoffs, letting out a guttural laugh.

"If I lose to you, then the fates have decided this war is not meant to happen." They smirk, "But I will not lose to the likes of you. This war is our destiny, it has been long since coming."

I began walking forward until I stood alone in the middle of the field.

Aslumnirr lets out a low growl as they slowly step forward to meet me in the middle of the field.

If I don't win -

No, losing is not an option. I must win...

I look at my foe on the field, though Aslumnirr is scrawny, she is battle hungry. With a dark gleam in her eyes. What is she trying to prove? What made her so battle hungry?

Right now that didn't matter.

I need to win this.

Vivienne widens her eyes as she sees me continue forward in my human form, she steps forward.

"Audrey no!"

I look at her, she spreads her wings out and mouths three words to me.

"Remember to fly."

My mouth falls open as I realize her meaning. I would need to fight this their way. *I would have to fight them as a dragonkin fighting for man.*

I need to shift. Right now.

Aslumnirr scoffs at my standing still, she doesn't wait and begins to charge across the field. I hold up my arm to defend myself and watch as it grows and shifts. Aslumnirr knocks it aside, hissing.

"No, the same trick will not work twice!"

Ducking beneath my growing arm, Aslumnirr bats me aside. I crash across the field, feeling my whole body ache. Dominique begins to shove his way forward on the other side but King Hraikon stops him.

I open my eyes and quickly look around for Aslumnirr as I hear a cry. I look back to the army, and see two sets of familiar eyes.

Fletcher and Remy!

Before I can say anything Aslumnirr crashes down from the sky and pins me down. I look up at her grin and clench my jaw. My vision was getting hazy and I felt my legs giving away as my heart beats fast and my hands shake.

I can't lose so fast!

"Audrey!" I hear screams of my name nearby, I can't turn but recognize my brother's voices.

If I die here, my brother's face a death sentence!

As I hear them continue to shout my name I feel my body begin shifting rapidly, Aslumnirr notices and begins to rear back, a red glow coming from their mouth. I panic as I realize her goal, I shove her off and scurry away as my limbs continue to grow and morph around me. Everything is blurry as I shift, all I can do is hope and pray I have enough time. My skin feels as though it is peeling as it turns into scales, wings sprout out of my back and I flex them slowly as my neck extends and my whole body grows.

As I stand on all four legs I spread my wings, shaking my head as I refocus on Aslumnirr. She rears back again, flames erupting from her open jaw and melting the snow. I narrowly avoid the flames as I jump away, the ground where my feet had been burned and snow is gone.

I look at her, she is preparing to breathe more flames. I take that moment to rush at her, barreling into her with my full weight she is knocked down and the glow of flames in her throat dies away.

As she falls she slashes at my wings, claws tear through the elastic skin of my wings. I hiss in pain but ignore it as I begin batting at her with my claws.

Aslumnirr was clearly taken by surprise, expecting nothing from this fight. Taking a few hits before she finally gets up Aslumnirr growls at me.

Hatred seethes from her as she begins advancing Clawing and biting anything she can reach. Scales and skin tear as she strikes and as I fight back.

I crouch down leaning back before leaping at her and barreling her back into the snow. Aslumnirr is easy to overpower with weight, but as I slash and strike at her while she is down she takes in enough air to breathe fire. My face burns and I am forced to jump away before my eyes are singed. Aslumnirr stands as I jump away, as I brace myself I realize she is slowing down immensely.

As I stop for that second I feel my body start to slow down as well. Wings suddenly heavy and tail dragging through the snow as I rush forward and strike her again. She spins, avoiding the hit and slamming her whip-thin tail into my side as she does. The breath is knocked out of me and I fall to the ground, and I try to heave in to gain it back. Looking up I can see Aslumnirr smiling down at me, but she too was panting. Blood covers many of her scales and she seems faint as she stands still.

I struggle to stand, forcing my weight onto my front legs as I try to stand and fall back onto the ground. Loud crunching of footsteps on snow can be heard behind me, I turn to see Julian running to my side. I widen my eyes at him and shake my head.

“Ju - Julian what are you doing?!” I force myself to stand and see Aslumnirr has targeted him. Licking her fangs before whipping around me to strike at Julian.

Quickly I tackle her aside and begin clawing at her without hesitation, I ignore her screeches of pain and continue striking her. I slowly stop as I look down at her and see her hardly reacting, as I do Aslumnirr snaps back to attention and rears up, shoving me away before swatting me down with her wings. I am knocked back onto the ground, but this time I cannot find the will to stand again.

As I lay on the ground, panting and out of breath, I feel my whole body draining of energy. Any adrenaline rush I had moments before is gone, replaced by the painful throbbing aches and pains across my body. I look over to see Aslumnirr fallen over as well, she still meets my gaze, wanting to fight more, but already battered and worn beyond her expectations.

"This is over," King Hraikon announces loudly, his deep voice booming across the field. "Surely this shows the battle should not happen?"

More dragonkin step out from the trees, nodding in agreement.

Aslumnirr tries to stand but falls back down, angrily she dips her head and begins to slink back to the other side.

"No, this isn't over." Prince Leon says, stepping forward. He walks over and stops, standing over me.

"This is not how this is destined to end," He says to me. "This war is what must happen."

"Why?!" I ask through heavy breaths.

"You seem to be forgetting to whom you speak." He growls as he looks down upon me. "Because I, the crown prince of Flaize, deem it so."

The prince turns to face the army he has amassed, holding up a sword he yells out.

"The time to fight is upon us! Soldiers! Ready your weapons."

39
ADVISORS WARDS

"The man who stands besides the one who rules is stronger than he who wears the crown. For he has the same strength, knowledge, and wisdom as the king and gladly chooses to stand on the sidelines in support of his king."
- Bryun F. Lumar

As the soldiers begin to march forward I feel my heart drop. *Was it all for nothing?*

All of the work I did, everything I tried, gained me nothing?

I look at the dragonkin, "Do not advance!" I try to shout, but my voice dies off as I feel myself running out of breath. The dragonkin casts glances between each other as the human army begins to move forward, uncertain if they are to fight or not.

King Hraikon looks to his people but keeps one of his two heads focused on the human army, his scales rattle as he flares out his wings and begins stepping forward, and another dragonkin shoves him aside.

As the soldiers begin to march, a dragonkin rushes forward across the field, as I look up, a large red dragonkin stands over me. It was Dominique.

"Can you stand?" He asks, leaning down to my level. I let out an annoyed hiss as I tried to push myself off the ground.

Prince Leon takes two steps back, pulling out his sword and pointing it at Dominique.

My whole body screamed at me to stop as I did. I cast a glance at the human army.

There were two small forms shoving their way through everyone else. My eyes well up with tears as I recognize two boys in armor two sizes too large.

"Fletcher - Remy..."

Dominique looks up as well, and his gaze falters as he recognizes who I was searching for. He lets out a deep growl before looking back to me.

"I need to heal you, we have to get out of here." He says quickly, he lets out a deep breath and a gold mist surrounds me, I suddenly feel rejuvenated, better than I had this whole year even. I stand and look at Dominique, his eyes are suddenly glazed over and he looks exhausted.

"Dominique? Dominique what's wrong?!" I lean down to him, and he lets out a pained laugh.

"Healing magic isn't easy you know," He says.

I widen my eyes, "Then why!? Why do it?"

I ask as I look back at the advancing army.

Why not just leave me?

I begin trying to nudge him to his feet, "We need to move!"

"HALT!" A booming shout echoes across the field, and the human army stops, staring at a single person. The prince spins around, angry.

Advisor Odell stands at the front of the army, she holds a fist up to signal the army to stop, and stands with her sword sheathed as she stares down the prince.

"This is not a fight we can - or should win."

Prince Leon watches baffled at his his advisor shaking her head as she walks toward him.

"What are you doing? I said advance!"

Despite the prince's commands, nobody moves. Everyone looks to the advisor for further direction.

"My prince, I must implore you," Advisor Odell speaks under her breath, "You must turn back from this war-hungry path you face. Kings of war may be remembered for centuries, but only in foul words of warning to future generations."

Prince Leon clenches his jaw, face flush as he realizes not a single soldier will listen to him over Advisor Odell. He holds his sword out and points it at me, fury in his eyes.

At this moment, two small figures break from the rest of the soldiers.

Please, I pray silently, *please allow the prince to see reason.*

There is no reason to this war.

"Auddie!"

I look over to see Fletcher and Remy running out onto the battlefield. The prince watches with wide eyes as my brothers stop beside me, not at all hesitating because of the dragonkin that stood over me, or at my dragonkin form for that matter.

I sit up slightly as the two rest against my neck, I wrap my wing over to slightly cover them as they hug me.

"You're alive!" Fletcher cries out. "We thought you were dead!"

Remy doesn't say anything as he holds on tight, and I hold them back as I look past at the soldiers casting glances between each other.

They all seemed weary to fight after the battle they just witnessed.

Some even cry as they see Fletcher and Remy with me.

Prince Leon stares down at my brothers, bewildered.

"She's... A dragonkin..." He says slowly to them, disgust clear in his tone of voice. "Can't you see that?! Why did you run to her?" He asks, raising his voice.

Fletcher and Remy look back at him, confused. Remy pulls away and stands up to the prince, as he does Dominique slowly gets to his feet, standing near him defensively.

"She's our sister," Remy says simply.

Prince Leon takes a step back, he looks at his surroundings horrified, it is almost as if it is the first time he truly looks at what was going on.

Aslumnirr slowly gets to her feet, hissing as she begrudgingly joins the other dragonkin by the border, the snow where we fought either melted or stained red with blood. Dragonkin flare their wings and huddle together by the treeline, and the human soldiers tremble at the mere sight of them. Prince Leon looks astonished by the sight of all of this.

He curls his lip in disgust and points his sword at me, as he does cries and shouts of dismay can be heard from both sides.

Odell shakes her head at him and turns away, motioning towards her men.

The prince turns back to his army, confused, as many soldiers advance.

He smiles as they do, “See Odell? This war is worth something -”

Before he can finish his words the advancing solders grab him from anything they can reach. Arms, legs shoulder, they drag him back in the direction of Yonnam, and those who don’t cheer the others on.

“There will be no more fighting today.” The advisor calls out as she watches the prince get dragged away by his people, by his own men.

“We had high hopes for Prince Leon, the King and I, but it seems *Princess Lorenne* will be far better suited to be next in line to rule.”

I notice that Advisor Odell smiles at this, as though this was what she had wanted all along.

“How will she be able to rule? She is a woman.” I ask.

Advisor Odell smiles, “Don’t worry, we will find a way to make sure everything goes well.” She turns to King Hraikon. “I give you the sincerest apologies on behalf of the King of Flaize, it would seem this was too much for the young prince to handle. You can expect an official envoy of the King’s as soon as humanly possible.”

Advisor Odell dips her head, a hint of a smile upon her face. Turning to the army she begins to walk through and leads them back.

The prince's screams and shouts echo for a while before they can no longer be heard. Leaving a single human soldier alone in the field just a few feet away from us, with the dragonkin army still by the forest border.

I notice the figure still standing across the field. I frown at them as they come closer, feeling a pit in my stomach grow as I recognize who it is.

Papa.

I slowly sit up and flare out my wings as he gets closer, showing my fangs. He sits his sword down beside him and puts his hands up.

"Why?"

I furrow my brows, confused. "Why, what?"

He sighs and looks down at me, "You're a dragonkin."

I sigh, "Yes, I am."

He curls his lip, "Why would you of all people fight for our side?"

"I am not for sides," I say, shaking my head, "I only want peace. For my brother's, for Vivienne, for all dragonkin, and selfishly; for me as well"

As I speak, King Hraikon slowly joins us, stopping at my side.

"I'm not here to fight you Audrey," He says quietly, wearily eyeing Dominique.

I snarl, "Then what are you here for?" I ask, wrapping my tail around to block him from the boys.

He sighs, "I'm not here for them either," He says looking at Fletcher and Remy. "I know they will be better off with you then with me."

I relax slightly, and notice Dominique bristling besides me. "Let's hear him out," I mutter to him.

"I had a feeling I would meet you here, so I kept this with me." He scoffs as he pulls out n envelope, "Though I had the feeling you would find it on my dead
body one day.

Remy grabs the envelope from him, and I frown.

"What is it?"

He sighs, "We found this with you when you were young. I... we never opened it. There is something from me as well."

I can't help but laugh at this, "And why are you giving it to me now? After everything you said and did?"

He hangs his head, "I don't expect you to be happy seeing me, I understand what I did was wrong. So I wanted to give you are your brother's a clean slate." He sighs. "You were - you *are* right. There should be peace for our people. War will not bring those who were lost back." He hands the letters to Remy.

"It is better this way." King Hraikon agrees solemnly. "This is not worth more blood being shed."

With that, papa dips his head to King Hraikon and begins to follow the rest of the army away.

Remy looks at me, waiting for a signal to open the letter, I shake my head. This was something I needed to see.

I slowly sit up, I needed to shift, I wanted to go back to my normal form, but I couldn't.

"You two will need to rest now," King Hraikon says, "Wait before shifting," He says with a glance at me. I dip my head.

"Thank you, King Hraikon," I say, making him chuckle.

"There is no need, I should be thanking you." He says, "I am told it is because of you Dominique achieved his goals here."

"Should I open it then?" Fletcher asks impatiently, making Remy scoff.

"I have it, I should open it -"

"You each can open one... just - show me what is inside." I say solemnly.

Remy hands Fletcher one of the two

envelopes and he opens it almost immediately. A thin paper slip falls out, I immediately recognize it as a check.

That must be the letter from papa.

I anxiously watch Remy as he carefully opens the other letter, this envelope was far more worn and old and required caution in opening. I'm slightly relieved Remy is opening this one.

Pulling out a piece of paper, Remy frowns. "It's just a picture?"

King Hraikon frowns, he leans in towards Remy, "Show it to me."

Dominique looks at his father, confused, but Remy turns the page towards us all anyways.

King Hraikon let's out a suprised gasp as he sees the image.

It is a sketch of a dragon with horns like that of a ram, with a large anthurium plant growing around it. Snapdragon. It isn't the best artwork, and is very old and smudges, yet the dragonkin king still seems taken aback by the image.

I frown, looking up to King Hraikon. "Does this mean anything to you?"

When King Hraikon doesn't respond Dominique bristles with annoyance. "What does it mean father?"

"That is Emperor Alzeron... the last ruler of all the dragonkin territories."

"Why... Why would I be given an image of him?" I ask slowly.

King Hraikon looks to me, "It all makes sense now, I wondered why your dragonic form looked so familiar. You are his daughter."

Dominique's eyes go wide and Fletcher and Remy gasp in awe while I sit there confused.

Daughter of an emperor? There is no way someone of such a position would end up where I have.

"If I am the daughter of an emperor as you think, why would I have been left for dead in the woods?" I ask.

King Hraikon dips his head as his advisor, Jorunmeer joins us with his head hanging.

"You were born on a very special night, there is only one like it ever thousands of years." Jorunmeer begins. "This is why you have been able to achieve everything that you have - you have exceptional abilities in brining calm wherever you go. You have unnatural abilities of charm when you believe you can."

I shake my head, "But that still doesn't tell me why I was left to the humans -"

King Hraikon glares at Jorunmeer, "You'd best be the one to tell her."

Jorunmeer sighs, "I was put in charge of watching you for a time... As a baby you tended to stay in your human form more than your dragonic form after an incident at the border allowed you to see humans. It got to the point where... you wouldn't change back often. Your abilities and your transformation made people... nervous. There was a rebellion and, well when your father left you to me I didn't know where else you could be safe."

Remy looks up at me, "Does that mean you can rule Dragnior?"

I shake my head quickly, "Of course not! But -" I look to King Hraikon. "Does this mean I will not be trusted within the territories?"

"I do not yet know." King Hraikon says solemnly. "It has been many years... I would have to speak with the rulers of the other territories."

"But it does mean one thing," Dominique says suddenly, standing up next to me. "There is no one better to work on the relations between dragonkin and humans."

I tilt my head at this, "How do you mean?"

"You're dragonkin royalty and the Lady of

District Yonnam, I couldn't think of anyone better for the job." He looks at his father, King Hraikon. "And one day I will be able to support you as leader of the Hylligard."

King Hraikon dips his head at Dominique, "My son is right, and after everything you have done for both sides, I believe you would still be suited to this position even without the titles you carry."

I stand and let out a deep breath as I finally manage to shift my scales. As I regain my human form I look to Dominique.

"All right then, where do we begin?"

40
GHOST WRITER

"“The last of the frost has finally thawed, leaving way to a bright spring ahead. After one of the longest winters Flaize has ever experienced, we begin this new season with word of a peace treaty between Flaize and our neighboring country Dragnior...”

- Flaize Daily

"Dominique! Come here for a moment.”

I watch as Dominique looks up from his reading, shutting the book he had been going through. He stands up off of the couch to join me at the table in the window room of the library I once worked at.

The warm sunglight filtered through the windows and left a cheerful glow on the pages scattered on the table in front of me. He sits across from me in Farah’s old seat, looking amused at all of the papers and books scattered about on the table in front of me. He laughs as he sees what I was looking over.

“Are those the floor plans for the new abbey... again?”

I look up from the papers, “We finally got in the new design architect, the abbey will be more modern like many other ruling houses of other districts. With all levels of workers and board members alike sharing the same spaces. No dramatic large wasteful spaces."

Dominique tilts his head as he looks down at the designs, "It looks good but..."

"But?" I frown, "Is there something off about it?"

Dominique sighs and leans back in his seat, pulling his hair back into a ponytail as he does. "You've been obsessing with this for a little while now, is there something on your mind?"

"Just... waiting for the King's envoy to get here to cross the border has been nerve wracking." I admit after a moment. "I know that when I meet them -"

"We will meet them when they get here." Dominique adds.

"Isn't that what I said?"

Dominique shakes his head and I sigh, "Alright *we* will be ready to meet them, well us and Julian."

When Dominique groans at the mentions of the other board member I chuckle, "He isn't as bad as before you know."

"I know, but hearing you say that makes it even worse."

I snort at this and look back at the papers in front of me. *This layout will make so much better use of the property given to the board, perhaps we can even consider building a school closer to the gate. That would be safer for the children of Yonnam -*

I am pulled out of my thoughts as Dominique shuts the book in front of me and stands. As I frown at him he extends a hand towards me.

"How about we take a break from all of this? I don't know about you, but I still feel like I'm burnt out from these past few months."

"But shouldn't we be preparing?"

"Building will not start for another month at least, and the King and his envoy won't be here for at least another week. You should relax a bit, maybe let Julian pick up a little more slack." As I start to open my mouth to speak he continues, "Don't worry about your brother's either, they are at the park with Mr. Abbott today. I suggested they go out now that the weather is better."

I look at Dominique's hand for a moment before I take it, "You really think of everything don't you?"

He flashes his teeth in smile, "But of course."

I follow Dominique out of the library and onto the streets, the roads and sidewalks were bustling with life now that the frost was gone. Businesses were booming and no one feared the sickness anymore. I can't help but smile as I walk down the sidewalk with Dominique.

"You know..." I begin slowly. "In spite of everything, I haven't felt like this in a long time."

"Like what?" Dominique asks.

"Well... Hopeful. Anxious, of course, that never goes away, but genuinely hopeful."

He skips around me to walk on the outer part of the sidewalk as he speaks, I chuckle at this.

Dominique dips his head in agreement, "I agree. I'm glad it was you."

I tilt my head at him, looking up at his flush face. "Glad it was me for what?"

"Everything. Without you, I could never have achieved even half of what you did."

I laugh, "It wasn't because of me, as much as I once wished I could say that. It was because of us."

"Us," Dominique smiles, "I like the way that sounds."

I can't help but smile as well. There is much ahead of us still, yet I feel more at peace than I had in years.

The battle may have been won, and tensions were out at ease on the field where the two sides met. Yet there are still problems to be dealt with.

The prince was no longer set in line to be the next ruler, but he still was outspoken about the evil of the dragonkin. Tensions were still high on the idea of peace with the dragonkin, if there is to one day be open borders between us many fears would need to be resolved.

We stopped the war, but there would still be problems between the countries.

What is easy and what is right are very different, and in order to work towards a more peaceful time between our people, much work must be done. Only now do I know that it cannot be done alone.

And I feel lucky with the people I have at my side going forward.

I can only hope Farah would be proud if she could see me now.

THE SPELLBOUND ABBEY

THE END

Acknowledgements

I would like to acknowledge my fantastic beta readers, Shane Fitzgerald and Jaclin Geiger. Your feedback on my story has been so valuable, and I greatly appreciated your motivating words. My cover artist, Stefanie Saw from Seventhstar Art, thank you for helping me get my vague ideas into a fantastic cover!

I want to acknowledge the professors in my college career who motivated me and supported my writing. Thank you for taking the time out of your busy teaching life to converse with a single student, your kindness helped this book reach completion.

I would not have gotten so far into my writing progress if not for my family supporting me. Even though you might not have understood my long ramblings about my book, thank you for listening and cheering me on. Most of all thank you for being ecstatic the tens of hundreds of times I announced the book is finished only to continue to add to it.

About the Author

Mason Monteith is an artist, writer, and college student from the East Coast.
She began to write in 2012, and while she has written many stories, The Spellbound Abbey is her first novel.
She currently lives in the midwest where she enjoys writing fantasy worlds to escape into with dark academia themes, morally grey characters, and deep and intriguing plots.
Mason hopes to write and complete her next novel soon, if only she can stop getting distracted by her many story ideas.
You can find her on socials under *@writingmasonmonteith.*